TO MAKE A MAN

BLOODY JOE MANNION BOOK FOUR

PETER BRANDVOLD

WOLFPACK
PUBLISHING
— EST 2013 —

To Make a Man
Paperback Edition
Copyright © 2022 Peter Brandvold

Wolfpack Publishing
5130 S. Fort Apache Rd. 215-380
Las Vegas, NV 89148

wolfpackpublishing.com

Paperback ISBN 978-1-63977-112-7
Large Print Hardcover ISBN 978-1-63977-113-4
eBook ISBN 978-1-63977-111-0

TO MAKE A MAN

TO MAKE A MAN

HENRY "STRINGBEAN" MCCALLISTER RAN AS FAST AS his long, thin legs could carry him among red desert rocks and prickly cactus as slugs chewed up the ground just behind his scissoring boots with their chinging, sun-glinting spurs.

"Christalmighty—how many shooters are there, anyways!" the young deputy exclaimed, vaulting off his feet, diving ahead, landing on his chest and belly, then rolling behind a large rock.

He didn't have a chance. Just way too many villainous Mexicans dogging his trail, wanting very badly to fill him full of hot lead and kick him out with a cold shovel.

Two more bullets caromed up the hill and slammed into the face of Stringbean's covering boulder, casting rock shards and dust in all directions and causing String-bean's ears to ring like cracked bells.

Sitting up against the boulder, he cast his desperate daze down the hill to the southeast. Three Mexicans were running toward him, meandering around the rocks and barrel cactus, occasionally stopping and dropping to a knee to fire the Winchesters they held in gloved hands.

Their colorful, Spanish-cut clothes glinted brightly in the Arizona sunshine.

"Three on that side," Stringbean said, breathless, hearing the fear and desperation in his voice. He turned his head forward and leaned slightly to his left to peer through a notch between two more boulders, toward the west. His pulse drummed in his ears when he saw four more Mexicans—including the big, bad, one-eyed hombre La Stiletta had called Manuel San Jacinto, Hidalgo's first lieutenant—were heading toward Stringbean from that side of the hill.

Somehow, they'd gotten around him.

He looked back in the direction from which he'd come, north, to see the stage lying in a twisted heap, the Jehu and shotgun messenger lying unmoving among the wreckage. The old cowboy, Ike, lay back along the trail somewhere, dead as a boot. The team had broken away and headed for the distant, rocky, scrub-covered Arizona hills. Stringbean didn't blame them.

Not one diddly-damn bit!

He'd even allow as much to Marshal "Bloody" Joe Mannion. In the middle of the Arizona desert and surrounded by Mexicans, this was no time for pride.

"Oh, Lordy, Lordy, Lordy," the young man complained. "I'm gonna die out here. Never gonna see Molly again, never get the chance to make things right between us."

Molly Hurdstrom was the sweetheart Stringbean had left back in his and her hometown of Del Norte, in the south-central Colorado Territory.

Rocks and sand dribbled down the face of a large boulder ahead and to Stringbean's right.

Stringbean looked up in a panic to see a short, broad-shouldered Mexican smiling down at him, aiming a saddle-ring carbine pressed up against his ruddy right cheek.

"Yikes!" Stringbean rolled to his right, certain he was crow bait.

But somehow, and to his own surprise, he managed to raise his own carbine, slamming it up against his cheek and shoulder, and fired just a hair after the Mexican's bullet had merely cut a small groove across the deputy's right shoulder, tearing his shirt. Stringbean's Winchester bucked and roared twice fast.

The Mexican staggered backward. The man's straw sombrero tumbled down to hang from its thong down his back, exposing a great, bald, savage head. He dropped his rifle and gave an agonized wail, clutching both hands over his belly before stumbling forward and tumbling straight down the face of the rock.

Stringbean had to throw himself back to his left or the big Mex would have landed on top of him. The man struck with an enormous *thud!*

Stringbean was damn lucky he'd thrown himself to his left. Just a second after the big Mexican had struck the ground, several shots were fired from behind the deputy to carom through the air where his back had faced them half a second before. Two of those bullets plunked into the big, dead Mexican's bald, bullet-shaped head.

"Oh, that's just nasty business, now!"

Stringbean could hear the three Mexicans running up behind him. He lay belly flat and snaked the Winchester around his covering boulder's right side, lined up the sights on one of his pursuers, and fired. The man went down with a wail.

Stringbean ejected the spent cartridge, seated fresh, lined up the sights on another man, and fired. The bullet blew a hole in the Mex's knee. Stringbean shot him again quickly, but now he could see the others moving up on his west flank.

Stringbean wasn't the most experienced lawman, but he'd been Bloody Joe's junior deputy long enough to know the lay of the land—leastways, up in Colorado. He'd never been to Arizona before and so far, he didn't like the heat or the people.

Not one diddly-dee damn bit!

He did know he was about to get caught in a whipsaw, however.

He clambered to his feet and took off running straight ahead as fast as his long, thin legs could carry him.

The Mexicans shouted behind him.

Rifles screeched. Bullets hummed nastily all around Stringbean's head, kicking up the red desert caliche around his boots. He ran down a low area where several slab-sided boulders tilted every which way. He ran into a little niche among the big rocks, turned around, dropped to a knee, and saw three Mexicans running toward him, maybe fifteen feet behind.

He dropped one of them with a bullet through the man's big Adam's apple. The man threw his two pistols straight up in the air and went down shouting something Stringbean couldn't understand but he had a feeling it was about Stringbean's bloodline, and it wasn't no compliment, neither.

The others ran to ground, yelling Mex curses.

Stringbean saw a narrow stone corridor dropping away on his left. He followed the cool, shaded declivity. When he emerged from the other side, he saw that one of the slab-sided boulders was tilted back up, sort of like a pitched roof, toward the Mexicans he'd just driven to ground—he thought there were three, maybe four left; he'd lost count—and were likely cooling their heels, having seen how bad it had gone for their amigos.

Stringbean didn't look like much—tall, thin, sort of long-faced and a little buck-toothed—but he'd given these Mexican hellions the what for, all right!

No time to congratulate yourself, ya dunderhead, he chastised himself and leaped up onto the slab-sided boulder, crouching low as he walked back toward where he'd been hunkered in the niche under the boulder's sheltering roof. As he moved, he thumbed fresh cartridges through his Winchester's loading gate.

When he'd nearly reached the peak of the "roof," he dropped to his knees, removed his hat, and crawled the rest of the way until he could look back toward where he'd run from the border bandits. One just then stepped out from the rock he'd been crouched behind. A big, shaggy-headed fella in a red sombrero and a fancily stitched red shirt and chaparreras. He glanced back toward where Stringbean could see part of the hatted heads of two others peeking out from behind their own covering rocks.

The shaggy-headed fella with gaudy fashion sense, Stringbean had to admit, gave a little whistle and motioned with his black-gloved hand for the two others to move through the rocks to Stringbean's left, as he faced the three men.

The shaggy-headed hombre turned back to Stringbean just as the other two stepped out from their own covers.

Stringbean grinned and knocked a bullet through the shaggy fella's forehead, just above his nose. He pumped a new round into the chamber, fired, pumped another new one, fired, and his grin broadened as the other two

6 / PETER BRANDVOLD

danced around, screaming and dropping their guns before piling up in bloody heaps in the red rocks.

The smile faded from Stringbean's face when a shadow slid across the rock to his right.

Ah, hell...

He swung around but not before the short, wiry little Mex with a thick, walrus mustache drilled one through Stringbean's right arm. He felt like he'd been kicked by a hot boot. He still managed to raise his own carbine and punch one through the little man's chest, knocking him flat before he rolled wildly down the slanted roof to the ground below with a clipped wail and a thud.

"Ah, hell," Stringbean said, looking down at the blood oozing from his arm, midway between the elbow and shoulder. Well, he was even now. He'd been shot in the left arm not three full days ago. "Ah, hell, hell, hell...now I've done it!"

He set his rifle down then unknotted his green bandanna from around his neck. He knotted it tightly around the wound, cursing through gritted teeth.

"Damn, damn, damn...too damn confident, and I should know better!"

He leaned back, wincing against the pain.

He spied movement to his left side. A big diamond-back was just then sliding its head out from a crack in the roof-like boulder, flicking its long, black, forked tongue, its beady eyes regarding Stringbean as though the deputy were his next meal.

"No, no, no," Stringbean said. "Go back to where you came from, granddaddy viper. I don't want to waste a shot on you. I'm runnin' short, and I still got a few miles left...and likely more men to ward off."

As though understanding, the big snake pulled its head back into the crack.

He picked up his rifle, set his hat on his head, and walked back down the slanting roof to the ground, stepping over the dead Mexican as he did. He was about to crouch over the dead Mex and see what caliber of ammo the man was carrying when he heard a girl's scream rip through the hot, dry, Arizona wind.

It was then he remembered he'd heard her scream once before, maybe ten minutes ago.

He'd been dodging so much lead, he'd forgotten.

Mathilda Calderon.

La Stiletta...

So much had happened, he'd forgotten.

He got his bearings and began making his way toward the sound of the girl's agony...

CHAPTER 2

TWO WEEKS BEFORE...

"SHE SURE IS PRETTY," SAID STRINGBEAN.

"Don't let her looks fool you, kid," warned String-bean's boss, "Bloody" Joe Mannion, town marshal of Del Norte in the south-central Colorado Territory. "That girl will carve your heart out and serve it to you on a cold platter."

The fire the pair were sitting around in the high country near the little mountain mining town of Tincup, snapped suddenly, sending gray ashes flying up onto the wanted circular Stringbean was holding in his gloved hands. He gave a grunt and blew the ashes off the likeness of the young Mexican woman penciled on the dodger, as though nothing should be allowed to blemish her beauty.

"Looks so dang...I don't know...*innocent*," Stringbean said, his eyes tracing the lines of the heart-shaped face with plump, well-turned lips, almond-shaped eyes with long, alluring lashes, wavy long hair framing her lovely countenance as it tumbled to her shoulders sort of messily, as though she'd just gotten out of bed in the morning or maybe after she'd removed her hat and given her head a good shake, her hair a tumble. In the drawing, a slender thong curved down over her chest and Stringbean could see a straw sombrero peaking up from behind her shoulders.

"She is anything but," Mannion said, pulling a small, hide-wrapped flask from a pocket of his wool-lined, black denim jacket, popping the cap on it, and tipping it over his freshly poured cup of coal-black coffee. "Only twenty-three years old—your age—and she's already got one helluva reputation down along the border," he said. "She's half-Mexican, half-Italian. They call her *La Stiletta* because of the style of weapon she wields. Runs with a bad bunch. Border banditos and revolutionarios. She'd just as soon stick a knife in you as share a fire with you."

The wanted circular as well as a notice had been sent up from the office of the U.S. marshal for the south-western district a few weeks earlier, when Mathilda Calderon, or La Stiletta, as she was more widely known, had given the marshals down there the slip when they'd been busy arresting her boyfriend, and was spotted heading north. U.S. Marshal Dwight Sullivan thought she intended to get lost in the Colorado mining camps until her trail cooled farther south.

Apparently, she'd done that before, knowing she'd be expected to head south into her home country of Old Mexico.

Mannion splashed a little more firewater into his mud. He could smell the aroma of the busthead mixing with that of the coffee. The Who-Hit-John took the sting out of the high-country cold, bone penetrating even in August and with the sun down only an hour.

But then, August was fall up here, damn near ten

thousand feet above sea level. On his and Stringbean's ride up from the San Juan Valley into the Sawatch, north of Del Norte, Mannion had spied several aspens well on their way to turning from their deep-summer green to the golden hues of fall. The Who-Hit-John took more than the sting of the cold out of the forty-six-year-old lawman's bones. It took the sting out of the fact that he was a married man with an absent wife.

Jane had run out on him, sure enough. After only four months of marriage.

But he was "Bloody Joe," after all. Why would any man with such a name, which he'd come by honestly, indeed, over his years of town taming in Kansas down to Texas during the grand old days of the great Texas cattle herds, expect anything less from any woman foolish enough to marry him?

The fact of Jane's leaving was never clearer than after the sun had gone down, even when he was at home with his daughter, Evangeline, "Vangie" for short, back in Del Norte.

He raised the flask, considered the smoking, black surface of the coffee lightly flecked with gray ash from the fire, then added another shot of the busthead. He'd purchased an entire crock jug of it from the old, hermetic Irish prospector, Theophilus O'Flanagan, whose own brand of mash Bloody Joe had for years favored over even labeled bottles from bona fide distilleries.

Theo was somewhat of a mad Irish poet who came to town from time to time, got drunk, and goaded men two or three times his puny size into fights and ended up the guest of honor at Hotel de Mannion, which was what Joe's office and jailhouse in Del Norte was locally called. Joe secretly and uncharacteristically—he always fined everybody—never fined old Theo, and he always released him after the man had slept it off. Theo almost always left Joe a poem scrawled in an amalgam of English and old Gaelic on the back of an age-yellowed wanted circular, most of which Joe didn't understand but which amused him nonetheless.

No one else liked Theo, but Joe did.

But then, damn few liked Bloody Joe. But Jane did.

Had for a while. Then she'd tired of his selfish, bullheaded ways, fell out of love with him, and left him, so now there was only Vangie, whose love didn't really count. Daughters were supposed to love their fathers despite how unlovable their fathers could be.

On the other hand, anyone could love Vangie. Vangie was easy. It was no great feat that Joe loved her more than life itself.

At least he had that. He had Vangie. And for what he was worth, which wasn't much, she had him.

Mannion capped the flask and returned it to his pocket. He glanced up to see Stringbean—tall and lean, as per his name, with a long, oval face and a perennial sheepish cast to his gaze—staring down at him. When his boss's eyes met his, the twenty-three-year-old deputy gave a startled grunt then returned his eyes to the wanted circular he held before him in his two gloved hands.

He stared down at it, frowning, moving a gloved index finger over the words and figures: "Wa...wanted...by Feder-all Auth...Auth...Auther..."

"Authorities," Mannion assisted.

Stringbean had been breaking wild horses for area ranchers when more privileged young men his age had been attending school, learning their letters and numbers. Recently, Stringbean had been working on his own education, however, teaching himself to read with help from the *National Police Gazette* and *Beadle's Dime Novels* sporting lurid, yellow pasteboard covers as well as the wanted circulars sent out by various government agencies and the Pinkertons and Wells Fargo.

"...by Federal Authorities," Stringbean read, "to test-if-i in fed-feder-all—*federal!*—cower...cower, no—"

"Federal court trial."

"Federal court trial against her border bandito accomplice Diego Hidalgo who stole three Gatling guns from the army outpost at Fort Bowie!" Stringbean held his head high, smiling proudly across the fire at Mannion, who just then sipped his dark, warming, nerve-numbing elixir that bathed his cold cheeks in its aromatic steam.

"You memorized the rest," Joe chuckled, pulling the cup down and running his tongue across his mustached upper lip. "Here I thought you were just staring at the picture all day."

Again, he chuckled.

Stringbean flushed and returned his gaze to the dodger in his hands. "Sure is pretty, though...to be on the run from the federals." He glanced at Mannion. "You sure we got the right gal, Marshal? I mean, we have only Dexter Strawberry's word on that, and he's three sheets to the wind by three in the afternoon."

Strawberry had just opened a new saloon in town, one favored by the track layers and gandy dancers working for a new narrow-gauge rail line crawling up the canyons from Colorado Springs—named the Rio Grande Southern. Strawberry's business benefited though the mostly vermin track layers, graders, and the human carrion eaters following their progress like hawks and buzzards hovering over half-dead cattle, were a thorn in Mannion's side.

They were the reason he and Stringbean hadn't been

able to get on the trail of Mathilda Calderon—La Stiletta —until said trail was nearly cold. An especially violent fight had broken out in the street between the Rio Grande Southern's men and a rival outfit laying track up from Colorado Springs via an alternate route—the Pueblo, Colorado Springs, and Del Norte Line. The race was on between the two outfits to get to Del Norte first. So far, they were running almost neck and neck, which made their workers sleep-deprived and especially hot-tempered and quick to use picks and shovels on each other right out on Main Street at high noon.

"He saw her, all right," Mannion said, meaning Strawberry. "He described her perfectly. Said he served a gal who looked just like the one in that picture and kept suspiciously to herself. At one point, she asked Strawberry for a job. Probably short on jingle. When Dex gave her what was no doubt a brazen look and told her she could put on something frilly and work upstairs...on her back...she'd threatened to gut him like the lowly bottom-feeding carp he was then finished her shot of tangleleg, went out, and promptly stole Wayne Ellison's copper-red sorrel from in front of the Three-Legged Dog.

"Rode out of Del Norte at a full gallop, nearly running over Wilfred Drake crossing the street from the post office with an armload of parcels. Those parcels went flying in all directions, piss-burning Drake even worse than that twisted ankle, as those packages were long overdue from the Montgomery Ward Company."

"Where do you suppose she's headed, Marshal? Miss Calderon."

"Leadville." Mannion sipped his flavored coffee and smacked his lips. "I'd bet the farm on it. She's low on money so she's desperate and looking for work. Since she doesn't want to perform mattress dances, she must be exploring other options—most of which she'd likely find in a village the size of Leadville. Con artist, I'd say. Those eyes say it all. I bet she's run them all—banking or mining fraud, diamond fraud, miracle elixirs, tarot cards. A girl who looks like that could turn a tidy profit in two or three nights. In a week, she'd likely have enough—maybe even a rich, half-drunk husband she'd fleece before leaving him with his throat cut in some tony hotel room—for a train ticket to Frisco."

Mannion took another deep drink of his lukewarm coffee, added some fresh, and dug the flask out of his coat pocket.

"Best go easy, Marshal," Stringbean said, casting his boss a cautionary glance over the top of the wanted dodger in his hands.

Mannion grinned as he popped the cap and turned the flask over the smoking mud. "Medicine, Stringbean, my lad," Joe said. He capped the flask, returned it to his pocket, and sagged back against his saddle with a sigh. "Medicine."

He did feel guilty, though. The night the cutthroats had burned his and Vangie's house and kidnapped his daughter, taking her away to rape her, Joe had been drunk. He'd vowed to stop drinking but then he reneged and vowed only to cut back. A man with his unbridled temperament needed the medicinal properties of the Who-Hit-John to restrain his strong emotions and his tendency to act out with his fists.

Although sometimes he had to admit it did just the latter...

"You're the one who always says we need to stay alert on the stalkin' trail," Stringbean said then winced, stealing himself against his boss's notorious wrath.

"I am alert." Unexpectedly, Bloody Joe smiled across

the fire at his junior deputy. "Besides, Señorita Calderon might be double-dee damned devilish, but she *is* just a girl. Nah, I 'spect we'll run her down by high noon tomorrow, have her back in Del Norte by noon the next day. I'll cable the federals to come for her, and we'll be free and clear of that little border bandita and can go back to concentrating on the track layers picking and shoveling each other on Main Street till the blood rises to the levels of the damned boardwalks!"

He gave a wry sigh and took another sip of his relaxing brew, noting he hadn't thought about Jane in several minutes.

"She sure is pretty," Stringbean said, looking down at the dodger again.

MIDMORNING THE NEXT DAY, MATHILDA CALDERON, aka *La Stiletta*, inspected her stolen horse's swollen ankle then straightened and chewed her thumbnail through the glove on her right hand.

"Mierda!" She stomped a foot and looked around.

She was on a high mountain, which a wooden sign below at the start of the long, steep rise, had identified as Cottonwood Pass. Pines towered around her on the relatively flat shelf she was on, a reprieve from the grueling climb. To the north lay more forest through which the graded trail twisted and turned, rising toward a crest Mathilda could not yet see. She'd been on the pass for hours and was beginning to wonder if she would ever crest it.

Maybe it didn't have a crest.

Maybe it was one of those mountains that went on and on forever, like in one of the fairy tales she'd read

when she'd been very young, and which had been confis-
cated by the nuns because everyone knew that girls
shouldn't read. Reading would only fill their silly, simple
heads with crazy ideas not unlike the very one that had
told young Mathilda to teach herself how to read in the
first place!

No, of course the mountain had a top. Not only a top
but another side. From the map she'd stowed away in her
saddlebags and which she'd stolen from a drunk government surveyor on a little ranch road in northern New
Mexico, the town on the other side of the pass was
Buena Vista. North of Buena Vista lay the town she was
heading for—Leadville.

On her travels up from Las Cruces, she'd heard much
about Leadville—namely, that it was a fast-growing
mining town rife with rich men from Denver as well as
places farther east in America. Rife with opportunity for
a beautiful young señorita as ambitious as Mathilda
Calderon. Besides, she had an uncle there, if she could
find him. The gold-hunting Uncle Tio would likely give
her shelter until she could find a shelter of her own.

Preferably, shelter owned by a rich man.

She smiled.

Si, si. She would look for a rich man with a big house
to support her until it was time to head back down to the
border which, despite the savagery with which she was
raised, was still home to her, after all...

But how she would reach Leadville now, she did not
know. She looked again at the copper-red sorrel horse
she'd stolen in Del Norte. The ankle was badly swollen;
the damn beast could put barely any weight on it. Time
would probably heal it, but Mathilda didn't have time.
She was short on trail supplies. Short on money, for that
matter, and, peering back in the direction from which

she'd come, due south, she saw nothing but thick forest and empty space trailing away to hazy, distant mountains.

"Mierda," she said again, removing the canteen from where it hung by a hemp lanyard from her saddle horn. She unscrewed the cap and tipped the canteen to her mouth, but there was barely enough water to dampen her lips.

She cursed again and let the canteen drop back down against the stirrup fender.

She peered south again. She didn't think anyone was following her, but she couldn't be too careful. The man whom she'd stolen the fine horse from would no doubt come looking for it or, worse, he might have sent the law.

She'd been careless to steal such a fine mount in broad daylight, but desperation and anger had made her act hastily, as it often did. To think the stupid gringo barkeep in Del Norte would invite her to whore for him!

Mathilda Calderon may have been many things, but she was not a puta!

She spat in distaste at the thought of having some bearded scoundrel thrusting himself between her spread knees. She lifted the straw sombrero from her head and ran a hand through her long, thick, curly, sweaty hair. She shuddered at how filthy she felt—every inch of her clad in a white blouse with a ruffled front and a long, black leather skirt and high-topped, silver-buckle boots with silver toe caps, felt caked with ground-in trail dirt and sweat.

She could use a long, hot bath as well as a hot meal.

But first she needed a healthy horse...

She lifted her chin suddenly, wrinkling the skin above her long, fine nose in sudden interest, her heart quickening.

She'd heard something. The sorrel had heard it, too.

The handsome animal gave its tail a quick switch then craned its neck to peer behind him and its rider and off toward where the trail climbed up through pines from below. The sorrel whickered deep in its chest, and then, meandering through the trees and occasionally drowned by the intermittent breeze causing the pine crowns to dance and make soft wheezing sounds, came the sound of a man singing.

The singing grew gradually louder.

The man was on the trail below her, heading toward her...

Probably on a horse.

Hmm.

CHAPTER 3

THE MAN WASN'T ON A HORSE. HE WAS IN AN OLD Conestoga-style wagon pulled by a mule.

A mule would do...

As he followed the switch-backing trail through the thick forest south of La Stiletta's position, she saw through the screening trees the mule pulling the covered wagon and heard the man sitting in the driver's boot, throwing his head back and singing loudly, proudly, and terribly:

> *"I've been the wild rover for many's a year*
> *And I spent all my money on whiskey and beer,*
> *And now I'm returning with gold in great store*
> *And I never will play the wild rover no more..."*

As he followed a switchback trail through the trees, angling generally toward Mathilda and the sorrel, which stood with its ears pricked and tail arched, the singer—if you could call it singing—continued at the tops of his lungs with:

> *"I went into an ale house I used to frequent*
> *And I told the landlady my money was spent—"*

He cut himself off abruptly when the mule pulled the rickety wagon around another turn in the trail and the little, gray-headed man in the driver's boot, wearing a bowler hat and shabby suit, turned his head toward Mathilda. As the mule continued at a good clip along the trail, the man turned his head forward once more and continued, even louder than before, with:

> *"On a hill far away stood an old rugged cross,*
> *The emblem of suffering and shame;*
> *And I love that old cross where the dearest*
> *   and best*
> *For a world of lost sinners was slain.*
> *So I'll cherish the old rugged cross,*
> *The...old...rug-ged...cross!...*
> *Till my trophies at last I lay down;*
> *I will cling to the old rugged cross,*
> *And exchange it someday for a crown!"*

The scratchy-voiced man, so badly out of tune that he made Mathilda grind her teeth, pulled back on the mule's reins. The wagon rocked to a stop on the trail. The little, gray-headed, potbellied man sitting on the driver's seat, padded with a shabby, red pillow with gold embroidering, grinned seedily down at her, doffing his hat and holding it over his chest, saying, "Well, hello there, señorita. Do my eyes deceive me or are you really standin' here on the trail before me—purely a vision, for sure?"

Inwardly, Mathilda rolled her eyes. Gringos.

Outwardly, she smiled broadly and let her long-lashed

lids flutter over dark-brown eyes. "No, no—I am really here, Señor." She gave a mock-embarrassed giggle behind the gloved hand she laid across her lips, fake-nervously swinging to-and-fro on her hips. "I couldn't be happier nor more grateful to Madre Maria for summoning you here to render possible assistance, Señor. As you can see, my poor horse has fallen lame. He set me afoot with very little to eat and drink, so far out here in the middle of nowhere!"

She looked out over the broad, empty valley opening to the south. In her current stranded condition, the view was like the broad yawn of a malevolent God. Mathilda stifled a not entirely manufactured sob.

She leaned out to one side to read the words stenciled in ornate green letters on the white wooden side panel of the little man's wagon:

Dr. J. Felix Bartlett
Road to Eternal Salvation
&
Founder of Bartlett's Own Patented Liver
and Gallbladder Tonic

A bullet hole all but obliterated the letter *r* in "liver."

Mathilda turned to the man grinning down at her, still holding his hat over his chest.

"Qué?" she said, incredulous.

"Ah, you readee zee Engleesh," the man said, chuckling, his eyes straying across her ruffle-fronted blouse as they'd been doing ever since he'd stopped the wagon. Mathilda had undone the first three buttons against the midmorning heat, revealing the first, high swells of what lay in such fulsome opulence below.

Inwardly, she again rolled her eyes. She said, "You're Doctor Bartlett?"

"Si, si, one and the same my dear young lady. Doctor of medicine, purveyor, patent holder of several healthful elixirs, as well as brother to Our Lord Jesus Christ whose word I have devoted my life to spreading far and wide and in all manner of terrain and weather."

"Mierda!" Mathilda said, unable to catch herself in time to keep the epithet from vaulting across her lips. "You've been a busy man, Doctor Bartlett!"

Bartlett threw his head back, laughing and carefully setting his hat back on his head capped in thin, blue-gray hair that hung down to brush his shoulders. It was greasy and weed seeds and trail dust clung to it. He wore a matching mustache with upswept, waxed ends.

"Where are you headed?" Mathilda asked. "As you can see, my horse is lame and I'm short on trail supplies and water. I don't want to be a burden, however, Doctor. I can see you're a busy man and probably in a hurry to reach your destination..."

Her eyes flicked to the mule in the wagon's traces. The brown beast was craning his head to look back at her. It gave a single flick of its bushy tail to which several burs clung, and a suspicious flick of its ears, as though reading the cunning in the young woman's mind.

"I'm never in a hurry, my dear child. Never in a hurry. Why, life is too short to hurry. My destination happens to be Buena Vista on the other side of Cottonwood Pass. Intend to speak a few words from the Good Book to the Ladies' Sobriety League, don't ya know. They're helping spread the Good Word as well as the glories of a sober life far and wide!"

He smiled broadly. "I, however, intend to layover for a day or two in my cabin near here, just up the pass another mile and then down a seldom used trail. I call the hovel—surely a humble one, indeed—mine, because I seem to be the only one who ever uses it. I suspect it was built by some old codger of the mountains—a mountain man, indeed. Long passed, alas. It's quite private. No one will pester you there, if you care for a respite, my dear. Mi casa, tu casa!"

He cackled out a laugh that was as hard on Mathilda's ears as his singing.

"To be sure, my larder is well stocked." Dr. Bartlett's eyes smoldered as they flicked to Mathilda's blouse before returning to her face, his own cheeks flushing a little, guiltily. "And I have a well with fresh water and a good stove to heat water for a bath. I bet you'd welcome a long, refreshing soak!"

His lips stretched as he smiled, and his eyes slitted before blinking once, slowly.

"A bath! ¡Qué no daría yo por un buen baño caliente!"

Dr. Bartlett laughed. "Si, si, señorita! I don't know what you just said—I do have quite a large Spanish vocabulary and some knowledge of Spanish grammar, but you spoke far too quickly for me!" He laughed. "I do take it from your tone, however, that you'd be delighted to be my guest at my humble little hovel"—he gave a slow, regal bow of his head—"and I know I couldn't be more delighted to serve as your host. A most gracious one at that."

Mathilda glanced at the mule staring back at her, suspicious of her motives. Or was she just imagining the beast's thoughts, being driven to paranoia by her own?

She lifted her hand and chewed the thumbnail through her glove, staring up at the little, gray-headed, potbellied man before her, grinning down at her like the snake mesmerizing the proverbial cottontail. She stretched her plump lips back from her perfect, white teeth and said, "Oh, but I don't think it would be proper, Doctor! What would Missus Bartlett say, and of course you would tell her!"

Inwardly, she giggled. She couldn't help toying with the good doctor a little. And why should she not? He was sitting up there undressing her with his eyes, was he not? Of course he was. Every man did. She couldn't blame them, for she'd admired herself in enough mirrors to know rather intimately the fine figure of a young woman she cut...

Modesty was not high on Mathilda Calderon's list of admirable attributes.

"Of course, I would tell her!" Dr. Bartlett intoned, laughing then sobering suddenly and casting the young lady a sly wink. "If I were married. Alas, I am not. And you can trust me for the gentleman I am...as well as a man of God," he added very soberly, almost gravely, indeed.

The lusty old goat!

"Well, in that case, could I tie my horse to the back of your wag—"

"Let me do that!" Dr. Bartlett wrapped his ribbons around the handle of the brake he'd set then clambered quickly but awkwardly down from the driver's boot, one of his worn half boots sliding off a wheel spoke and nearly sending him sprawling onto the trail. He managed to throw his arms out and to regain his balance at the last second. Flushing with embarrassment, he lifted his chin high, reset the angle of the hat on his head, and pulled up his baggy, age-coppered, wash-worn broadcloth trousers. He stepped forward to take the sorrel's dangling reins.

"Easy, boy. Easy, boy—here we go," he said, casting Mathilda another wry, smoldering smile, his eyes wandering brazenly once more as though of their own accord—the old sot just couldn't help himself!—as he led the limping horse around behind the wagon.

As he did, he glanced at the sorrel appraisingly and said, "Nice horse you have here, señorita. Funny thing, Wayne Ellison from Del Norte had one that looks just like him!" He chuckled as he brushed a hand down the blaze on the sorrel's long, fine snout and slid a fleeting, cockeyed look to Mathilda, who, flushing, turned away quickly to make her way around to the other side of the wagon.

Twenty minutes later, Bartlett had regained his seat in the driver's boot, released the brake, and taken up the reins. He pulled the wagon off onto a forking side trail with the sorrel limping along behind. Fortunately, the trail was packed hard between rocks shoving up from the earth below. That was good. The mule, the sorrel, and the wagon likely wouldn't leave much of a trail for any possible shadowers.

Mathilda leaned out from the right side of the wagon to peer back along the trail behind her. Again, she was relieved to spy no one lurking around back there.

"Not to worry, dear child," said Dr. Bartlett. "The cabin's well off the trail. A nice little hidey-hole, sure enough. No bad folks...or anyone else," he added, meaningfully, leaning toward her and offering a knowing half grin, "will pester you out here. I'll see to it!" He glanced beneath the splintered wooden seat. "Got me a loaded double-bore down yonder, an' I know how to use it, too!"

He winked, and his grin turned foxy.

Mathilda leaned forward to peer beneath the seat. Sure enough, Bartlett had a gun sheathed under the seat, a scratched walnut stock protruding from the open end.

She could see the delineation of the shotgun's double barrels through the leather.

She gave the man a disbelieving scowl. "You...a man of the cloth...?"

"Hah!" Bartlett threw his head back with a laugh. "In this world, my dear, only fools turn the other cheek, an' only if they want the second one slapped even harder than the first. Hah! I maybe be a believer, but I'm no fool!" He shook the reins over the mule's back and said, "Giddyup there, Scoundrel—we're damn...er, I mean *darn*...near home!"

He slid another foxy look to Mathilda and chuckled.

The mule brayed and shook its head as it followed a bend in the rocky trail. A sun-dappled clearing lay ahead, and as the sun found the mule and then the wagon, Mathilda shaded her eyes to inspect the low-slung shack sitting ahead and to her right, its shake-shingled roof green with moss and almost thoroughly concealed by needles that had fallen from the surrounding pines.

The cabin wasn't much larger than a large box, but it looked sound, with a stoop with an awning set on peeled pine poles running along half of its front wall and a hide-bottom chair sitting to the left of the door. Ancient, paper-thin skins were nailed to the cabin's walls; bleached skulls adorned the awning support posts. The skull of what appeared to be a large bear, probably a grizzly, hung over the front door, snarling as if to warn visitors away.

Mathilda winced.

Yes, the place looked sound enough, but it bespoke male savagery. How well she knew the subject!

Oh well—beggars couldn't be choosers. She needed that mule. She wasn't sure how she was going to get it away from Bartlett, but she'd come up with something. Mathilda had been alone on the frontier—both Mexican and American—since she'd fled the sisters at *Mission de St. Agnes Para Niñas Rebeles*, St. Agnes's Mission for Wayward Girls, east of Durango. The orphan had learned early a thing or two about parting men with their belongings. She'd been at it since she was ten years old.

She knew a thing or two about parting men with their lives as well. She had an obsidian-handled stiletto and two small revolvers in the war bag hanging from the sorrel's saddle horn. She'd come by the "wayward girl" moniker honestly enough, she couldn't help snickering to herself.

She glanced at the old reprobate sitting to her left. He was ogling her again with his lusty gaze as he reined the mule to a halt fronting the cabin. He had his old gray head canted slightly forward, his gray-blue eyes owning a shiny, lusty cast as he studied the front of her blouse.

Mathilda turned to him as he set the brake. "How did you ever find this place so concealed from the trail?"

Bartlett looked at the cabin, brows raised. "Oh, well, uh..." He smiled again, flushing slightly. "Let's just say that before I became a devout man of the cloth and inventor and purveyor of potent, life-enhancing and life-lengthening elixirs, I was a...a, uh..." He looked again at the cabin, a strained expression on his craggy, sagging features as he searched for the words he was looking for.

Mathilda helped him with a foxy smile of her own. "Bandido, perhaps, Doctor Bartlett...?"

"Ah!" Bartlett slapped his thigh and gave a nervous laugh. "I reckon you might say that, señorita. Si, si. The good doctor did have some oats to sow before he turned to the path of righteousness..." He chuckled again. "Why don't you go on inside and I'll tend ol' Scoundrel here and your sorrel then skin up onto the roof and take that old coffee can off the chimney pipe—keeps the birds and squirrels out, don't ya know—then build a fire, cook us some vittles, an' heat you some water for a nice, hot bath? Bet you'd like that just fine, wouldn't ya, young lady?"

Si, I would like it just fine. And wouldn't you, as well, you goatish old lobo? Mathilda did not say out loud.

CHAPTER 4

MATHILDA HAD TO ADMIT THE MEAL THE OLD Bartlett threw together was not half bad.

He used some tinned meat, tomatoes, a couple of potatoes and an onion he found in his cellar, and a can of pinto beans. While he cooked, he sang hymns which did not fool Mathilda one bit. She knew that despite the words stenciled on the side of his wagon, and those he was wailing out off-key enough to choke a hog, he was about as religious as she, a victim of thuggish nuns, was.

And just as guileless.

While Bartlett sang and cooked and heated water for Mathilda's bath, she sat on the hide-bottom chair on the porch, keeping a sharp eye on the woods surrounding the cabin. Bartlett had unsaddled and tended the sorrel and stabled him with his mule. Mathilda had piled her gear on the stoop at her feet. She considered the possibility of trading the sorrel for the mule but nixed the idea. Dr. Bartlett, or whoever the graybeard really was, knew it was stolen. Besides, it had a bum foot and wouldn't be able to pull the old rascal's wagon for another week or two.

Sounded like he had some church ladies to fleece over in Buena Vista the next day, and he wouldn't want to miss out on that...

Mathilda had to find another way to separate the old fool from the mule.

She glanced down at the canvas war bag residing next to her right boot. The top was open just enough that she could see the old, rusty knife and her two small revolvers —Merwin .32s with silver chasing, three-and-a-half-inch barrels, and gutta percha grips. Each was a seven-shot.

Of course, she'd need only drill one bullet through Dr. Bartlett's seedy, old head.

She was contemplating that now when Bartlett opened the door to her left and stepped out, setting his hat on his head. He hefted his double-bore shotgun in his hands and grinned down at her while steam wafted out around him from the potbelly stove behind him.

"Your water's ready anytime, mi lady," he said with a courtly bow. "There's a bucket of cool beside the tub, another of hot simmering on the stove. You go on in and enjoy yourself and I'll just sit out here and clean Ol' Rufus. Never know when the barn blaster is gonna come in handy, what with all the highwaymen haunting these mountain trails. You might just want to consider lettin' me drive you on into Buena Vista tomorrow. The trails aren't safe for a purty young lady alone."

He grinned, showing his yellow teeth, and winked.

"Si, si, muchas gracias for your hospitality, Doctor Bartlett," Mathilda said demurely, quickly closing her war bag and hoisting it onto her shoulder.

As she turned to the door, Bartlett said, "I set two towels on a chair there by the tub. Help yourself, dearie, and take all the time you need." He grinned and pinched the narrow brim of his shabby bowler to her.

"Gracias," Mathilda said again, and squeezed past him through the half-open door.

She closed the door behind her and stood regarding the square, corrugated tin washtub sitting on a braided rug. The tub was half full of steaming water. Like Bartlett had said, a bucket of cold sat on the floor beside the tub and another of hot steamed on the stove. Two towels, very frayed but appearing relatively clean, were folded neatly on a chair angled toward the tub.

"Dios mio," Mathilda said quietly to herself, turning to the door behind her. Through some missing chinking between two logs to the right of the door, she could see Dr. Bartlett sitting in the chair, his back to the cabin. He was humming softly to himself as he cleaned his shotgun, Ol' Rufus. "What hospitality."

And here I've only been thinking about how I can rob the old devil blind...

Mathilda felt a rare pang of guilt.

Yes, indeed, it was rare.

Most of the men she'd robbed, and worse—and there were a good many—had tried to rob or do worse to her. Dr. Bartlett might have cast her a few goatish stares, undressing her with his eyes, but could she really blame him? What man with any taste at all could help himself? Besides, she'd been pondering ways to separate the old man from his mule. Those ways were not restricted to nonviolence. No, a few of those ways, involving either the pigsticker or the two short-barreled revolvers in her war bag were definitely not restricted to nonviolence.

Again, guilt stabbed her low on her right side.

She found herself in a pickle. She was low on food and money, she had no mount, and she found herself stranded high in the Rocky Mountains, still a good two days' ride from her destination. Also, because she'd made the foolish mistake of stealing a good horse off the Main Street in Del Norte in broad daylight, she likely had a man or men following her, wishing her great harm, indeed.

Or time in prison, which was one and the same, to her way of thinking.

Crestfallen, she set down the war bag, removed her sombrero, hooked it over an arm of the chair, then glanced toward the sparse chinking between the logs. Dr. Bartlett still sat with his back to the cabin, humming to himself while he cleaned Ol' Rufus.

Oh well, Mathilda thought as she began unbuttoning her blouse. Maybe she'd set out on foot first thing in the morning and meet some other unsuspecting man along the trail. A man with a good mount she could take—a man who would give her no qualms about sticking that rusty knife in his guts or popping a .32-round through his brain plate.

How god-awful was guilt! She'd never realized it before. But then, she'd so rarely had occasion to.

Keeping her back to the door and the front of the cabin, she finished undressing then pinned up her hair. Holding one arm across her breasts, she hooked her skirt and chemise over the other arm of the chair. She glanced once more to peer through the loose chinking. Bartlett was still humming while cleaning the shotgun. Mathilda felt comfortable enough now to remove her arm from her breasts and to stick one toe in the water.

"Ahh," she said, her full lips pulling back from her teeth.

Just right.

She turned to face the cabin then stepped into the tub. She wanted to face forward to keep an eye on the door. After all, it was not only Bartlett she had to be cautious of, but any man or men riding up to the cabin from the main trail. She'd set the war bag containing the guns and the knife close against the tub's right side, within an easy reach.

Dr. Bartlett had provided a cake of lye soap on the seat of the chair. Mathilda sank deep into the tub. She washed her face first then soaked everything else. She took the soap and began rubbing it over her body—under and down each arm, up over her bosoms, across her belly, down and up each leg as she lifted each well-turned limb up out of the water, bent at the knee, the water making a musical splashing sound to enhance the rare feeling of serenity the girl felt, all wet and soaped, the grit and grime peeling off her fine, olive-hued skin in layers.

She set her right foot back down in the water and dropped her rump to the bottom of the tub, letting the sudsy hot water wash over every inch of her body below her neck. She set the soap on the seat of the chair then rested back against the tub, arms draped over its sides, and closed her eyes, giving a long, luxurious sigh.

A creaking sound rose.

She opened her eyes only halfway. She peered through the loose chinking between the logs.

Dr. Bartlett was no longer sitting in the chair.

She glanced to the left. Her heart thudded; her lower jaw dropped in shock.

There was a knot the size of a marble roughly halfway down the door, a foot to the right of the metal latch. The knot was filled with a marble-like, wide, gray-blue, unblinking eye.

"Mierda!" she cried, slapping her hands to the side of the tub then heaving herself to her feet.

She'd just started to reach for the war bag when a strangling sound rose from the other side of the door.

She'd placed her right arm over her breasts, and now, straightening, she cast her puzzled look toward the door again.

The eye appeared even wider than before, white ringed and bloodshot.

The strangling sound grew louder.

"What the...?"

Her frown grew more severe. It sounded as though Dr. Bartlett was choking out there.

The eye pulled slightly away from the knot, jostling a little as the lusty old coot fought for balance. There could be no doubt about what the old man, seemingly strangling on his own tongue, was staring at.

A wolfish grin crooked Mathilda's mouth corners.

"I see," she said as the strangling sounds on the other side of the door grew louder. Slowly, she lowered her arm from her breasts. "Go ahead, and take a good long look, amigo. Choke on them!"

A loud wheezing sound replaced the strangling sound and the eye pulled back away from the knot. Then it was gone. There was the sound of a body striking the ground.

Frowning incredulously, Mathilda stepped out of the tub and onto the braided rug. She picked up one of the two towels on the chair and wrapped it around her long, fine, high-busted body. She crouched to pick up one of the Merwin .32s from the war bag, cocked it, and walked to the door. She opened the door and stepped out. She stared down at Dr. Bartlett sprawled half on and half off the stoop, arms and legs spread wide. Both eyes stared up in shock.

He wasn't moving but his eyes and mouth still formed an amazed half smile.

Dead.

Mathilda gave a wry chuff and depressed the

Merwin's hammer. She lowered the gun to her side. Still staring down at the so-called doctor, she said, "*Esa es una forma de despellejar a un gato.*"

That's one way to skin a cat.

AT THE SAME TIME, MARSHAL JOE MANNION STEPPED down from Red's back, thumbed his Stetson up off his forehead, dropped to a knee, and looked around closely at the ground where a secondary trail forked off of the main one.

"Hard to tell for sure," he said, "the ground being so rocky, but I'd say whoever picked our girl up in that wagon turned off here."

Roughly a mile back, he and Stringbean had spied the place on the trail where the tracks of a wagon had intersected those of the girl's sorrel, which, judging by tracks farther on down the pass, had gradually been growing lame for a good half a mile. Mannion had seen where the prints of two people mingled with those of two mounts and the wagon and had deemed that whoever was driving the wagon had rescued the girl and Wayne Ellison's sorrel.

He'd caught a devil by the tail, in other words. Lord only knew what the poor fool was going through at this very moment...

"Say, I know this place," Stringbean said, glancing on up the secondary two-track. I was hunting up here one summer with Wendell Craven from the Bar-V back when I was still breaking broncs. We got stuck in a storm and followed this trail, hoping to find shelter. We sure enough did. There's a little shack a little ways up that trail, likely built by some old prospector or mountain man. It was long abandoned but still tight, last time I was there."

"Hmm." Joe raked a gloved thumb down the long line of his jaw carpeted in two days' growth of gray-brown beard stubble, contemplating the secondary trail well-shaded by overhanging pines and aspens. "Well, looks like it's not so abandoned anymore." He pulled his hat down lower on his head and stepped back into the saddle.

"Let's give it a look-see."

Mannion swung Red onto the secondary trail, and Stringbean fell in behind him on his coyote dun. After ten minutes of slow, cautious walking, the two lawmen stopped their horses, swung down from their saddles, and tied the mounts to shrubs alongside the trail. The trail appeared to curve around to the left roughly a hundred feet beyond. Mannion and his deputy climbed the wooded rise off the trail's left side.

At the top of the rise, they moved forward and down a gradual declivity until a clearing opened before them. They dropped to knees behind a single broad aspen and peered down at the humble cabin flanked by an old, lean-to stable and falling-down corral. A wagon was parked outside the corral.

"Ahh," Joe said quietly, recognizing the wagon.

He also recognized the handsome sorrel standing nose to tail beside a big mule, which he also recognized, inside the corral.

"What is it?" Stringbean whispered to the lawman kneeling to his right.

Leaning forward against his 1866 Yellowboy Winchester repeater, which he held butt down against the ground, Mannion turned to Stringbean. "That rig belongs to a fella calls himself Doctor J. Felix Bartlett. He's no more a sawbones than I am. Nor a preacher. And the only thing that's in his liver tonic is laudanum and gunpowder. After a few swills of that, if you light a cigar, you'd likely blow your head plum off your shoulders."

"Wonder why I ain't never seen him."

"You were probably sleeping in."

As Mannion's junior deputy, Stringbean usually took the night shift before being relieved by Mannion's senior and only other deputy, Rio Waite. At least, that's how it *had been* before Mannion had hired Cletus Booker, who'd worked for Forsythe Town Marshal Curt Bishop until Booker, a bit of a head breaker, got crossways with a few of the businessmen up Forsythe way.

Bishop had to cut the deputy loose. Mannion had hired him pronto. He didn't mind head breakers. Hell, he was a head breaker himself. And, with Del Norte growing as quickly as it was and with two warring railroads pulling into town, he badly needed more help.

Head breakers, especially.

Cletus Booker was just the ticket. He was back in Del Norte now, helping Rio Waite keep a lid on the place.

Mannion continued with: "The so-called Doctor Bartlett sells his tonic and preaches a few words to the suckers dumb enough to fall for his ploy and then moves on. He knows I don't want him hanging around long. Con men have a way of getting found out, and trouble usually ensues. I've seen enough of them tarred and feathered. Besides, I have a soft spot for old Bartlett. He ran a grog shop back in Abilene when I was deputy marshal. He throws his heart and soul into his cons—I'll give him that. Hard to fault a con man who's that good of an actor—so good I swear he half believes the con himself. Picks pockets clean without even sticking his hand in."

Mannion chuckled. He sobered when, raking the

clearing with his gaze, he saw what appeared to be a body lying out front of the cabin's closed door. "Oh-oh."

"What is it?"

"Take a look at the stoop in front of the door there. I do believe the good doctor has come to his Waterloo...in the shapely form of Señorita Calderon."

Stringbean followed his boss's gaze, squinting.

He whistled softly.

"Do believe you might be right, Marshal."

Mannion grimaced, hardening his jaws. He rose and began moving slowly down the decline toward the yard opening below. As he did, he could hear someone singing inside the cabin.

Sounded female. Sounded like Spanish.

Be careful, Joe, he told himself. *She might be a girl but like the U.S. marshal out of Arizona said, she's a wolf in sheep's clothing...er, in that of a pretty señorita.*

That made her even more deadly.

CHAPTER 5

THE SINGING INSIDE THE CABIN GREW LOUDER AS Mannion and Stringbean descended the slope, wending their way around cedars, pines, and aspens. They'd each removed their spurs before leaving their horses, so they moved relatively quietly into the yard of the small cabin, keeping the cabin between them and the small stable flanking it, so neither the sorrel nor the mule would give away the interlopers' presence.

Fortunately, the stable was upwind of the cabin.

Just as fortunately, the shutters were closed over the cabin's two front windows.

Mannion and Stringbean stopped behind a small cedar that was roughly a hundred feet from the cabin. Joe could clearly see that the gent lying belly up in front of the door was indeed Felix Bartlett. She'd probably killed him so she could switch her lame sorrel for the man's mule.

Cold-blooded.

The girl was still singing. Her singing was accompanied by the intermittent sounds of gently splashing water.

Taking her time with her bath with Bartlett lying dead only a few feet away.

Yep, cold-blooded.

"There a back door to this place?" Joe asked his deputy, keeping his voice low.

"Not that I recollect—no, sir."

"All right, then. Let's go in and get her."

"Just like that?"

Mannion shrugged a shoulder. "Why not? She's bathing. Seems to be right enjoying herself. We'll surprise her, throw the cuffs on her."

"You don't think we oughta...give her a chance to get dressed. I mean, if she's bathing, she's..."

"Naked?"

Stringbean ran his tongue along the underside of his upper lip, atop which he was trying to grow a mustache with little success. It was a fine layer of red-blond down. "Uh, well...yes, sir."

Mannion chuckled. "I commend you on your gallantry, Deputy, but we got a job to do. Now, get focused. We can't underestimate this gal. She killed old Bartlett. She might be soaking in that tub, but we have to tread carefully. She's likely got a gun close. Our orders are to bring her in alive, but let's do it in such a way we don't get *ourselves* beefed."

Stringbean drew his mouth corners down and nodded. "Reckon you're right, Marshal."

"Stay focused, move slow, and be quiet. Real quiet. Apache quiet."

"Apache quiet. You got it."

"You head for the left side of the door. I'll take the right."

Again, Stringbean nodded.

Mannion stepped out from behind the cedar, angling right. Stringbean stepped out from behind the cedar, angling left. They moved slowly, purposely toward the front of the cabin. Inside, the girl was still singing casually, sonorously, dreamily...really enjoying herself.

Mannion stepped around old Felix Bartlett, who lay flat on his back, arms and legs spread wide, as though the poor old sot had been dropped from the sky. Joe would be damned if the old con artist didn't appear to have a sort of smile quirking his mouth and even showing in his otherwise dead gaze.

Stay focused, Mannion, the marshal reminded himself.

Don't underestimate this gal, which is obviously what old Bartlett had done.

Odd, though. Bartlett didn't appear to have a mark on him...

Mannion stepped up to the cabin, right of the door. He put his back up against the age-silvered logs. On the other side of the door, Stringbean did the same.

Inside, the girl was still singing.

Mannion locked meaningful gazes with Stringbean. He stepped in front of the door and, holding the Yellowboy up high across his chest, raised his right knee. He had just started to thrust the flat of his foot forward, toward the door, when he realized that while the girl was still singing, he hadn't heard any splashing for a while.

It was too late to stop the kick.

As it connected with the door, just right of the latch, the door flew inward to reveal the girl standing naked before him, seven feet away, aiming a long, double-barreled shotgun out from her right side. Yep, as naked as the day she was born but a whole lot better filled out. Her lips stopped moving, and the ballad she'd been singing in Spanish fell silent.

A jeering smile touched her full, red lips.

Joe flung himself hard to his right.

Both shotgun barrels blossomed red.

The explosion rocked the whole cabin and made the ground beneath Mannion's feet pitch just as he left them, feeling the tooth-gnashing sting of buckshot pellets ripping into his left arm. He struck the ground on his right side and rolled onto his back, half sitting up. Stringbean stared down at him in hang-jawed shock, holding his own repeater straight up and down in his gloved hands.

"Get that catamount!" Mannion bellowed, hardening his jaws and squeezing his bloody left arm with his right hand.

Stringbean turned his head to look into the cabin. His eyes widened as he said to Mannion, "Yep, she's buck naked, all right!"

It had done the trick, too, Mannion was afraid to say. He'd never seen a pretty, dark-haired, dark-eyed beauty wielding a shotgun naked before. She'd figured on that, as most ringtails of her stripe would. She'd known that would make any man hesitate. It had, all right. Hell, despite his orders to take her alive so she could testify at the trial in Tucson, he would have shot her to save his and his deputy's lives but seeing her in there...in her condition...naked and wielding a shotgun as well as a cat-like grin...had made him damn near swallow his tongue.

Now, he shouted, "That didn't keep her from damn near blowing a hole in me big enough to drive a train through! *Get her!*"

Stringbean hesitated only half a second more then ran into the cabin, shouting, "Hold it right there, Miss! Don't you dare pick that up or I'll...I'll—"

He was cut off by the girl's shrill scream.

There was a hard thud as though of a gun striking a table.

She screamed again. There was a clattering thud, and Mannion knew Stringbean had dropped his carbine. Loud grunts and the sound of a violent skirmish.

Stringbean yelled in a strangled voice, "Oh, no you don't—get back here, you—"

She screamed again and cut loose with a spew of Spanish and then Stringbean and the woman came out of the cabin together, Stringbean holding her up off the ground from behind while she kicked and punched at him, making sounds like those of a she-cat caught in a leg trap.

Her hair danced and flew around both their heads, sliding between Stringbean's lips.

"You were right—she's a wild one, that's for sure, Marshal!" Stringbean yelled.

He tripped over the so-called Dr. Bartlett sprawled dead before the door, and he and the girl fell in a pile, the girl giving another scream as she struck the ground and rolled.

"Throw your cuffs on her, Stringbean!" Mannion yelled, half sitting up against the cabin wall, clutching his bloody left arm and gritting his teeth against the searing pain.

"Easier said than done, Marshal!" Stringbean said as he grabbed one of the girl's ankles as she started to rise.

That tripped her. She went face down with another wild yell.

Stringbean gained his feet and faced her, hatless now, his hair hanging down over his ears and in his eyes. He held his head a little to one side as though trying not to look at her, since she was naked and all. He jutted a commanding finger at her and said, "Now, you just hold it right there, Miss. You're under arrest and there ain't no ifs, ands, or buts—*oafffhahhhh!*" he bellowed as one of her bare feet shot up to connect with the young deputy's groin.

Stringbean gave another strangled wail as he jack-knifed, thrusting his arms between his legs, and dropped to his knees. "Oh, Lordy!"

She stomped past him, fuming, heading for the cabin.

Stringbean reached out and grabbed her left ankle, tripping her again.

"*Mierda!*" she cursed and struck the ground on her belly.

Lightning quick, she was back on her feet. This time she had a length of split cordwood in her right hand. Stringbean was gaining his feet, his face a bright-red mask of agony. "Hey!" he yelled as she laid into him with the stove wood.

He managed to get one arm up to stave off the full force of the blows, but she still laid into him pretty good, delivering two glancing blows to his head, causing him to stagger backward on the heels of his undershot boots.

"*Stupid lousy bastardo son of a puta mother who was nothing but a low-down dirty gringo whore!*" she shrieked at him, leaning forward at her waist, one arm over her breasts.

She swung around sharply and stopped suddenly, Spanish black eyes widening in shock. Mannion pressed the barrel of one of his two silver-chased, walnut-gripped, .44-caliber, top-break Russian revolvers against her forehead, and clicked the hammer back. He narrowed one of his hawkish, gray eyes and said with even, quiet menace, "Stand down, señorita, or I *will* drill a hole through your head, pretty as it is."

She looked up at the revolver's long barrel.

Then she followed the man's wrist and arm, clad in dark-brown corduroy under a black leather vest, to his eyes shaded by the broad brim of his high-crowned black Stetson that contrasted sharply with the long, liberally silver-streaked, dark-brown hair hanging down from the hat to brush his broad shoulders.

She flared a nostril and lifted her chin in noble defiance and announced, "I would rather die with a bullet in my head than be raped by you two curs. So go ahead. Finish me now and do what you will to my corpse!"

"We're not gonna rape you. Feel like tanning your purty behind over my knee, but we're not gonna rape you." Mannion brushed his left hand, smeared red from the blood running down the inside of his shirt from the dozen or more shotgun pellets lodged in his upper arm and elbow, across the silver, five-pointed star pinned to his shirt and peeking out from behind the vest. "Joe Mannion, Del Norte town marshal with a deputy sheriff's commission, which gives me jurisdiction out here in the high-and-rocky. You're under arrest for aiding and abetting a known criminal—namely, Diego Hidalgo—after he and his gang of desperado *revolutionarios* wiped out an army contingent and stole the three Gatling guns the soldiers were transporting across the Arizona desert, north of the border. You aided and abetted him, all right, and you likely know what he did with those Gatling guns after he left your rancho. That's what the U.S. marshal wants you to palaver about at Hidalgo's trial in Tucson. You give him the information he wants, you'll be released. Otherwise, you'll go to prison. We aim to make sure you get to Tucson...unless you want a bullet in your head, instead."

Mannion hardened his jaws and pressed the barrel of the Russian a little more firmly against her forehead.

"Make up your mind. I'm not in the mood for any more nonsense."

"To testify against Diego Hidalgo is a death sentence, so you might as well kill me here!" she barked out at Mannion, dark eyes flashing in the midday, high-country light.

"Have it your way," Mannion said.

He tightened his index finger against the Russian's trigger.

She saw the move and wrinkled the skin above the bridge of her nose. Fear touched her eyes. Her lips parted but she studied Mannion's eyes in silence, a gambler trying to read her opponent.

Her eyes widened and her lips continued to part as she continued to study Mannion and apparently decided she didn't like what she saw there. "All right," she said finally. She crossed her arms over her breasts; defiance still shone in her eyes. "Have it your way."

Mannion depressed the Russian's hammer and lowered the revolver to his side. "Let's go inside and get you dressed." He stepped to one side and turned to Stringbean who stood bent forward at the waist, hands on his knees. He was looking up at Mannion, pain still showing in his eyes.

"How you doin', kid?"

Stringbean gave his head a single shake. "She got me good."

"How many guns inside?"

"I saw two...then again, I didn't have much time to get a thorough look around." Stringbean glowered, shook his head again, and dropped his chin to stare at the ground, waiting for the agony to pass.

It would take a while. Like the kid had said, she'd gotten him good. Mannion could feel that kick himself.

He turned to the girl who was sneering at him, nostrils flared, both arms crossed on her breasts, one knee bent over the other. Her hair had tumbled down from the top of her head to hang in pretty tangles, half concealing her face.

"Inside, señorita. Nice an' slow..."

CHAPTER 6

MANNION SENT STRINGBEAN FOR THE HORSES.

The kid didn't look well. Joe wasn't sure if it was because of the groining the señorita from hell had given him or the fact he hadn't been able to subdue her.

Maybe both.

Unlike himself, Stringbean was the sensitive sort. Or unlike the way Mannion *used to* be. He wasn't sure how he was or was not anymore, and he wasn't sure how much, if anything, that it had to do with the former preacher, Ezekial Storm, having laid hands on him a few months back, pulling him back from the dead and damn near healing his broken body almost overnight.

That still haunted Joe. He'd never thought about men having or not having souls before. He'd been too busy with the things of this world to think about such impractical nonsense. But Storm had made him start wondering if he had one—a soul—until Storm had joined forces with some dark being, specter, maybe a ghost, something not of this world, anyway...to pull Joe back from death and set him back on the killing trail.

At the cost of the soul he'd never thought much

about having until that crazy time he'd hunted the killer, Frank Lord, who'd murdered one of Mannion's few friends, Jeremiah Claggett, town constable of the nearby ghost town of Fury.

Could you have a soul and not know it and then lose it and feel empty...changed...without it? To feel a darkness at the periphery of your being for having had it plucked out and tendered like cash in exchange for your life?

"Stop staring at me," the girl said.

That snapped Mannion out of his reverie. He'd been cleaning his arm over a bowl of steaming water at Felix Bartlett's kitchen table, having cut off the bloody sleeve with his bowie knife.

"I wasn't staring," he said, averting his gaze. "Leastways, at nothing save your hands." He'd thrown all the weapons he'd found in the cabin out into the brush, but he wasn't taking any chances. Not with this little catamount.

"You were, too." She'd stepped into her skirt and had donned a thin, silk chemise and was now shaking a white blouse out before her, an angry scowl furling her brows. "I saw you staring at me like a randy old dog."

Mannion gave a dry chuckle and went back to gently swabbing the nasty little holes that had been torn in his arm by the girl and Bartlett's shotgun. "A man with an arm this sore doesn't stare at anyone like a randy old dog. Besides, I have a daughter only a little younger than you."

"So?"

"It matters."

He wasn't sure how, but it did. Not that he felt any fatherly sense of protection for this insufferable little hellion. But he sure didn't feel any attraction to her. Girls her age might be easy on the eyes, but they were no longer targets of his lust. Of course, that might have something to do with how his daughter, Vangie, had been so badly savaged by Whip Helton, the now-dead firebrand son of a once high-and-mighty, local rancher. It was hard to look at a girl Vangie's age and not think of what had happened to her. The physical and mental torment. The desecration of her innocence. Thank God for her horses. They'd pulled her through.

Her horses and Jane—who was gone now because of him.

"Ouch, *goddammit!*" he groaned now as he used the tip of his bowie to work a pellet out of his left arm, just above the elbow.

"Serves you right!" the girl said, buttoning her blouse. "If you send me to testify against Diego, he will kill me slowly. If I utter one word about anything he did, he will kill me slowly and enjoy hearing me howl!"

"He's in jail."

"No jail can hold Diego. And if not him, he will have his men do it. Maybe his first lieutenant, Manuel San Jacinto. He would love to have a good, long go at me, make me really suffer while he enjoyed himself."

"Nice fella, this guy you threw in with. Sounds like true love." Joe laughed dryly.

"Go to hell," she said, throwing her arms out for balance as she stepped into a boot. She swung toward him angrily. "What would you know about it?"

"Damned little—you're right." Mannion groaned again as he used the knife to lever out another pellet. It dropped onto the wooden table, bounced, and rolled. He looked at her staring at him from near the tub full of now-cold water. He kicked out a chair on the far side of the table. "Have a seat."

She flared a nostril, shook her hair back, and sat down.

"Give me your hands."

"What?"

"Give me your hands."

"Why?"

Mannion pulled a set of handcuffs out of a pocket of the corduroy jacket hanging from the back of the chair to his left.

She scowled and pulled her hands down off the table, crossed her arms over her breasts. "I will not be cuffed."

"Hands on the table or I'll throw you down and hog-tie you!"

Her face and eyes pinched up most unbeautifully. "You're a gringo pig! I hate you!"

She slid her hands across the table.

Mannion closed the bracelets around each slender wrist in turn.

"You move fast for an old man," she snapped out. "Otherwise, I would have shredded your heart!"

"Otherwise, you would have," Mannion had to admit.

He'd found a roll of relatively clean felt in an army footlocker under Bartlett's bed, which also contained other medical supplies including a small, flat bottle of whiskey. He picked up the bottle and popped the cork.

She smiled mockingly. "Got an eyeful, didn't you?"

He held his bare, wounded arm over the washbasin and poured whiskey over it.

The pain bit him like a wild dog with razor-edged canines. He sucked sharply through gritted teeth.

"Did you like what you saw?"

"Honey, this is not the time to be fishing around for compliments," Mannion raked out, voice pinched with pain against the fire in his arm.

She leaned across the table, her cuffed hands on the table before her, and gave a slow, coquettish blink of her eyes. "Free me, and I will make you feel better, uh? Before the skinny one returns!"

"You must think I'm even dumber than I look," Mannion laughed.

She pounded the table with the ends of her cuffed fists. "Dog!"

She glanced at the bowie knife resting across the side of the washbasin. A furtive cunning shown in her eyes. Mannion was wrapping the felt around his pellet-torn upper arm. He'd caught the girl's glance at the knife. He sighed, paused in his work to pluck the bowie off the washbasin and set it down close to him at the edge of the table.

She sat back in her chair and flared her nostrils at him. "You are a gringo pig!"

Mannion awkwardly knotted the felt with one hand. "You're soon going to run out of animals."

He frowned as he turned to where Stringbean had wrapped old Bartlett in a blanket from the cabin's only cot and laid him on the stoop in front of the door. They'd haul the old con artist to Del Norte and have him buried on Boot Hill. He was the sort who'd like company on that long, quiet ride through the ages. Besides, Mannion didn't want to take time to bury him, or take the time for Stringbean to bury him. He couldn't do it because of the arm.

He turned to the girl, frowning curiously. "What'd you do to the good doctor there, anyway? I didn't see a mark on him."

Mathilda smiled snootily. "Let's just say he got an eyeful and liked what he saw."

Her smile turned cold.

"Well, that's one way to skin a cat," Joe said.

———

"WHAT THE HELL'S THE MATTER, STRINGBEAN?" JOE asked his junior deputy as they rode back along the shaded trail through the pines toward the main road.

Mannion and the girl were riding double. They'd left her...er, *Wayne Ellison's*...red-copper sorrel in Bartlett's stable. They'd send Ellison out for the mount once they reached Del Norte. With a little doctoring, the horse would be good in a week or two. The girl rode with her hands cuffed behind her back. Stringbean was leading Bartlett's mule, the good doctor himself riding belly down across the big animal's broad back, hands loosely tied to his ankles so the blanket-wrapped corpse wouldn't fall off and add insult to injury, as it were.

Mannion glanced back at the girl riding behind him, chin down, black eyes on him, coldly staring. There was a perpetual fierceness to her gaze. He turned to Stringbean riding his coyote dun to Mannion's right. The kid still had a sour look.

Stringbean hadn't ventured a reply to his question, so Mannion repeated it, more or less. "You look two days off your feed and only buck brush in the crib. Come on—out with it, kid."

Stringbean sighed and kept his gaze straight ahead along the sun-dappled trail. "I messed up again. Played the fool."

"What're you talking about?"

"Leastways, I didn't run." Stringbean was referring to how he'd once run when the posse he'd been leading after bank robbers and killers had been ambushed. He glanced over his shoulder at the girl then turned his sour expression back forward, staring at the trail over his dun's twitching ears. "But I let her get the best of me. Her, just a girl."

"Just a girl, eh, amigo?" La Stiletta said in her snotty way. "You're just a boy. A man-child."

"Shut up, Princess," Mannion said.

"What kind of a man is called Stringbean?" the girl said with a sneer at Stringbean's back.

Mannion glanced at his deputy. Stringbean wasn't taking her jeering well at all. The deputy rode stiffly in his saddle, chin down, staring straight ahead, cheeks dimpling where his jaws hinged.

"You did fine," Mannion said.

"She caught me off guard!"

Joe laughed. "Hell, she caught *me* off guard!" He winced as he raised his wounded wing, which was still barking under the sleeve of his corduroy jacket. "Some women...well, they're like witches." He glanced over his shoulder at the girl who was smiling with great satisfaction at him. "They catch you off guard. So, you lay the law down on 'em. Now she's cuffed and tied." He turned to Stringbean again. "You'll do better next time. We *both* will."

"I was a damn fool about it. Should not have hesitated. Should have knocked her down and thrown the cuffs on her like you said!"

"You were hurting too bad," the girl said, smiling. "And your eyes were having too much fun."

"I told you to shut up, Princess."

"I don't take orders from old men!"

Mannion wasn't sure why that tickled his funny bone, but it did. He threw his head back, laughing. "Oh, the federals are gonna have a fine time with you, honey!"

"*What* federals?"

"The federals the U.S. marshal for the southwestern district will likely send north to fetch you and give me and my deputy here—"

"*String-bean*," she said, with a delighted glare at the deputy's slender back.

"—some badly needed relief. Only known you an hour but it feels like a lifetime."

"It was pure luck that you caught me. You know that —don't you, old man?"

"Oh, I always get my man...er, *girl*," Mannion said, casting a jeering smile of his own over his right shoulder at the ring-tailed polecat behind him.

"The federals will never get me to Tucson," she said, her tone bitter now.

"They'll do just fine."

"Diego's men will rescue me. And they will die *slowly*."

Her tone was so menacing that Stringbean turned to his boss, darkly frowning. Mannion smiled and gave a dismissive shrug. "She's just being a dramatic chili pepper," he explained.

"Si," she said in the same bitter tone. "We will see how dramatic I am being when Manuel San Jacinto gets his hands on those federales. They'd better send a dozen or they won't have a chance!"

Mannion chuckled as he glanced at Stringbean. "She's exaggerating."

They'd just leveled out at the bottom of Cottonwood Pass. Behind them on the forested pass rose the rumbling of many hooves and the pistol-like cracks of a whip.

Mannion stopped Red and curveted the mount to stare up through the pines. He spied shadowy movement in the trees roughly a hundred yards up the pale, two-track trail and glanced at Stringbean. "Here comes the

Wednesday stage. We'll hop it, make better time that way. Should be home by nightfall."

He'd be relieved as hell to get the señorita from hell in a cage, the rest of the pellets dug out of his arm, and a bottle of pain-relieving busthead down his craw.

He did not, however, look forward to going to bed without Jane.

What a damn fool he'd been to have messed up his life this way.

CHAPTER 7

MANNION HELD UP HIS RIGHT HAND AS THE STAGE, pulled by a six-horse hitch, swung around a curve in the switch-backing trail and thundered down out of the pines, the team straightening out and the carriage falling into line behind it, a great, tan-colored dust cloud billowing up around it.

"Whoahh!" yelled the jehu, Lyle Horton, leaning back against his seat and planting his boots on the dashboard as he pulled back on the ribbons in his gloved hands. "*Whoahh! Whoahh! Whoahh, ya mangy cay-ooses!*"

Sitting to Horton's left, the shotgun messenger, his face hidden by a green bandanna with white polka dots drawn up over his nose, straightened in his seat, taking the nasty-looking, sawed-off, double-barreled Richards coach gun in both his gloved hands and angling his right index finger through the trigger guard.

Mannion couldn't see either face clearly, for the jehu wore a bandanna up over his mouth and nose as well, but he saw the recognition in both men's eyes as the stage came on down the rise, slowing, the team digging their heels in, skidding, the carriage rocking on its leather thoroughbraces, before halting roughly fifty feet from Mannion, Stringbean, and their female charge riding double with Mannion on Red's back.

The shotgun guard opened and closed his hands around the gut shredder, then smiled as he pulled his bandanna down beneath his chin. The jehu pulled his own bandanna down from his wedge-shaped nose that had a big, dark mole bristling from its right side. A straggly, colorless beard hung nearly halfway down his chest. Horton took the ribbons in one hand, set the brake with the other hand with a grunt, then glanced at the dead man riding over the mule's back before turning to Mannion with a lopsided grin.

"Well, well—if it ain't Bloody Joe his own nasty self," he said, glancing at the shotgunner riding to his right and whose name was Magnus Haroldson and who looked just like you'd think a Magnus Haroldson would look—blond, craggy-faced, his hard-bitten features sun seared, and with frosty gray eyes that bore holes right through you. "And he's got himself some fresh beef, looks like."

The driver canted his head a little to one side, scrutinizing the pretty face of La Stiletta peeking up from behind Mannion's right shoulder. "And a purty girl... Er, *señor-ita*...?"

True to character, the "purty señorita" told the middle-aged, bearded, brown-eyed jehu to perform a physically impossible maneuver.

"And a foul-mouthed one at that!" Horton said to his longtime, shotgun messenger partner, Haroldson, slapping a gloved right hand to his right thigh.

Both men laughed.

"You got room for the three of us, Lyle?" Mannion

glanced toward the mule standing on the trail behind Stringbean's dun. "Er...*four*. The good doctor won't mind riding up top as long as we strap him down so he don't roll off."

Horton pinched up his face. So did Haroldson, but the big Norwegian characteristically let his longtime partner do the talking. "Doctor?"

"So-called," Mannion said. "Bartlett."

"Ah, shit!" Horton spat chaw down the side of the carriage to his left, grazing the iron-shoed front wheel, and brushed the back of his gloved, right hand across his bearded mouth. "He took the deep dive, did he?"

"Reckon so."

"How?"

Mannion cut his eyes to the girl behind him. "Let's not waste time on details. You got room or not?"

"I got two ladies in the coach. I mean, *ladies*." Horton stuck his arm and pointing finger straight out from his right shoulder at La Stiletta. "Her tongue may not be welcome."

As if on cue, two picture-hatted countenances poked out from windows on either side of the stage, gloved hands holding hats on the immaculately coifed, middle-aged heads. Eyes wide with incredulity.

Mannion glanced at the girl. She sneered over his right shoulder at him. "Can you hold your tongue, or do I have to cut it out? Which I *will* do. That's how bad my arm hurts."

La Stiletta wrinkled her nose at him but said nothing.

Mannion glanced at Stringbean then swung down from the leather. In minutes, he and his deputy had unsaddled both his and Mannion's mounts and the mule, set the saddles and the good doctor's body on the brass-railed top of the stage, and seated themselves in the coach with one rat-faced drummer in a cheap, checked suit, a mustached cowboy in a red shirt and cream Stetson, and the two picture-hatted ladies—one in frilly pink, the other in frilly lime green.

They were big women, probably sisters, and they couldn't stop frowning at Mannion, his beautiful but surly-looking Mexican charge, and his reedy, raggedy-heeled deputy with the soot-smudge mustache. Mannion and La Stiletta sat facing front, Mannion on the right side near the door, Mathilda Calderon between him and the rat-faced drummer, who kept his lewd gaze on the prisoner.

His goatish smile revealed a missing front tooth.

The cowboy and the two picture-hatted ladies sat facing Mannion, Mathilda, and the rat-faced drummer, to the right of Stringbean, who still looked a good two or three days off his feed and facing the prospect of a crib full of foxtails. Mannion had cuffed his prisoner's hands in front of her. She sat with an indignant scowl on her pretty, heart-shaped face.

The cowboy, who sat directly across from Joe, sat looking at her without expression.

Mannion and Stringbean let their horses and the mule run free behind the stage. Not wanting to be far from their riders, Red and the coyote dun would keep up. Whether the mule did or not was anyone's guess, but Mannion guessed the mule would keep up. Mules were as social as horses and wouldn't want to be left behind, especially knowing its owner, albeit dead, was riding for free on the roof.

Lyle Horton hoorahed his team and cracked his blacksnake over their backs, and the carriage rocked and lunged forward, heading off along the graded trail across the Taylor Valley threaded by the Taylor River curving through its deep bed off the trail's right side. The two picture-hatted biddies gave Mannion and his savagely lovely charge the woolly eyeball.

The one in pink said, "Good Lord—how dare you transport a prisoner of her...of her obvious *ilk*...on a stage of otherwise God-fearing folk." She glanced at La Stiletta's well-filled blouse, rolled her eyes, wagged her head, and clucked her disapproval.

The one in lime green said primly, "For my letter of complaint, which I intend to send to the stage line, I'll be needing your name, Marshal..."

"Mannion." The cowboy grinned knowingly at Joe. "Bloody Joe Mannion." He glanced at the ladies riding beside him on his right. "And me..." He shrugged a shoulder and cast his cool-eyed glance at Mannion's prisoner. "I don't mind a bit. Imagine findin' myself on the same stage as *La Stiletta* her own purty self."

He grinned more broadly, and his own lusty gaze found the señorita's irresistible blouse.

La Stiletta turned to him and canted her head toward her jailor. "Kill him for me. I'll make it worth your time, amigo." She smiled.

The two old biddies gasped and covered their mouths.

Stringbean turned his hang-jawed gaze to his boss.

Mannion looked at the cowboy, whose smile had tightened considerably, a flush rising in his cheeks above his mustache.

The rat-faced drummer turned to Mannion then, too, his own eyes widening with apprehension.

Mannion looked at the horn-gripped, .45 Colt residing in the black leather holster riding high on the cowboy's right hip. As he did, the cowboy turned his taut smile to him.

"She's not worth dying for," Mannion said.

"See? See?" The pink-clad biddy's blue eyes widened and rounded in exasperation. "This is the very thing I was worried about! Why, if you two go to *swapping lead,* as the gaudy periodicals so colorfully call it, one of us *innocent bystanders* might very well catch a bad case of *lead poisoning!*"

"I wouldn't know," the cowboy said, sliding his taut smile to La Stiletta once more. "Never had the pleasure."

Again, the biddies gasped. La Stiletta stared at him as though he were something left by a dog on a boardwalk.

"Oh, you know," La Stiletta said, softly, huskily. "You know."

Again, the biddies gasped and turned exasperated gazes to each other.

The cowboy turned to Mannion again. "How you doin', Joe?"

"Same ol', same ol'," Mannion said, hiking a shoulder. "How 'bout you, Ed?"

It was the cowboy's turn to shrug. "Tumblin' tumbleweed. The Kitchen Sink got bought up by some Englishman. I hate Englishmen. Thought I'd look over Del Norte way."

"Max Lundeen's hiring," Mannion said. "From the Circle-Six."

"Lundeen, eh?" Ed Plummer slid his hand toward his right side.

Mannion stiffened a little, flexed his trigger finger.

In the periphery of his gaze, he saw Stringbean stiffen, too.

Plummer stuck his hand in the pocket of his blue denim jacket and pulled out a small pencil and a small, thin, pasteboard notebook so worn it resembled scrap leather. He opened the notebook, flipped through the pages until he found a clean leaf then moistened the pencil's tip with his tongue.

"Max Lundeen, eh?" he said.

"Max Lundeen," Mannion said.

"Max Lun-deen," Plummer said slowly, scowling as he scratched the pencil across the leaf before him. "Circle-Six." He tapped the pencil point against the page as though to punctuate the note. "Obliged."

He closed the notebook and returned it and the pencil to his pocket.

Smiling good-naturedly, he sank back in his seat.

He kept his gaze on Mannion.

The coach rocked and pitched on its thoroughbraces, bounced over potholes and stones. The passengers swayed and jerked with the coach's sometimes violent jostling.

Mannion kept his gaze on Plummer.

The others kept their gazes on Mannion and the cowboy. A sweat bead popped out on one side of the drummer's forehead and ran down through the two- or three-days' worth of ginger-gray beard stubble.

Mannion lowered his gaze from Plummer's face to the silver-chased gun on his right hip. When the man had returned the notebook and pencil to his pocket, he'd kept his hand there, casually draped over the handle of his gun, fingers curving down over the front of the holster. He had a gold ring with a square obsidian stone on the middle finger. The stone had a gold G etched in it.

While the cowboy had been fiddling with the pencil and notebook, Mannion had slowly slid his own hand down over the handle of the .44 Russian holstered on his own right side. He had it there now. The cowboy knew it.

He'd very subtly and fleetingly dropped his gaze in that direction. Now he sat, rocking with the coach, keeping his gaze on the lawman, that gaze gradually losing its good-natured smile.

Sitting to Mannion's left, her shoulder nudging his with the coach's rock and sway, La Stiletta, looking at the cowboy, said just loudly enough to be heard above the coach's steady clatter, "Like I said, I'll make it worth your time, amigo."

In the periphery of his vision, Mannion saw her shape a slow, alluring smile.

The two old biddies switched their gazes to the vixen then exchanged another round of scandalized glances.

Mannion heard a loud, high-pitched whistle out the stage to his left. Stringbean turned his head to stare out the window then jerked his wide, round eyes to Mannion.

"Trouble, boss!"

Mannion turned his head slightly to see three or four riders galloping down from a wooded ridge, heading on what appeared an interception course with the stage.

"More over there!" cried the drummer, pointing out the window on the coach's right side.

In the periphery of his vision, Mannion saw more riders galloping toward the stage on the opposite side of the trail from the others. He didn't take time to count them. He kept his gaze on Ed Plummer.

As if to validate Joe's suspicion about Plummer's change of occupations, the man's right hand moved in a blur of fast motion and pulled up the big .45 from the hard leather holster. Having anticipated the move as soon as he'd heard the whistle, Mannion's Russian was already in his hand. He jerked it straight out before him, clicking the hammer back.

The two biddies screamed as the Russian filled the

coach with ear-rattling thunder. Smoke and flames stabbed from the barrel, setting the front of Plummer's shirt on fire as the cowboy groaned and thumped back in his seat, firing his Colt into the coach floor, the bullet nipping the side of the drummer's left half boot.

The drummer yipped and jerked that foot up off the floor.

"Mierda!" La Stiletta bellowed, regarding the burning cowboy who slumped against the pink-clad biddy.

She cowered away from him, howling, trying to crawl on top of the green-clad biddy.

Outside, guns popped and the rumble of many horses rose.

A man shouted, "Rein in, Horton, or we'll blow you and your messenger out of the damn driver's boot!"

"Go to hell!" Horton shouted.

More pistols popped. A bullet tore into the side of the coach nearest the drummer, nicking his ear before cleaving a hole in the writhing, burning cowboy's forehead, ending the man's fiery torment. Plummer rolled off the seat onto the floor, the floor somewhat smothering the flames of his burning shirt, the smell of burning flesh mixing with the rotten-egg smell of cordite.

"Mierda!" the girl yelled again, staring down in revulsion at the smoking, dead cowboy lying belly down at her feet.

Mannion turned toward the window on his right then turned to Stringbean on the coach's opposite side. "It's a holdup—give 'em hell, kid!"

Mannion poked his Russian out the window on the coach's right side, lined up the sights on the jostling figure of a rider approaching from that side of the trail, and fired.

"Gotta feelin' this ain't gonna end well, boss!" String-

bean yelled as he fired out the door on the other side of
the coach.

"No!" Mannion watched his bullet only blow the hat
off the head of the man he'd been aiming at. "It never
does!"

CHAPTER 8

MANNION PULLED HIS HEAD BACK FROM THE WINDOW as the man he'd just left hatless shifted his attention, previously focused on the stage driver and shotgun messenger, to Joe himself. He swung a Winchester carbine around as he did, stretching his lips back from his teeth and levering a live round in the action.

The rifle thundered, flames stabbing.

The bullet smashed into the side of the window Mannion had fired out of; it caromed through the carriage and how it refrained from striking any of the flesh jostling around inside, Joe had no idea. It must have come close to the señorita, though, because she turned her fiery eyes to Mannion and cut loose with a string of Spanish invectives that sounded nothing so much as the Spanish opera he'd once heard in an opera house on the outskirts of Clyde, Oklahoma, when he'd first started cracking heads in his early years as a town tamer of growing renown.

The Spanish opera singer had had to fairly shout to be heard above the raucous din of the unruly mob who hadn't paid two bits to hear her sing but to see her tits gallblastit!

That's whom La Stiletta sounded like now, shouting at the tops of her lungs while glaring at Mannion, tossing her head so that her dark brown, curly tresses blew around her face, obscuring it, strands occasionally getting caught between her lips so that she had to spit them out while at the same time spitting more vitriol at the lawdog whom she blamed for putting her in this position—handcuffed and helpless in what was essentially a large matchbox getting honeycombed by the lead being slung by common gringo road agents.

And she, a beautiful Mexican princessa—La Stiletta herself—cloaked in her own brand of legendary notoriety down around the border country!

Leastways, that was what Joe assumed she was saying, though at the moment he had to admit he didn't have a whole lot of time to ponder on it, what with bullets being slung at him from both sides of the coach and him emptying one Russian as he returned fire and then quickly reached for the other. The driver wailed at his team, cracking the blacksnake over their backs, urging more and more speed. Joe thought they must be almost blown by now. The carriage was badly fishtailing in loose gravel and several times nearly slid off the trail and into a shallow ravine dropping sharply off his side of the carriage, in which three riders were racing along beside him, still flinging lead.

Joe poked his second Russian out the window, lined up his sights, and fired.

He grinned savagely as the lead rider threw his hands up, dropping his reins and the pistols in his hands, and rolled back over the arched tail of his galloping Steeldust stallion. One of the horses of the two riders galloping behind him kicked him in the head just after he'd struck the ground, spinning him violently. Both riders slowed their mounts and looked up at Mannion.

The one on the right, whose horse had kicked the man Joe had shot, stretched his lips back from his teeth and shouted something Joe couldn't hear above the din of guns still being fired on the opposite side of the stage and of the cursing messenger's thundering sawed-off, the pounding of the coach wheels and of the team itself. Both riders reined their horses sharply up out of the ravine, toward the trail, and then the coach sped on beyond them, heading down a gradual decline, which might help the fagged team.

Mannion looked past the still raging La Stiletta kneeling on the back of the no-longer-smoking, dead cowboy—the two biddies were cowering together in a corner while the drummer cowered in another corner, looking ashen—to Stringbean who was now firing his Winchester carbine out the window on his side of the coach.

"How many over there?" Mannion yelled.

Stringbean fired the Winchester and, racking another round into the action, cast a lopsided grin over his right shoulder at his boss. The wind was bending the brim of his tan Stetson. "Just got me one more—the second one I perforated. That leaves two more!"

"Don't get cocky, kid!" Mannion yelled. "There's two comin' up behind us. That leaves four!"

The "four" had just left the lawman's mouth when he felt something slam against the stage from behind. He frowned then turned to look out the window on his side of the stage. The ravine had disappeared and out across the rolling sagebrush now a riderless horse, reins bouncing along the ground to each side, angled away from the trail, galloping hard, snout raised, whinnying shrilly.

Riderless horse...

Mannion heard a thump on the coach roof. He looked up. There was another thump on the roof.

"Behind us!" the driver shouted.

Ah, shit!

Above Mannion, a gun crashed loudly—once, twice, three times.

He heard Lyle Horton and Magnus Haroldson groan loudly. A shadow dropped over the coach's left side. Another shadow dropped down over the coach's right side. The heavy thuds of bodies striking the ground rose beneath the coach's din. The big, brown Stetson of Lyle Horton blew up into Mannion's field of vision and then away on the wind.

Gritting his teeth and bellowing curses, Mannion grabbed his Winchester up off the forward-facing seat, pumped a cartridge into the action, aimed the long gun at the ceiling, and fired three rounds, each one a little forward of the last.

There was another groan and then the thump of a body striking the coach roof.

Mannion looked to his left as a black-mustached man in a long, black duster and red-and-white checked shirt and billowing green neckerchief dropped down from the top of the coach. The man hit the ground, bounced once, and rolled wildly off the side of the trail and into the brush.

"Ah, shit," Joe said, poking his head out the window on his side of the coach.

He saw the bodies of the driver and the shotgun messenger dwindle into the distance on each side of the trail, beyond the man Joe had just shot and who was still rolling into the mountain sage off the side of the trail, his black duster flapping like the wings of a fallen and desperately struggling crow.

"We're on a runaway!" Mannion yelled. "Stringbean, cover me!"

"What're you gonna do, Mar—"

Stringbean stopped. Mannion was already out the door on his side of the coach, leaping up to grab the brass rail on the roof with both his gloved hands. In all the commotion, he'd forgotten his wounded arm. He remembered it now and gave a wail of unadulterated agony.

The wind pushed against him.

He wailed again, gritting his teeth as steel claws of pain ground into his upper left arm. Despite the pain, unable to suppress it but to use it somehow, he hoisted himself up with both gloved hands. They slipped with every jolt and pitch of the coach, which, Mannion saw now as he peered forward, was angling off the trail and heading toward the canyon cut by the Taylor River.

He looked over the rail toward the other side of the coach.

Three more outlaws were galloping toward the stage, returning fire at Stringbean slinging lead at them from the coach's far side. One—a big, red-bearded man in a buckskin jacket with long whang strings blowing in the wind—just then snapped a shot off at Stringbean.

The young deputy did not return fire. He was probably out of ammo.

Mannion gave a loud, bellowing roar as he put every ounce of strength he had into his hands and forearms, pulling his six foot four, 220-pound bulk up and over the brass rail. He rolled over Dr. J. Felix Bartlett's blanketed corpse and onto his back, giving another tooth-gnashing wail, his hat blowing off his head and throwing it back into the scrub behind him.

He clawed the Russian from the holster angled for the cross-draw on his left hip. He broke open the gun and quickly, awkwardly, the coach pitching crazily beneath him as the canyon of the Taylor River yawned wider and wider before him, thumbed three shells from his cartridge belt into the gun's open wheel.

The pain sweat bathing him was cold as fresh snowmelt.

He closed the weapon and rolled onto his right side, extended the .44 straight out to the side of the coach, and—*Bam! Bam! Bam!*—emptied the saddles of all three horses running alongside the coach.

All three outlaws went flying off into the sage, rolling, coats flapping, hats blowing off in the wind.

The three horses galloped off away from the coach, making slow turns away from the canyon, reins leaping over the sage tufts alongside them.

Mannion peered over the bobbing heads of the coach team's six-horse hitch. His eyes widened.

The team was within sixty yards of the canyon now.

Joe holstered the Russian, pushed up onto his knees, and crawled toward the front of the coach. The wind lashed him. He felt as though rough hands were clawing at him from all sides, trying to unseat him, to toss him off into the sage with the men he'd just killed—all while the razored-edge teeth of a dozen rabid wolves were grinding into the flesh of his upper left arm, which under his coat was bathed in fresh, cold blood.

The team was within forty yards of the canyon now...

Joe dropped down into the driver's boot.

The team was within twenty yards of the canyon now...

Joe looked for the reins.

Even if they'd been in the box and not being dragged along on the ground behind the team, leaping and bouncing when the team stepped on them or the coach's wheels rolled over them, which they were, he was out of time.

The two lead horses dropped down over the side of the canyon at the bottom of which the Taylor River, nearly three hundred feet wide, curved like a giant, dark-blue snake.

"Oh, shit!" Joe yelled. "Hold on, everybody—*we're goin' for a swim!*"

His guts knotted when he saw the middle team, the "swing team," drop over the side of the cliff to be followed by the big "wheelers," followed by Joe himself, the driver's seat dropping out from under him.

"I can't swim," he heard Stringbean bellow from inside the carriage.

"Hell," Joe yelled as he dropped into the canyon, his heart leaping into his throat, "the fall'll prob'ly kill ya!"

The horses screamed like a dozen terrified little girls as they flew out away from the cliff and dropped in a steep arc out over the cobalt waters of the river glinting in the high-altitude sunshine below. Mannion found himself seated in midair, the team and the coach drop-ping away beneath him. He heard beneath the screams of the horses the screams of the two biddies inside the coach just before the team plunged into the river in a gigantic, white splash.

Joe flew out to the right side of the team, between the team and the coach, the water coming up fast until it hammered into him as he plunged through its crystalline surface, feet first. The frigid snowmelt enveloped him in the embrace of a cold, cold lover, sucking the air from his lungs. He twisted around to see through the clear water the stage slanting into the river behind him, breaking apart, bodies emerging from the wreckage. One of those bodies was Stringbean, swimming up out of the wreckage, air bubbles rising from his nose and mouth.

Mannion pushed off the stream's sandy bottom and swam to the surface, his head breaking free of the river just as his young deputy's did a few feet to his right.

Teeth clacking, Stringbean said, "Suh-suh...so *cold!*"

"Where's our prisoner!"

"Hell, if I know—prob'ly dead with the others!"

"Ah, Jesus!"

Mannion drew a deep breath then plunged back into the river. He dove down toward the stage that the river's strong current had pulled him away from. He fought the current as three bodies caromed toward him from the stage lying crumpled at the river's bottom, in pieces. One body was clad in lime green, another in pink. The two old biddies came toward Mannion with eyes wide and glassy in death, missing their hats, hair no longer as neatly coifed as before, both sporting bullet holes—one from her cheek, another from the side of her head and from which blood still leaked to be torn away by the river's current.

They were followed by the cowboy, Plummer, floating on his back, lolling gently to-and-fro in the current, blond hair streaming forward over his slack-jawed head. He seemed to have a dreamy smile on his face, as though he couldn't be having a better time.

Another body came flying up from the piecemeal wreckage.

This was the drummer, the man's eyes cast wide in astonishment and horror. Unlike the biddies, he appeared to have avoided the lead that had been punched into the carriage. The coach's impact with the river had probably killed him.

Joe ducked, letting the drummer float over and away from him.

Then he saw the girl—*Señorita La Stiletta*...

She was drifting toward him with pieces of the stage wreckage, fiercely kicking her legs, hands still cuffed in front of her, eyes fierce, air bubbles escaping moving lips as she continued to castigate her jailor—even under water and half drowned!

Mannion grabbed her and swam to the surface. Both his and her heads broke the surface of the river and he saw the slumped bodies of the old biddies, the cowboy, and the drummer drifting on downstream while Stringbean, clinging to a stage door, was kicking his way toward a rocky tongue extending out from the river's left bank.

Mannion and La Stiletta gained the gravelly shallows aproning out from the rocky tongue. Stringbean cast his life-raft door away and came splashing out to Mannion and the señorita, shivering. "Dang, Marshal—I done told you this weren't gonna end well!"

"You oughta take up fortune-telling!" Mannion said.

He hooked his injured left arm around Stringbean's right one and let the younger man pull him and the outlaw princess, whom he had his right arm hooked around, onto the rocky tongue. Mannion collapsed. So did the girl.

She sat up, vomiting water, then turned her infuriated gaze to him again and cut loose with more Spanish bile.

"Ah, shut up!" Mannion said.

He smashed his right fist against her jaw.

She fell back against the rocks, out like a doused flame.

Mannion turned to Stringbean sitting beside him, shivering, lower jaw hanging in shock.

"One way to skin a cat," Joe said, and collapsed in exhaustion.

CHAPTER 9

THE WIND WAS BLOWING FIERCELY.

Dust and leaves blew.

Mannion stood in his and his wife's house in Kansas, staring down into their backyard, at the cottonwood up which his wife had climbed after looping a rope over a stout branch and tying it off near the bottom of the trunk. Mannion stared down in shock, unable to move his feet as Sarah stood in the fork of the old cottonwood, looking down.

He wanted to move in the worst way, but he could not.

He wanted, at least, to hammer the window, to shout at Sarah to stop, but he couldn't move his hands.

Dressed in a simple cambric day dress, she smiled up at him and while he could not hear her words, he could read her lips: "*Why didn't you save me, Joe?*"

Sarah's head became a crow's head. She cawed angrily as she reached out for the noose, slid it over her head, cawed at him once more, turning her angry crow's face to him, then dropped down out of the fork of the tree, the slack quickly coming out of the rope and snapping her neck with a violent jerk of her entire body. Her light-brown hair ripped loose of the French braid she always wore and danced about her head and shoulders.

A baby cried shrilly.

"*Sarah!*"

Mannion jerked his chin up from his chest, his own scream echoing around inside his head.

Caw! Caw! Caw!

Mannion jerked with a start and turned to peer over the rolltop desk in his office on Main Street in Del Norte at a large crow peering in through the dusty window at him.

Caw! Caw! Caw! came the bird's castigation once more.

It turned away from the window, spread its wings, and flew away, cawing, over the false fronts and rooftops of the buildings on the other side of the street.

"Oh, go to hell," Joe said and ran a hand down his face.

He shook his head as though to clear the dream. It lingered, haunting.

He'd been having the dream ever since Ezekial Storm had saved his life, supernaturally. At least, it had seemed supernatural—being healed that fast.

But at what cost?

"Who is Sarah?" The woman's voice came up the stairs from the basement cellblock. Mannion had left the cellblock door open because he was expecting Stringbean to deliver his sole prisoner's lunch from a local café, Ida Becker's Good Food, at any time.

He had only one prisoner because the last batch of track layers had been hauled off to the state pen in a jail wagon by two deputy U.S. marshals just that morning. The others he'd fined and released.

Mannion rose wearily from his chair, wincing at the pain in his left arm, which he now wore in a sling. It had been three days since he and Stringbean and La Stiletta had returned from their near-death plunge into the Taylor River, having caught a ride on a dray from one of the several lumber camps in the Sawatch Range. The local sawbones had plucked the remaining pellets out of Mannion's arm, medicated and wrapped the wound, and suspended the limb in a sling across his chest.

The pain remained.

Joe supposed he should count himself lucky. The stage driver and messenger as well as the two old biddies and the drummer hadn't fared nearly as well that fateful day. Neither had Ed Plummer, who had apparently thrown in with the road agents to rob the stage, which Joe had learned later had been carrying only a mail sack likely carried away on the current with the rest of the strewn wreckage. The horses had survived the plunge, having broken away from the hitch and the harness, and had swum to safety on the other side of the river.

Plummer and his gang, all former cow punchers, had been damn fools. But then, Mannion had never known a cow puncher not a little soft in his thinker box.

He walked to the top of the stairs and stared down into the shadows. His prisoner lay on the cot in the cell at the bottom of the stairs. She had her arms bent behind her head and her long legs crossed at the ankles. The usual scowl in place. She'd gotten over the tap Joe had given her. He hadn't given her much of one, just enough to shut her up for a few minutes.

Physically, she'd gotten over it. He knew, however, that she'd love nothing more than to make Joe pay for it with the stiletto of her moniker plunged deep in his guts and twisted a few times.

"Who is Sarah, old man?" she repeated the question.

"No one. Leastways, not anymore."

"Your wife?"

Mannion started to turn away, but the girl's voice pulled him back. "How did she die?"

Joe turned back to her, incredulous.

Yes, how, Joe thought? Sarah had killed herself in the first few weeks after Vangie's birth. He'd been told by a doctor that emotional doldrums, sometimes suicidal, was a common affliction for young mothers. Joe should have been home to help pull his young wife out of it, but he'd been too busy toting the badge, trying to keep the lid on a booming western town lest it should be torn asunder by cow punchers up from Texas.

He could still hear that baby crying, little Vangie, as though the baby, only a few weeks old, had somehow sensed she was suddenly without her mother. And whose fault was that? Joe hadn't been there. Only in dreams, staring out through a window, eternally helpless, eternally guilty.

Mannion stared down into the cellblock.

Yes, how?

La Stiletta arched a brow. "You're a dark man, Marshal."

Mannion glared at her.

"You don't want to talk about it." She shrugged. "Just making conversation...passing the time till the marshals get here." She flared a nostril. "*If* they get here."

"They'll get he—"

He stopped when the office door opened suddenly and Mannion's senior-most deputy, Rio Waite, hurried in, followed by Mannion's newest deputy, the big, taciturn, Cletus Booker, whom Joe's friend Curt Bishop had had to let go up in the mountain mining town of Forsythe because several rich mucky-mucks hadn't approved of Booker's none-too-by-the-book-like, head-breaking ways. Booker was an expressionless, heavy-lidded man.

Joe didn't like nor dislike him. Booker was Booker—a walking chunk of granite who got the job done. He was in his late thirties and likely, if he lived to ninety, would never rise from his position as a deputy town marshal. Mannion figured that was just fine with the big man, a couple inches taller than Mannion's own six-four and broad as a barn door.

Just as dumb as a barn door, too. But in a booming town like Del Norte, growing more violent by the day, dumb was just fine to Marshal Joe Mannion, as long as it came with a good pair of fists and the willingness to use a bung starter or shotgun when needed.

And in Cletus Booker, it did.

"What the hell's got your drawers in a twist?" Joe asked Rio, who headed straight for the gun rack on the office's back wall, beside a framed map of the southern Colorado Territory with a red star placing Del Norte surrounded by three mountain ranges—the Sangre de Christos, the San Juans, and the Sawatch Range.

Mannion turned to the big, sleepy-eyed Booker. "Yours, too?"

They'd come in together, fast. Booker had stopped, his big frame filling the front door. He had to stand slightly crouched or the ceiling would have brushed off his short-crowned, broad-brimmed hat that was the color of old, badly weathered canvas.

"Yep," was all Booker had to say, blinking his heavy-lidded eyes and leaving it to Rio Waite to tell the story.

Rio unlocked the chain over the gun rack and pulled down his double-barreled shotgun. As he did, his black-and-white cat, Buster, who'd been snoozing in his straw-lined wicker basket on the cabinet beneath the rack, rose to yawn and then paw at his beloved master for affection. Buster had a furry black bowtie, which always made him look all dressed up with no date to take to the ball.

One helluva good mouser, though. The upstairs office of Hotel de Mannion as well as its basement cellblock were usually free of mice and rats though a few blood stains remained to tell the tale of Buster's nocturnal savagery.

"Not now, Buster," Rio said and turned to Mannion. "Trouble over to the Three-Legged Dog, boss. A faction each from the Rio Grande Southern's Line and the Pueblo Line are over there, about to bust each other's heads wide open! Two are arm-rassling and while it was all peaches and cream and friendly-like a minute ago, when me and Cletus walked by, it's likely to go south as soon as those two bruisers finish business. One's a Swede, the other's Norwegian. They're fighting over broken beer bottles"—Rio wagged his fleshy, craggy-faced head as he broke open the shotgun—"and that always ends bad!"

"Ah, shit." Mannion closed and locked the cellblock door.

"Wait!" yelled the outlaw señorita from the shadows below. "You were just starting to entertain me! Besides, where is my lunch?"

"Shut up," Mannion said through the little barred window in the cellblock door.

"We Mexicans get hungry!" she said, grinning and rubbing her belly.

"Your bread and water will get here when it gets here," Mannion said through the little barred window in the door.

He grabbed his shell belt and two holsters off the arm of the chair he'd fallen asleep in, wrapped the belt around his waist, cinched the buckle, and looked at his two deputies—one shorter, one taller than he. "Let's go."

———————

AT THE SAME TIME, DEPUTY STRINGBEAN McCallister walked out of Ida Becker's Good Food with an oilcloth-covered basket hooked over his right arm.

He smelled the savory aroma of the fried chicken, best in town, with mashed potatoes and Miss Ida's good, rich, creamy gravy wafting up from beneath the oilcloth and wondered why on God's green earth he was delivering such a fine meal to a hellion like Señorita Mathilda Calderon, or La Stiletta, as she was more widely known down around the border country.

The vile little filly had dang near caved in Stringbean's oysters not three days ago! Planted that booted foot up soundly between his legs!

And made him look the fool in the eyes of Stringbean's hero, Bloody Joe Mannion, a man he wanted so much to please.

Then again, she'd looked mighty sportin', clad as she'd been in nothing but a shotgun and a cold, dark, Mexican smile...

Señorita La Stiletta...

Just the same, though, Stringbean thought as he turned and headed toward Main Street, still smelling that greasy fried chicken and gravy wafting up to his nose from the basket hooked over his arm, *with my finances bein' as low as they are, I'll likely be washing some bits of old, tough beef jerky down with water while the señorita will be dining in high style down in the cellblock at ol' Hotel de Mannion, as everyone called Bloody Joe's office and jailhouse here in rollicking Del Norte.*

"Henry!"

Stringbean stopped just before he would have run full steam into his pretty li'l miss, as he thought of the small, comely, gray-eyed brunette, Molly Hurdstrom. Clad in a purple blouse with a black belt and black skirt, the daughter of one of Del Norte's wealthiest mucky-mucks stopped abruptly, clamping her round, straw hat on her head with one, black-gloved hand. She smiled up at Stringbean, her peaches-and-cream cheeks flushed beautifully, eyes glittering with love and recognition.

"Where are you off to in such a hurry, Deputy, that you almost ran your betrothed off the boardwalk and into the dust!" She tittered a laugh.

"I'm sorry, Molly, I reckon I didn't see you an'...well... I reckon I was daydreamin' again, as usual. You know how I am!"

"What were you daydreaming about? You had such a smile on your face, dear Henry, I swear!" Molly looked down at the basket hooked over his arm then frowned up at him, suspicious. "Why, you're taking food over to your and Bloody Joe's prisoner, aren't you?"

"Well...yeah...bein' the junior deputy, I reckon such lowly chores are in my job description," he couldn't help saying with some self-righteous indignation.

"You appear to be enjoying it."

"Wh-what's that, my darling?"

"You seem to be enjoying your lowly chore." Molly canted her pretty head, with a splash of freckles across her pert nose, to one side and scowled up at him again, even more suspicious than before. "Or—maybe you were thinking about your prisoner...and how pretty she is, in a dusky-skinned, south-of-the-border sort of way, and how nicely she fills out a nice, tight white blouse!"

She bunched her lips and pressed her right, gloved fist

to her jutting right hip. She tapped the ankle boot of that foot against the boardwalk.

Despite his chagrin, Stringbean smiled and placed his left hand on his beloved's right forearm. "Molly, don't be silly. You know you're the only girl for me!"

She was, too.

They'd been through a lot together, Molly and Stringbean. Such an unlikely pair. Her father and mother ran a freighting business—one of the biggest in the southern Colorado Territory. Stringbean hailed from dirt-poor farmers back in Oklahoma and, short on food and room back home, had come west to break horses, which he'd done fairly well, if he didn't mind saying so his own self, until one particular surly bronc had thrown him on the point of one hip and proceeded to stomp him into the dirt, which the bronc had done with Stringbean-acknowledged aplomb.

The pummeling had ended Stringbean's horse-breaking career right then and there.

After being laid up in a Del Norte boarding house for nigh on three months (a bill he was still paying and probably would for another year or two) he'd applied for a deputy town marshal's position with none other than the (in)famous Bloody Joe Mannion his ownself. Since no one else seemed to want to work with the ornery lawman of Texas-to-Oklahoma town-taming fame, Stringbean had gotten the job complete with a badge pinned to his chest by none other than Bloody Joe himself.

Yessir, things had been looking up for Henry "Stringbean" McCallister.

And now he was set to marry Molly Hurdstrom—against her corrupt, moneyed parents' wishes, of course —and he wasn't about to let anything...or any*one*...get in his way. He truly did love the girl.

"Then I will see you over to Hotel de Mannion, Mister McCallister," Molly said, forthrightly hooking her arm through Stringbean's. "And oversee your tending of your prisoner's needs!"

Oh, dang, Stringbean said to himself as he marched along beside his betrothed. *I gotta feelin' this is another scene that ain't gonna end well...*

CHAPTER 10

"NOW, MOLLY, I GOTTA BE REAL CAREFUL," Stringbean said five minutes later as he mounted the small wooden stoop fronting the jailhouse.

Rio Waite's big cat, Buster, lay on the railing, on his side, facing along the street to the south, toward the Three-Legged Dog Saloon. Buster was anxiously curling his tail as though worried about some doings down that way. Stringbean gave the cat only passing notice as he used his key to unlock the jailhouse door. Molly ran her hand absently along the cat's sprawled body as she turned to her husband-to-be.

"I mean," Stringbean added with his own brand of anxiousness, "there can be no foolin' around here. This is official business."

"What is? Feeding your prisoner?"

"Yes, that exactly. She is no ordinary prisoner, Molly. Take it from me."

"Yes, that's what I heard!" Molly said, testily.

Molly hadn't heard the details of Stringbean's and Marshal Mannion's arrest of the pretty, dangerous woman. Neither had let the cat out of the bag, as it were.

Both would have been too embarrassed for anyone to have learned the infamous, notorious Bloody Joe himself and his deputy, Henry "Stringbean" McCallister, had been so nearly thoroughly thwarted by the pretty prisoner and her wily ways—specifically, that she'd confronted them both wearing nothing more than a loaded shotgun and a smile.

That image was a little hard for Stringbean to get out of his mind, try as he might. As he got the jailhouse door open, his hand shaking with the prospect of confronting the intrepid vixen housed in the cellblock once more, Molly said, "Every man in town has been talking about the beautiful *Mejicana* you and Bloody Joe have locked up, Henry McCallister. Does feeding every prisoner you have housed down there make you so nervous? If you're not careful, Henry, I'm gonna get right jealous!"

Stringbean had tossed his jailhouse key onto Marshal Mannion's desk. He'd plucked the cellblock key off the spike embedded in a stout ceiling support post and was walking toward the cellblock door, the covered wicker basket still steaming warmly where it was hooked over his arm. "Please, Molly. Not now. I got a job to do!"

"One that makes you nervous!"

"Well sure it does," Stringbean said as he unlocked the cellblock door. "If you only knew..." he did not mean to add aloud.

"Let me take it down to her."

Stringbean stopped, the stout cellblock door partway open.

"What?"

"Let me take it down to Señorita La Stiletta!"

Stringbean's lower jaw hung. "Oh, nah...no, no, no..."

"Si, let the fiery little gringa bring it down to me,"

came the huskily sexy, female voice from the shadows at the bottom of the cellblock steps.

"Nah, no," Stringbean said with a nervous chuckle. "That wouldn't be a good idea."

"If she makes you so darn nervous, Henry, let me deliver the food!"

"She doesn't make me nervous!"

"Yes, she does! Look at you. Why, Henry J. McCallister, I do believe you're sweating and it's not even hot outside!"

"I think the chiquita is right, Henry." Like a cat, the long limbed, high-busted La Stiletta rose from the cot and came up to the door, placing each hand on a bar. "You *are* sweating. I can see it from here."

"Henry!" Molly said with no little accusing. "So that's what you have down there!"

"English is my second language," said La Stiletta, "but I believe the correct word is *who*."

"I will be taking that lunch down to *that*, thank you very much!" Before Stringbean could stop her, Molly had grabbed the wicker basket off his arm.

"*Molly, no!*"

Stringbean reached for the basket. But Molly had already started down the stairs. While grabbing the basket, Stringbean got his feet tangled up with both of Molly's. Molly screamed.

"*Oh, dang!*" Stringbean yelled as he suddenly found himself tumbling head over heels down the stairs, Molly tumbling down behind him, her skirt rising above her knees to show her filly, white and pink undergarments.

Stringbean struck the stone floor at the foot of the steps. Half an eye wink later, Molly gave a scream and landed on top of him.

He looked up. Molly lay atop him, her brown hair lying in coils across his face.

"Oh," Molly said.

"Oh," Stringbean said.

There was a ratcheting clicking sound.

Stringbean lifted his head and slid Molly's hair aside to see the barrel of a gun—the barrel of his *own* gun, an old-model Remington .44—staring him right in the face.

Right between the eyes, in fact.

He followed the barrel to the olive-colored wrist whose hand was wrapped around the gun handle. He followed the olive-colored wrist back up to the pretty, olive-colored, black-eyed face smiling at him from between the bars of the cell door.

"The key, *Henry*." La Stiletta glanced at the key ring lying on the stone floor to Stringbean's right, Molly's hair partly obscuring it. "Or your life."

La Stiletta smiled more broadly, showing her fine, white teeth.

———

THE BIG NORWEGIAN, KNUT HAMSUN, SLAMMED THE hand of the big Swede, Lars Nordstrom, down into the glass shards forming a not-so-neat pile on the scarred wooden table in the Three-Legged Dog Saloon.

Hamsun stretched his lips back from yellow, crooked teeth as he ground the Swede's hand into the glass, chuckling as the jagged, brown glass tore into the freckled, sun-browned hand of the Swede, who opened his mouth wide, showing nearly all his own, crooked, yellow teeth as he hurled an agonized wail at the Three-Legged Dog's soot-stained ceiling.

"Take that, Swedish dog!" Hamsun shouted, leaping out of his chair.

Another gent—big, bearded, and shaggy-headed—leaped out of his own chair behind Hamsun. The chair went flying into another occupied chair, evoking an indignant curse from a cross-eyed Russian who'd been playing poker with four Chinese. The big, bearded, shaggy-headed man broke a beer bottle over the edge of the table he'd been sitting at with four others—four Swedes and a humpbacked Cossack who cooked for the Del Norte Line—and lurched toward Hamsun, shouting in a thick Scandinavian brogue, "Jhah—that tears it! You motherless dogs from the Rio Grande Southern are gonna go down *bloody*!"

Joe Mannion smashed a hide-wrapped bung starter over the big, bearded man's shaggy head with a resolute *thud!*

"The only one going down bloody, Hans Zimmerman, is you!" Joe bellowed.

Zimmerman, a gandy dancer for the Pueblo, Colorado Springs, and Del Norte Line, scrunched up his sun-wizened face and struck the floor like a sack of grain dropped from a loading dock—out cold and with a chuff of expelled air from his lungs.

Half the clientele leaped from their chairs, glaring at Mannion and the two deputies—Rio Waite and the hulking Cletus Booker—flanking him, both armed with double-barreled shotguns.

"We'll settle our own scores, Mannion!" bellowed a square-faced, black-haired, lantern-jawed gent—a ramrod for the Rio Grande Southern Line.

He'd just leaped out of his own chair and pulled a big, horn-gripped .44 from a shoulder holster half hidden by his elk hide jacket. Bloody Joe had taken the bung starter in his left hand. Now with his right hand he pulled his right-side Russian from the holster thonged on his right thigh—a quick blur of motion almost no one in the Three-Legged Dog had caught—and cocked and triggered the big, impressive popper.

The thunder of the Russian's explosion made the whole room jump. A bottle tumbled from a back bar shelf and dropped to the floor with a screech of breaking glass.

"*Jay-zuzzz!*" someone exclaimed.

The .44 went flying out of the Rio Grande Southern ramrod's hand and through a window behind him with another screech of breaking glass as well as a female shriek from the boardwalk fronting the saloon.

"*My hand!*" the Rio Grande Southern ramrod wailed, clutching the limb of topic sporting a ragged hole in the palm and from which dark, red blood oozed to drip onto the square toe of the man's right, cork-soled boot. "Jesus Christ, Mannion, you bloody son of a bitch!"

"That's going to be carved on my headstone, Marvin," Joe said. "Now sit down in your damn chair and wait for the sawbones." He glanced at a short, wide-eyed, bespectacled gent standing just inside the batwings, having no doubt entered to see what all the commotion was about. "Shorty, send for the pillroller before Marvin here bleeds out through his hand. Wouldn't want to leave the Rio Grande Southern without its ramrod, now, would we?"

"Go to hell, Mannion!" Marvin O'Bannion said as he dropped into the chair he'd vacated, all eyes of the men at the table he'd been playing Yellow Dog with gazing in shock at O'Bannion's bloody hand. The blood was now spilling onto the table and into a half-empty shot glass, making the sunlit side of the glass turn red.

"If I had a dime for every time I been told that…"

Joe glanced around the room, at the angry eyes riveted on him. "Everybody, cool your drawers and sit back down in your chairs." He holstered the big, still-smoking Russian then hiked his right boot onto an empty chair, took the bung starter in his right hand and tapped it, meaningfully, against the palm of his left. Leaning forward over his right knee, he said, "There will be no more fighting between the Rio Grande Southern and the Pueblo, Colorado Springs, and Del Norte Lines."

He continued casting his gaze around the smoke-hazy room while the Rio Grande Southern ramrod sat grunting in his chair, clutching his bleeding right hand, staring down at the ruined limb in misery.

"Leastways, not in my town," Mannion continued. "Not in Del Norte. If there is, you'll be charged fifty dollars. That's right—fifty dollars apiece for any foofaraw...or one month behind bars. And you'll be buying your own food or you'll starve," he added with a nod, acknowledging the collective, indignant, exasperated chuffs issuing from around the large room filled with sunlight angling in through the Three-Legged Dog's several, large, dust-streaked windows. "Fifty dollars or a month at Hotel de Mannion, room service on yourselves."

Joe grinned, showing all his large, square teeth beneath his brushy, salt-and-pepper mustache. "You heard it here and right now, and my word is bond!"

"Goddamn you, Mannion!" said a man in a red-and-white checked shirt to Mannion's right, pounding both his large, brown fists on the table before him and gritting his teeth. "You can't do that! A judge calls the damn punishment!"

Big Cletus Booker was standing beside the man. Cletus smiled coldly and rammed the butt of his big, steel, double-barreled coach gun into the man's thick-lipped, mustached mouth. It was a quick but casual move, the skin around Cletus's mouth tightening slightly but the grim smile remaining on his lips. The check-shirted man's lips exploded like overripe tomatoes, and he leaned back in his chair, cursing and spitting blood at the ceiling.

He cursed Booker then lowered his chin and glared at Mannion, blue eyes glowing frostily in the harsh light from a near window. "That's crazy and savage even for you, Bloody Joe!"

"That's just for starters," Mannion said, casually, giving his newest deputy, the large, hulking, heavy-lidded Cletus Booker an approving smile.

Standing to Booker's left, Rio Waite, six inches shorter than the new deputy, ten years older and soft and lumpy but still a proven man, grinned and winked his own approval at Bloody Joe.

"I might go to setting Cletus there loose on the whole lot of ya. Then you'll think my punishment is nothing more than a swim in a pretty creek at sunset!"

Mannion turned to the sawbones, Marcus P. Bohannon, MD, who'd just pushed through the batwings. The short, gray-headed oldster in a worn suit stopped and took one look around the saloon and said, "Good Christ!"

"Ain't been no Christ, good or bad, around here, Doc." Joe slid his snake-eyed grin to his deputies, one short and lumpy, one big and square-shouldered, and said, "Arrest these scrappers an' haul 'em over to Hotel de Mannion. If their pockets are empty, they'll be dining on the tabs of their respective rail lines until their ramrods come callin' for 'em, their hats in their hands..."

Mannion swung around and headed for the door.

He pushed through the batwings and stepped off the

boardwalk, blinking against the dust rising from the street before him kicked up by one set of mules or horses and large, rolling, iron-shod wheels after another. When he finally found a break in the traffic, he made his way over to the other side of the street, mounted the stoop of Hotel de Mannion, tripped the steel latch, and strode inside.

He'd only taken two steps when a strange feeling needled him.

He went back to the door and opened it. Rio Waite's cat, Buster, was sitting on the porch rail to Mannion's left. Nothing unusual about that. The big, black-and-white mouser was always sitting out there, taking the sun, usually with his lord and master, Rio Waite, kicked back in the hide-bottom chair to the right of the door. Now, however, Buster had an owly disposition, one that Mannion had sensed more than witnessed as he'd crossed the porch a minute ago.

The cat sat facing the open jailhouse door, flicking his tail and meowing deep in his throat.

Buster lifted his gaze to Mannion, gave his black-and-white tail another anxious flip, turned to glance over his shoulder toward the street, and meowed a little louder.

"What is it, Buster?" Mannion said, peering along the congested, dusty street. "What's goin'—?" Then he saw it. Or didn't see it, rather—his horse. He'd left the big bay tied at the hitchrack fronting the jailhouse.

Red was no longer there.

Mannion raked a thumb down along the line of his jaw, scowling and looking around at the congested and busy midday street. Who would have taken Mannion's horse? No one was fool enough to take Bloody Joe's horse!

Muttering confoundedly under his breath, he swung around and stepped back into his office.

"Ummm, Marshal...?" came a reedy, tentative voice on the other side of the cellblock door, echoing a little as it rose from the cellblock basement.

Mannion turned to the door. "Stringbean, what for the love of Pete is—" Again, he stopped. The key for the cellblock was in the door.

Mannion's heart thudded.

He hurried to the door, unlocked it, and gazed down into the dingy cellblock. Stringbean and his comely young girlfriend, the auburn-haired and gray-eyed Molly Hurdstrom, stood inside the cell where Mannion had left La Stiletta twenty minutes ago. They each had their hands on the bars of the door, peering up the stairs at Mannion like two kids caught rolling in their Sunday best in the churchyard on Sunday morning. The wreck of a meal lay on the floor fronting the cell.

"Christ!" Mannion swung around and ran back onto the stoop. "She couldn't get far on ol' Red. No, sir—that hoss is a one man—"

Just then, still on the rail to Mannion's left, Buster meowed and gave his tail another flip. A girl screamed on the street and Mannion turned to see the señorita—in a leather skirt and tight, white blouse her ownself—riding hell-for-leather past the jailhouse.

On Red's back.

Or *sort of* on his back.

With each passing second, she was somewhere different entirely and about to come off, Red crow hopping and sunfishing wildly beneath her, a great cloud of tan dust roiling up around them.

"Stop!" La Stiletta screamed and whipped the rein

ends against the bay's left wither. "Stop it, you mangy bronco from hell! You cayuse! *Bastardo!*"

Mannion grinned and crossed his arms on his chest. He glanced at Buster who appeared nearly as amused as Joe at the spectacle playing out before them.

The girl managed to hold on for a few more seconds.

Then Red stopped suddenly. He turned on a dime to face the exact opposite direction from half a second ago and lifted his front hooves far up off the ground, clawing at the sky and giving a deep, burly whinny. The girl gave one more, shrill cry then, hair and skirt flying inside that billowing cloud, she fell straight back off the saddle to land with a loud splash in the stock tank fronting John Dunham's barbershop.

Several passersby had stopped to watch the show—some on foot, some on horseback, some in wagons.

Wild laughter rose as the dust sifted.

John Dunham, who'd been reading the paper and smoking a meerschaum pipe on the chair fronting his tonsorial parlor, grinned broadly at Red who stood regarding the girl, tail arched, ears pinned back, as though he might like to give her another go.

"I'll be hanged if ol' Red don't still have some pitch!"

Mannion crossed the street to the stock trough.

"Didn't you ever teach that broom trail to ride?" she grouched from the water, wringing it out of her hair. "Dios mio—he damn near killed me!"

"Oh, I taught him to ride just fine," Mannion said. "But with only me on his back."

He pulled her out of the stock trough and gave her a kick to the seat of her pants, sending her off in the direction of the jailhouse. She went along, sulking, shoulders slouched. Quite a few of the men stood watching as she and Mannion mounted the jailhouse stoop. She was purely a sight to see in that clinging white blouse that left little to the imagination.

Mannion followed her into the basement cellblock and glowered at his deputy and Molly. Both looked duly chagrined. Especially Stringbean. He famously wanted nothing more than to please his boss, whom he tended to hero-worship, which made Mannion uncomfortable.

Bloody Joe was no hero. Just a lawman who didn't mind fudging the lines of what was lawful and what was not in the charge of performing his town-taming duties.

"You two out," he ordered Stringbean and Miss Hurd-strom. Turning to the señorita, he said, "You, in. You ever pull a stunt like that again, I'll shoot ya. You're more trouble than you're worth...and don't tell me you haven't heard that before!"

He closed and locked the door then followed his sullen deputy and the Hurdstrom girl up to his office. He turned to Stringbean and the Hurdstrom girl facing him as before—cheeks mottled red with embarrassment.

"I don't even want to hear it," Joe said. "Get a mop and a bucket and clean up that food down there. Both of you. Good *Christ*!"

"You got it, boss," Stringbean said.

"Yessir, Marshal Mannion," Molly said.

Mannion sighed and ran a hand through his hair. He was about to turn to his desk when quick footsteps sounded on the street. They grew louder until shoes tapped on the stoop. It was Farley Grissom, Western Union agent, clad in his usual blue wool trousers, collar-less pinstriped shirt with the sleeves rolled up his skinny forearms, and suspenders. He was a slight man with spectacles forever perched low on his nose, a green eyeshade on his forehead.

He had a yellow telegraph flimsy in his right hand, a pencil tucked behind his ear.

"Trouble, Marshal," the man said, regret showing in his slender, hawkish features. "You know those three federals the chief marshal in Arizona was gonna send to fetch your prisoner?"

"What about 'em?" Dread touched Mannion.

Grissom handed Mannion the flimsy. "All three were found with their throats cut in a Pullman car in Las Cruces early this morning. Here's the kicker."

"What's the kicker?"

"The chief marshal down there says he's shorthanded. He wants you to find a way to get the girl down to Tucson."

Mannion's face crumpled in exasperation. He didn't have a man to spare, especially himself, to run an errand for the feds. If he himself left Del Norte, the two factions of warring track layers would blow it up like a powder keg. He could send Rio Waite or Cletus Booker, he supposed.

But then he turned a wistful look at Stringbean hauling a wooden bucket of soapy water and a mop toward the cellblock door. His girlfriend followed him glumly with a broom.

Mannion turned back to Grissom. "Tell 'im I got just the man for the job!"

CHAPTER 11

MOLLY HURDSTROM WAS STILL LOOKING GLUM SEVERAL hours later.

She and Stringbean were sitting on a log along Burial Rock Creek. They were both fishing, dangling lines from skinned cottonwood branches into the slowly moving, clear, brown water. They'd taken their shoes and socks off and were dangling them in the water as well, gently kicking.

Occasionally, a minnow would swim up from the creek's depths to kiss their toes.

It was not proper, of course, for a young lady and a young man, not married, to be off on their own, unattended by a chaperone. It was even less proper, of course, for a young lady and a young man, not married, to be showing so much flesh. Stringbean had rolled up the cuffs of his faded blue denims to nearly his knees and Molly had done that same thing with the skirt of her yellow cotton day dress, which was conservatively fitted and edged with white lace at the collar and sleeves.

But then, neither no longer gave much thought to such proprieties. Molly was estranged from her family and had taken an apartment in a little house in Del Norte owned by a prim and proper older lady who had trouble keeping up with the girl but who'd taken her in because she'd felt sorry for Molly's bad turn of fortune. Molly's father had forbidden Molly from marrying Stringbean, who hailed from, in his eyes, a lowly station. He'd wanted Molly to marry the son of a corrupt business associate— Adam McClarksville. Molly had refused and tragedy had struck when her proposed beau and an equally thuggish friend, both on leave from a military academy in the east, had attacked Stringbean.

Molly had taken Stringbean's gun and shot Adam dead to save Stringbean's life.

Of course, it had been a town-wide scandal that had not yet completely settled down.

But neither Molly nor Stringbean much cared about what people thought anymore.

So they sat on the log, letting their bare feet dangle in the stream, looking glum, occasionally casting each other glum looks over their embarrassing display back at Hotel de Mannion.

Neither had said anything for nearly a half hour when Molly said suddenly, "It's not fair, Henry. That vile man is only trying to get back at the both of us for allowing that pretty señorita to get loose! Vile! Just vile!"

"You mean Marshal Mannion?"

"Of course I mean Marshal Mannion. I know you have nothing but respect and admiration for him, but his sending you off to deliver that nasty girl to the authorities in Tucson is just spiteful and mean and...and...well, it's just wrong! I wish you would quit!"

"Oh, I can't quit on Marshal Mannion, Molly. He gave me a job when no one else would have me on account of my bum hip. Besides, I like my job...and...well, I like working for Marshal Mannion, despite what you think of him..."

"He's a vile old fool, Henry. I know you don't see it, but everyone else does."

"Rio doesn't."

"Bloody Joe has got Rio Waite hornswoggled, too!"

"Ah, that's just not right, Molly!"

"Bloody Joe going to get you killed!" She turned to Stringbean, and large tears shown in her large gray eyes framed by auburn curls tumbling to her shoulders. "And since I'm estranged from my parents...for very good reason, I might add...I'll be all alone in the world!"

"Ah, Molly, no..." Stringbean wrapped his arm around the small but shapely girl and drew her against him. "I wish you'd have more confidence in me than that. I'll get her down to Tucson pronto. The marshal gave me maps to get us through the mountains—well off the beaten path so her gang won't find us. Besides, they won't be expecting her to be hauled down there by just one man—a lowly town marshal's deputy, no less!"

He gave the girl a reassuring smile.

"Besides," Molly said, scowling into the water from which a small red-throated trout had just leaped, making a silvery splash, "I've seen how she looks, and I have to admit I just don't know if I can trust you with her. I couldn't trust any man with a girl who looks like that, Henry!"

Despite their current row, he liked that she called him by his given name. She was the only one he knew who did. He wished more would. A twenty-three-year-old deputy town marshal should be above the lowly moniker of "Stringbean."

But then, after what happened earlier, he guessed the

childish nickname fit just fine. He didn't deserve anything more.

"I got to admit that she does cut a fine figure, but believe you me, Molly, she's got a black heart. I wouldn't trust her as far as I could throw her uphill against a Texas cyclone." That was one of Marshal Mannion's expressions. Again, Stringbean smiled, trying to lighten his girl's mood.

It did no such thing.

Molly turned to him again and gave an expression of dire pleading. "Please, Henry—won't you refuse the assignment? If the marshal won't allow it, then you quit!"

Stringbean winced and shook his head. "I'm sorry, honey. I just can't do that. He's the marshal. He asked me to do a job, and I have to do it."

"He's punishing you."

Again, Stringbean shook his head. "He's testing me. He wants me to prove to both him and me that I can do it."

If he could prove that he could do it, could he be called by his given name?

"All right, then." Molly set her fishing pole aside and pulled her bare legs out of the stream. "I guess you've made your decision."

"Molly," Stringbean said, awestruck. "You're not makin' me choose between you and the marshal, are you?"

"Yes, I guess I am," she said sullenly, drying her feet off in the grass.

She picked up her shoes and stockings and then strode off along the path that led back to town.

Stringbean rose and stared after her, heartbroken. They'd been planning to get married. "Molly, please don't do this!"

She glanced over her shoulder at him. "You've made your decision, Henry McCallister." She turned her head forward and continued walking away. "And I've made mine."

She followed a tree-lined bend in the trail and was gone.

The only person who called him by his given name —gone.

———

BLOODY JOE WAS HAVING HIS OWN PERSONAL PROBLEMS. He didn't like them anymore than Stringbean did, but there you had it.

Joe was faced with a wife who'd left him—a second one. He had no idea if Jane would ever return. He also had an angry daughter.

Ever since he'd arrived home late for supper, in the little cottage he'd bought nearly directly across the lane from his and Vangie's old, burned-out place, Vangie hadn't spoken two words to him. Evangeline Mannion had always been a quiet girl—she'd picked up that from her father—but tonight she was especially tight-lipped. She served him a good supper like she usually did—pot roast with all the trimmings including a rich, dark-brown gravy ladled over mashed potatoes—but she wouldn't speak to him as they sat down and ate it together.

She wouldn't even look at him.

Of course, Mannion knew what was eating his daughter.

His assigning Stringbean to escort the pretty but black-hearted Mexican princess down to Tucson so she could testify against her beau, Diego Hidalgo. Joe knew his daughter's moods. They could be as dark as his own. He didn't try to force conversation.

After supper, instead of helping her with the dishes like he usually did, sensing she wanted to be alone, he secretly poured half a cup of Theo's busthead—he used a cup so that if Vangie saw it she'd think it was coffee—and took his makings sack and went out and sat on one of the two chairs he kept outside so he could watch the creek curling through the trees, glinting in the light of the first shimmering stars.

Vangie usually sat in the other chair.

He wasn't sure if she would tonight or not.

He was surprised when she did, coming out in a light jacket and sitting down beside him. She was dressed as usual in denims and stockmen's boots, her hair pulled back in a French braid behind her head, like the one her mother used to wear. Vangie had seen it in the few pictures they had of Sarah.

"Would you like me to build a fire?" he asked her. There was a stone ring between the two chairs and the creek. The water murmured softly beyond the trees. It lifted a knife-edge chill that was soothing after the warm day.

Vangie shook her head and crossed her arms on her chest. "I'm not going to stay out long."

"Look, honey, I know you don't like it that I'm sending Stringbean to Tucson, but I've made up my mind and I'm not going to change it."

"No, you never do."

"He'll make a man one of these days, if he's tested enough. His problem is lack of confidence due to dunder-headed mistakes."

Vangie turned to him. "That's not your problem, though, is it, Poppa? Confidence."

"You'd be surprised."

"Really?"

Joe smiled. "I'm just a man, honey. With all the faults and frailties and failures of courage and character. I just try to let on as little as possible. In my line of work, you have to. Especially when I was first starting out."

"You're not starting out anymore, Pa."

"No, but I have a town to run. Stringbean does, too. It may not be as bad as Hayes back in the old days, or as bad as Abilene, Wichita Falls...Amarillo. But it's growing in a bad way."

"What are you going to do about Jane?"

The change of subject took him aback. "What?"

"Are you just going to sit out here, sipping Mister O'Flanagan's tarantula juice, looking at the creek, waiting for her to return of her own accord?"

Joe's cheeks warmed shamefully as he looked down at the cup in his hands. "She didn't have to leave."

"She knows your job is more important to you than she is."

"That's not true."

Vangie gave a caustic laugh. "Did you ever think about proving that to her?"

"You don't think that do you?" Joe asked his daughter. "I mean about my job meaning more to me than you do?"

Vangie shook her head then turned to stare at the creek glinting in the trees. "No, I've never worried about that, Papa. Still, you're a lonely man, Bloody Joe Mannion. And you're going to die alone unless you can swallow your pride and prove to the right woman...to Jane Ford Mannion...that you love her and need her. Because you do, you know? I see it in your eyes...your sad, angry, lonely eyes...every day."

Joe turned to look up at the first stars twinkling to

life above the crowns of the ponderosas lining the creek. "Well, I guess you let me have it—didn't you?"

"It's been a long time coming." Vangie turned to him and smiled. "And there's so much more, Bloody Joe."

He gave a grim smile and nodded.

Vangie rose and came over and sat down on his lap, turning to face him, wrapping her arms around his neck. "I love you, you know?"

"How could you?"

"Because we're a lot alike, you and me. Set apart from others to foil our chances for happiness. On the other hand, you have given me horses. Cochise is my best friend. We're soul mates." Cochise was the blue roan Mannion had captured for her out of the wild—as wild as his namesake—until Vangie had gentled him slowly, one hour, one day at a time, like few others could do.

She was acquainted with wild hearts, this girl.

"He's only a horse, though, honey."

"He's enough. For now." Vangie kissed his cheek then climbed up out of his lap.

She thumbed his nose, gave him a taunting smile, then flounced off to the house, the lower story front windows lit with the light of hurricane lanterns turned low. Mannion could still smell the succulent aromas of her pot roast wafting on the cool night breeze.

She planted one foot on the front step then turned back to him. "Go to her, Papa. Bring her back. And I don't mean tie her up and throw her over your shoulder like a sack of grain." Vangie laughed. "Let it be her choice. Because if you can manage the right words, she'll come, you know. She will."

Vangie took one more step then stopped again and turned back to her father. "Please reconsider about Stringbean? For me?" She didn't wait for a response but continued up the steps and across the stoop, boots thudding on the rough pine boards. "Good night."

The door clicked shut.

Mannion sighed. He sipped his whiskey, set it on the arm of the chair Vangie had vacated, then dug into his makings sack for his tobacco and papers. He began to build a smoke, muttering, "Why do all the damn women in my life have to be so much smarter than me?"

CHAPTER 12

"WHATEVER YOU DO, YOU KEEP THAT HELLION handcuffed. Either to you or something solid, and never... and I mean *never*...turn your back on her. When you're riding, keep her cuffed to that saddle, and I mean *tight*!"

Joe looked at La Stiletta and said, "Oh, and another thing." He turned to Stringbean. "Don't be afraid to shoot her!"

He turned back to the girl and gave a devilish smile.

"All right, Marshal," Stringbean said uncertainly. He glanced at the prison and then at Mannion and in the starlight, Joe could see the apprehension and lack of confidence in the young man's eyes. "Are you sure I'm really the right one for this job?"

Mannion, Stringbean, and the hellion were on horse-back. Mannion had waited till after dark to move his pris-oner out of town and to get Stringbean and the girl headed off on an old Spanish freight trail toward Tucson. He didn't want anyone in town to know they'd left the jail. Since La Stiletta had a two-thousand-dollar reward on her hand...and looked like she did...the threesome might be followed.

"No, I'm the one who should be doing it," Mannion said. "But I'm needed in town." He reached over and squeezed the deputy's shoulder. "You can do it. I believe in you."

"Even after—"

"Yes, even after the debacle in the basement cell-block. Maybe *because* of it. Now you have something to prove. Do this the way *I'd* do it"—Mannion hooked a wry smile—"and you'll make a man."

"You are making a big mistake, Mannion," said La Stiletta, grinning cunningly at Stringbean. "I'm going to carve this little fool up in tiny pieces and feed him to the wildcats!"

Stringbean winced.

"Don't let her get to you. She's going to try. Just keep her tied and don't let her get into your head."

"Hah!" said La Stiletta. "I get into every man's head. Maybe not yours," she said, looking at Joe, "but if I had a little more time, you, too, would be eating out of my hand."

"Yeah," Mannion said, chuckling. "You'd be eating rat poison out of it!" He turned to his deputy. "Like I said—don't let her get into your head, kid. It's over a week's ride to Tucson. That's if you're not interrupted. Just follow those maps and the directions I gave you and stay off the main trails. Once they get wind you're escorting Hidalgo's gal to Tucson—and we have to believe they will, sooner or later—Hidalgo's men will likely be scouring the main trails, stage, and rail lines for you. Bounty hunters might try to get her away from you too. Other men, too, once they get a look at her."

Mannion had little doubt that Hidalgo's men knew that La Stiletta had been locked up in Del Norte. That was a secret that could not be kept. Spies were no doubt already on the lurk—headed this way or maybe already in Del Norte, waiting for Mannion to make a move with his prisoner.

He gave the girl a hard look. She smiled back at him.

"Keep a finger on your trigger and one eye on your back trail," Mannion told his deputy.

"You can take all the precautions you want, lawman," said La Stiletta. "Diego's men led by Manuel San Jacinto will free me—don't you worry." She gave another white-toothed grin in the darkness. She turned to Stringbean. "And he will cut this one's throat but only after he'd been made to scream for an hour!"

Again, Stringbean winced.

Mannion kept his gaze on his deputy. "All right—head out. Remember, you'll be swinging west of the Black Range and then east around the Gilas and west around the Superstitions. It's gonna be a grueling ride, but she needs to testify at Hidalgo's trial." He turned to the prisoner. "To tell the federals where Hidalgo hid the Gatling guns. Lives are at stake, kid. That said, don't be afraid to shoot her if you have to."

The girl laughed. "Diego's men will free me, and we will head to Mexico—with the Gatling guns—leaving the vultures to dine on this simple fool!" Again, she glanced at Stringbean, who suppressed a wince this time though he felt as though he'd drunk a belly full of sour milk.

"Get moving, kid," Joe said. "We're burnin' starlight."

He heard something in the rugged, night-cloaked country back in the direction of Del Norte, which was roughly four miles away. "Wait." He slipped the '66 Winchester from its scabbard as his eyes raked the darkness behind them.

He heard it again, the clomp of a hoof then the jangle of a bridle chain in the quiet night.

"Someone's behind us. We might've been followed despite my precautions, dammit." Mannion turned to Stringbean. "Get moving, kid. I'll watch your back trail and clear it if I have to." He gritted his teeth in frustration. "Something tells me I'm gonna have to."

"All right, Marshal," Stringbean said, jerking the girl's rented sorrel along behind him by its bridle reins. She rode stiffly in the saddle, hands cuffed to the horn, feet tied to her stirrups. She wore her white blouse under a black leather jacket, and her black leather skirt. Her straw hat was perched on her head. A soogan with a rain slicker was lashed behind her saddle. Trail possibles in a canvas sack hung from her saddle horn.

She glanced behind her at Mannion. "This kid will be dead in a day—mark my words!"

Possibly, Mannion thought. He might have made a big mistake sending the kid with the girl. On the other hand, it was too long and rough a ride for Rio Waite, and Mannion did not yet know Cletus Booker well enough to trust that the big man would not get himself seduced and his throat cut for his trouble. Joe was sure that wouldn't happen to Stringbean. The kid had learned his lesson. Besides, he was head over heels for Molly Hurdstrom.

If the kid did what Joe had told him, and did it the *way* Joe would do it, he'd get the job done.

When Stringbean and the girl had drifted off in the darkness, Mannion swung down from his saddle, ground reined Red, then climbed a low, pine-stippled rise on his left. He kept his hand around the Yellowboy's brass receiver to keep it from reflecting starlight.

He hunkered behind a pine and stared down the other side of the rise, into a shallow canyon through which the old freight trail wound. Rocks shown pale in the starlight, and the pine needles were blue touched with silver. He waited, worrying his thumb against the rifle's hammer.

The hoof thuds continued to grow louder. Now he could hear the squawk of tack and men talking in low tones. Finally, four riders came around a bend in the canyon and out in the open. Men and horses were silhouetted against the starlit sky behind them. Still, Mannion saw that one wore a cream Stetson with a red neckerchief. Another was clad in black. One was big and beefy and wore a sugarloaf sombrero. The fourth was a small, wiry man.

All four wore dusters.

Rifles bristled from saddle scabbards.

"Damn fools," Joe muttered under his breath, scowling as the riders drew near, following the base of the canyon on his lower right.

He recognized all four. Market hunters for one of the track-laying railroads. A lowly lot. Now it appears they were fortune hunting. And woman hunting.

Mannion straightened and loudly jacked a round into the Winchester's breech. "All right—that's far enough!"

The men jerked their horses' heads up with starts so that the eyes of the mounts were white ringed in the darkness. The men cast their own startled gazes up at the big, rifle-wielding man on the ridge wearing a corduroy jacket and a big, high-crowned black hat.

"Who the hell is that?" the biggest one exclaimed.

"Who else—it's Mannion!" said the one in the cream Stetson.

"I'm gonna have to kill you four idiots," Mannion said. "I doubt just a tongue-lashing would do!"

The man in black said, "Go ahead and try, Mannion! You might get one or two of us, but you won't get us all!"

Joe grinned. "I wouldn't count on it, you coyote-faced devil."

The big man—Chester Norby, Joe thought was his name—threw up his gloved hands and said, "Hold on, now. You got us dead to rights."

The little, snake-eyed gent riding a sidestepping dun flanking Norby, said, "Chester's right. We'll just ride on back to Del Norte and forget the whole thing. No harm done."

"All right, you do that," Mannion said through a cunning grin.

He started to lower the Yellowboy but snapped it to his shoulder when all four men slapped gun leather, raising revolvers. Gun metal glinted in the starlight. Mannion went to work with the Yellowboy, shooting and cocking, shooting and cocking, the rifle screeching and lighting up the canyon with the orange light of the flames.

All four tinhorns were knocked off their horses in quick succession, howling.

They'd gotten a few shots off, but their horses were moving around too much for accurate shooting.

Mannion had killed Norby and the man in black, Wilfred Engle, outright. But the little fella and the man in the cream Stetson, whose named Mannion didn't know, were still howling. Mannion killed the man in the cream Stetson with another shot to the chest. The snake-eyed little devil, Willie Brush, rose to a knee, howling like a banshee and raising his Colt. He'd lost his hat in the tumble and his blond hair hung in his eyes.

Mannion shot him with a single bullet to the middle

of his forehead. Willie rocked back, triggering the Colt into his right boot. He dropped the Colt with a clattering thud in the rocks. His eyes rolled back in their sockets, showing the whites, and then he lay down on his back and shook his life out.

Joe lowered the Yellowboy and stared into the canyon through his own wafting powder smoke. "Damn idiots."

Oh well. The world had lost greater men. It wouldn't miss these and would be a better place in the bloody bargain.

But now he had to take the time to pack them back to town, turn them over to the undertaker. He could just leave them—wolves had to eat too—but he'd best go by the book and bring them back. Someone would likely be asking about them. Mannion had nothing to hide. Besides, he was already at odds with the town council, had been for most of his five-year tenure in Del Norte.

Damn the luck!

He went and fetched Red and led the bay into the canyon still smelling of the rotten-egg odor of gun smoke. All four horses had run but he managed to chase down two and lifted two dead men over each, letting them drape belly down across their saddles. He mounted Red and, leading the four horses by their lead lines, headed back to town.

"There's getting to be so many tinhorns in Del Norte these days you can toss a single horse apple and hit three!" he muttered, feeling foul, which he could do better than most.

He was also feeling bad about Stringbean.

It was a helluva mission he'd sent the kid on.

IT WAS STARTING TO GET LIGHT BY THE TIME HE RODE back into town, his grisly cargo trailing along behind him. Some watering holes were still hopping, however, what with all the track layers in town these days.

"More fresh beef—eh, Joe?" a man called from outside the Wooden Nickel Saloon. Others laughed.

Joe ignored the man. His incurring comments from onlookers every time he rode into town with bodies of dead men riding belly down across their saddles had gotten old a long time ago.

He rode up to Hotel de Mannion. Big Cletus Booker was sitting in a brocade armchair on the front porch. There was a smaller, hide-bottom chair on the porch, beside the brocade one. Joe and Rio Waite sat in the smaller one, but Booker had almost broken it when he'd once tried to sit in it. He'd seen the brocade one—old and badly faded and threadbare—in an alley beside a hurdy-gurdy house. He'd hauled the larger chair over to the jailhouse on his back and planted it to the left of the door.

He sat in it now, denim-clad legs spread wide, holding a hide-wrapped bung starter across his lap. The bung starter had dried blood on it.

"Hello, Cletus," Joe greeted the man. "How are you?"

Booker blinked his heavy-lidded eyes slowly, his face customarily expressionless. He grunted and hiked a shoulder.

"How was the night?"

"Had to crack a few heads. Got three more track layers locked up downstairs." Booker jerked his big chin toward the door of the jailhouse flanking him.

"Figures."

Mannion swung down from his saddle. "Take this beef

over to Bellringer, will you, then stable the horses. Then you can call it a night. I'll take over until Rio gets here." Mortimer Bellringer was the local undertaker. Joe kept a smile on the man's face and jingle in his pockets. Bellringer appreciated that.

As Booker began leading the horses away, a man's voice sounded from the opposite side of the street, in the direction of the former Jane Ford's San Juan Hotel and Saloon. "Say there—stop! Stop, I say, I want a look at those horses."

Mannion turned to see a slender, gray-headed, graymustached man in an impeccable gray suit stride along the boardwalk over there and then slant across the street to Hotel de Mannion. He strode quickly on his thin legs. He wore a grim expression on his pert, neat face, gray eyes mantled by ridged, gray brows.

"What's my beef to you?" Joe asked, still feeling a might off his feed about Stringbean and Jane and everything else.

Then he saw the town's prissy mayor, Charlie McQueen, also a prominent attorney in Del Norte, following the older gent, looking none too unconcerned himself. Joe sort of saw McQueen as his nemesis, as McQueen often and vociferously reacted to the town's marshal's uncouth ways. Mannion grimaced as he watched the little, neat-bearded, bespectacled gent in a three-piece suit walking quickly toward him on his short legs and brogan-clad feet, a few feet off the heels of the older gent, who could have been McQueen's stern father. McQueen's small, round spectacles glinted in the growing light.

Joe always marveled at the fact the mayor never seemed to have a speck of dust on his finely tailored suits. How that could be in a town as dusty as Del Norte was almost magical.

Mannion sized up these two men, the older gent a stranger, and determined that this new day was going to go from bad to worse.

CHAPTER 13

THE OLDER GENT STEPPED UP TO MANNION AND, looking up angrily at the taller man, planted his walking stick in the dirt of the street and announced, "I am H. Jerome Libby, superintendent of the Rio Grande Southern Line. I think I know...or *knew*...these men."

While Charlie McQueen flanked the man, looking constipated, H. Jerome Libby bent down to get a look at the faces of the four men sprawled belly down across the two horses. He straightened, his scowl growing more severe as he returned it to Mannion. "Sure enough—I know them...or *knew* them, all right. These men work...or *worked*...for me. They supplied game meat for my railroad crew just now laying track east of Del Norte!"

"Well," Mannion said, "they won't be doing that anymore."

"I've heard of you, Mannion." H. Jerome Libby pointed his cane at Joe, wielding it like a rifle. "I've heard of your bloody ways. And I know that you at one time or another have had many of my track layers housed in your jail when they should have been out laying track. Now you've jailed my ramrod, Marvin O'Bannion! We're in a race with another company, and if that other company arrives in Del Norte first, my company will be out thousands!"

Charlie McQueen stepped forthrightly up. "Why did you kill these men, Marshal Mannion?"

"Can you keep it under your hat?"

McQueen scowled. "*What?*"

"If you keep it under your hat...yours, too, Libby...I'll tell you. If not, no."

"Marshal, this is no time for your customary intransigence," McQueen said.

Mannion glanced at the horses and Cletus Booker and said, "Take them away." He walked up the steps of the jailhouse stoop.

"Marshal *Mannion!*" McQueen said, incensed. Mannion heard him stomp a shoe in the dirt. "Do not walk away from me when I am talking to you! I sign your checks!"

Joe curled a wry smile as he continued across the porch and into his jailhouse office.

He kicked the door closed behind him, hooked his hat on a wall peg, removed his cartridge belt and .44s, and hooked them over the peg by his hat. He walked to the washstand on the far side of the room, pulling his shirttails out of his pants. He'd removed his brown corduroy shirt and was washing at the stand, using semiwarm water from the cracked stone pitcher, when angry footsteps sounded on the porch outside the door.

McQueen said, "I'd better visit with him alone, Jerome. It's damned hard to talk to him when he's in one of his moods, but I'll be damned if he won't listen to me. I *do* sign his checks!"

"Yes, well good luck. I'll be waiting over at the San Juan anticipating the success of your conversation, Charlie. A more colicky man...not to mention disrespectful... I've never met. He needs to release my ramrod posthaste!" Footsteps tapped angrily down the porch steps.

Outside the door, McQueen cleared his throat, knocked once, and came inside. Mannion turned to him as he soaped his chest and armpits. McQueen stopped short, flushing. Mannion might have been pushing fifty, but he was still a large, well-built man—most impressive across the broad chest, hub-like shoulders, and he had only a little middle-aged tallow across his narrow waist.

"Oh...well, uh...excuse me," the mayor said, removing his hat and averting his gaze.

"Come on in, Mister Mayor. You know the man out there quite well, I take it." Joe grinned. "Don't tell me you've invested in the Rio Grande Southern!"

Again, McQueen flushed. "That's none of your damn business!" He kicked the door closed.

"Those four dead men out there were hounding the trail of my deputy and his prisoner." Toweling himself, Mannion stepped up to the diminutive McQueen. "Stringbean is taking her to Tucson. They started out under cover of darkness. Somehow, those four tinhorns got wind of our plan and followed us likely with the intent of kidnapping and raping the girl and turning her into Tucson themselves for the bounty on her head."

Mannion draped the towel over a chair back and glanced over his shoulder at the mayor. "You keep that under your hat. You may sign my checks, but if it gets around town about Stringbean and the girl, I'm gonna dirty your suit."

McQueen looked down at his suit then up at Mannion, scowling. "Is that a threat?"

"Damn tootin'."

"Mannion, you're impossible. Those four men were providing meat for Jerome's...*Mister Libby's*...work crew. Without food they can't work! Without Mister Libby's ramrod, his work crew is hamstrung!"

Mannion had donned his shirt and was buttoning it, facing the little mayor glaring back at him through his spectacles. "Jerome's just gonna have to hire new hunters and a new ramrod. The man pulled a gun on me. O'Bannion's fate is up to the circuit court judge, whenever he gets here."

McQueen stepped sharply forward, cheeks red above his neatly cropped, brown beard. "Why do you have to be so damned hard to work with?"

"Just my way, Charlie."

"The Del Norte Line has a larger crew. Without their ramrod, they could very likely get here first, ahead of the Rio Grande."

"That's your problem. If I don't keep the lid on things, there's gonna be an all-out war on the streets before either line gets here—including the one you have an interest in—and that'll be *my* problem." Mannion was pouring himself a cup of coffee at the potbelly stove. "Progress—crap!"

"I understand you need to keep the peace, Marshal. That's your job. But within *reason*!"

Mannion chuckled. "You mean, just arrest men from the Del Norte Line."

"That's not what I meant at all. I fully understand that if you can't keep the peace there won't be much of a town left by the time—"

"Jerome's line."

"By the time *either line* arrives here. I have to admit I have a small interest in the Rio Grande Southern, but either line is going to mean a major business inoculation into Del Norte's economy. Hell, business is already booming from the work crews and with the prospect of one of the two lines arriving. I hear from prospective business investors, cattle ranchers, and mine operators every day. The opera house in and of itself is doing a booming business." McQueen added more quietly and meaningfully, "Not to mention the San Juan."

That was Jane's business, of course. Was McQueen getting a dig in, knowing Jane had left Joe and Vangie?

"I'll do my job, Mayor. You do yours. I might have to hire more deputies."

"That might be problematic. You know how tight the town council is."

"Which you're head of," Joe pointed out.

"I'll talk to them about it." McQueen sniffed again and opened the door. "Please consider merely fining and releasing Libby's man. I'm sure there was plenty of blame to go around concerning those fights in the Three-Legged Dog. You know, Joe—Libby and the entire Rio Grande Southern Line is powerful, and they have great interest in reaching Del Norte ahead of the Del Norte Line. They're going to need O'Bannion."

Mannion had hiked his hip on the edge of his desk. He sipped his coffee—intending to pour some of Theo O'Flanagan's busthead into it as soon as McQueen left—and laughed. "Is that a threat, Mister Mayor? Are you threatening the man whose checks you sign?"

McQueen flushed again, sheepishly, as though saying what was good for the goose was good for the gander. "All I'm saying, Marshal," he said, pausing to clear his throat, "is that while of course it's necessary to keep the peace, it is also necessary for you to not get carried away, as we both know you can do."

He opened the door and went out.

Mannion shook his head. Amazing what money will do to people. Rich men had tried to line his pockets a time or two. Or three or four over the years. He'd had none of that. Say what you will about Bloody Joe Mannion, he could not be bought. His self-respect wasn't for sale.

Obviously, McQueen's was.

Holding his coffee, he walked to the door and stepped out onto the stoop, looking up and down the busy street. It was only eight o'clock, but already men and women of every stripe were milling about, driving wagons, walking up and down the boardwalks, riding horseback.

Line girls dressed in colorful frillies milled with the men on the boardwalks, bleary-eyed from all-night frolics and poker games.

Blue smoke from breakfast fires hung in ragged clouds over the street. The smell of bacon and morning coffee, some cooked right out on the street, permeated the air.

He noticed white men, Mexicans, Chinese, Blacks, and Old Worlders—Germans and Scandinavians, most of whom who either worked in the mines or for the two approaching railroads. As he continued to look around, one face in particular caught his eye. The face and the rusty red hair piled high atop her head as her two-seater carriage pulled up, driven by a Black man in a three-piece suit, red cravat, and black top hat, in front of the San Juan Hotel and Saloon.

Mannion's heart thudded. A knot formed in his throat.

Jane.

He stared at his estranged wife in mute shock.

She was dressed to the nines as usual, in a butternut traveling suit with matching waistcoat and a long, pleated skirt. She wore a flowered picture hat pinned to the side of her piled-up hair. As the driver helped her out of the carriage, she stepped onto the boardwalk fronting the San Juan and swung her gaze toward Hotel de Mannion.

Joe felt himself flinch, gut tightening, when she looked straight at him.

They shared a long, stony look and then she swung around and mounted the San Juan's high, broad wooden veranda. She didn't look at Joe again before she pushed through the San Juan's stout oak doors and was followed inside by her Black driver, who was carrying two portmanteaus, one under each arm.

The door swung closed.

Joe stepped back into his office, closed the door, set his coffee on his desk, and ran his hands brusquely through his hair, groaning miserably.

———

"HEY, PENDEJO," SAID LA STILETTA RIDING BEHIND Stringbean, "I have a nature call."

Stringbean hipped around in his saddle to peer back at the hellion riding her long-legged sorrel, the morning sun glistening in her rich, brown hair tumbling down from her straw sombrero. "What's that?"

"I have to *pee*."

Letting his coyote dun keep walking along the floor of the ancient, rocky riverbed they'd been following for the past hour, Stringbean pondered, confounded. Of course, she was going to have to tend nature. For some reason, he hadn't thought of that. Marshal Mannion must not have thought about it, either, because he hadn't given Stringbean instructions on how he was supposed to handle such a situation. The marshal had told him to keep his prisoner handcuffed at all times.

What about when she was tending nature?

She scowled at him scowling back at her. "Hey, pendejo, did you hear me? Don't give me that stupid look. I need to stop and make water. I could also do with some food and a cup of coffee. We've been riding all night and it is almost midmorning, after all. I am hungry!"

Stringbean looked around, glowering, before returning his gaze to the girl. "Would you keep your voice down?" He looked around again, anxiously. There likely wasn't anyone else out here, not this far off the beaten track the marshal had him following, but there was no point in taking chances.

She lifted her head suddenly and cut loose with a shrill cry at the sparkling, blue morning sky, letting the scream die, echoing off the near ridges. Then she laid in with a just as loud and shrill, "*I have to tend nature, pendejo! And I need a cup of coffee!*"

Coff-ee...

Ccof-fee...

Coff-ee-ee-ee...

echoed the girl's angry wail, dwindling gradually to be replaced by the ratcheting screech of a hawk making slow, lazy circles straight above them.

Stringbean was exasperated. "Hush up, now, dammit!"

He checked the dun down abruptly, swung his right leg over the saddle horn, and dropped straight down to the ground. He threw down the reins of both horses and walked over to the girl, his eyes and cheeks blazing with exasperation. "You cause too much trouble, I'll shoot you. Marshal's orders!"

She leaned out from her saddle to grin down at him

jeeringly, her mud-brown eyes glistening in the sunshine. "You won't do it, though, pendejo. You don't have it in you. The marshal you respect so much couldn't have chosen a worse man...just a *boy*, really...for the job!"

"Ah, hell," Stringbean said and drew his Barlow knife from his pants pocket.

She was right. He didn't have it in him. Marshal Mannion couldn't have chosen a worse man...or *boy*...for the job.

Stringbean cut her black-booted feet from the stirrups then reached up and cut her cuffed hands from her saddle horn. He stepped back, drew his old Remington from the holster riding high on his right hip, and aimed it at her. "Any sudden moves and I will put a bullet in you. You're right—it ain't gonna be easy, but I'll do it, by God. Marshal's orders, and I follow the marshal's orders!"

She rolled her eyes then swung her right leg over the horn of the saddle. Her skirt rose up around her legs, showing her long, white pantalettes underneath, as she dropped to stand before Stringbean, smiling her mocking smile up at him, who stood a little over a head taller than she.

"Don't you gringos have a saying? Never send a boy to do a man's job!"

She laughed her mocking laugh through her teeth.

CHAPTER 14

DANG, THIS GIRL WAS A PIECE OF WORK, STRINGBEAN thought.

He'd so much rather be back in Del Norte with his dear Molly, even though she was mad at him for accepting this crazy job, than having to endure the endless mocking and complication of La Stiletta. When she'd left Arizona, why couldn't she have gone south into Mexico instead of north into Colorado only to make Stringbean's life a living hell?

He didn't respond to the hellion's mockery. That's what she wanted him to do. He wasn't going to give her that. If he didn't respond to her, maybe she'd eventually get bored and keep her mouth shut.

He looked at her cuffed hands, remembering the marshal's order to keep her cuffed. What would the marshal propose in this situation?

Stringbean had to figure it out on his own. And he did.

Keeping the old Remy aimed at her belly, he pulled his handcuff keys out of his jeans pocket. Sliding his gaze between the girl's brown hands to her eyes, looking for sign of an imminent pounce, he unlocked the cuff from around her right hand then quickly closed it over his own left wrist.

She gave a caustic laugh. "You're going to help me *pee*, pendejo?"

Stringbean holstered the Remington and led her into the brush beside the trail, looking for a good place for her to tend nature without running out on him.

"What are you *doing*, pendejo?" she asked. "I am *not* going to drop my drawers with your hand cuffed to mine. Oh, you'd like that, wouldn't you?"

"Stop calling me pendejo," he said, leading her through the brush and stunt cedars. "I know what it means." It meant idiot in Spanish. It might be fitting, but he was tired of being reminded of it.

She threw her head back and cackled her witch's laugh.

"Here we go." He had found what he was looking for —a pine with a lower branch roughly as thick as his forearm. He smiled in satisfaction as he unlocked the cuff over his left wrist. The branch was about three feet up from the base of the pine's trunk. Still smiling in satisfaction, he started to close the cuff over the branch.

He had just started to squeeze the bracelet closed when she pounced with a feral scream—the scream of a wildcat with bloody murder on its mind. La Stiletta slammed into him, ramming her forehead into his chin. She bulled him over with surprising power for a girl her size. He struck the ground on his back, and then she was struggling on top of him, hammering his face with the end of her cuffed right wrist, grunting with each enraged blow, her jaws hard, eyes glinting with fury.

Amid the attack, Stringbean glanced down to see that with her free, left hand she was sliding his Remington from its cracked leather holster.

Without thinking about his next move but only reacting to the situation, he grabbed that wrist with his right hand and slammed the heel of his left hand against her right cheek, just beneath her eye.

She screamed and flew off him and lay still on the ground, out like a blown lamp. Her hair, tangled and peppered with pine needles, lay like a rich, dark-brown pillow on the ground beneath her head.

Stringbean sat up, breathless. Satisfaction touched him.

He'd staved off her first attack.

"Whew," he said, running his right wrist across his sweaty forehead. "Well, now, Miss La Stiletta," he said to the unconscious girl. "I hope you got a big bladder, because you'll be holdin' it for the whole rest of the trip!"

He cuffed her hands behind her back then walked to his horse and poured water from his canteen over his face. It burned where she'd cut him, in several places on his cheeks and lips. He'd bet if he had a looking glass his face would look like that of a bare-knuckle fighter at the end of a long Saturday night on Fourth Avenue in Del Norte. That's where they held the fights, which always erupted into the crowd of onlookers and bettors.

Del Norte. As rowdy as it was, he missed the place already.

He capped the canteen and returned it to his saddle.

Licking the blood from his lips, he gathered wood, started a fire, and had a pot of coffee gurgling by the time she stirred. Lying belly down ten feet from the fire, she turned to him, dirt and sand on her cheeks. Her left eye was already swelling.

"Release me, damn you, pendejo."

"Hah!" Stringbean dropped a handful of Arbuckles he'd just ground on a rock with his pistol butt into the boiling pot.

"Damn you!"

"Damn me?" Stringbean said, satisfaction overwhelming him. "Damn you. You really busted my chops for me!" He licked his lips and worked his jaws.

"Help me up, at least. I ache all over."

When the coffee returned to a boil, Stringbean took it off the fire and poured water from his canteen into the coffee pot to settle the grounds. As he did, he wondered what Marshal Mannion would do in such a situation—having staved off a savage attack from La Stiletta. He grinned as he returned the pot's lid to the pot with a leather swatch. He knew, all right. He'd let her lay there a good, long time.

"Nope. You're a ringtail, and you deserve no such thing. In fact, I might have you ridin' belly down across your saddle a ways, give you time to consider your misdeeds. Learn your lesson, so to speak." He could hear the words as though they were pouring out of Bloody Joe Mannion's mouth.

"Go to hell!" she said, spitting grit from her lips. "You're a pig! A jackass fool!"

"I ain't the one layin' cuffed belly down on the ground."

"My eye hurts."

What would the marshal say?

Stringbean grinned as it came to him. "Yep, you gotta nice shiner comin' up. My lips don't feel none too special, neither."

Stringbean poured himself a cup of the hot, piping java, the steam wafting aromatically into his face. He sat and drank a cup, enjoying the girl's eyes on him, hatefully. Under normal circumstances he'd feel guilty, but he didn't feel one bit guilty under these.

Would Bloody Joe?

Hell no.

He likely shouldn't give her a cup, but after Stringbean had finished his first cup, the tenderhearted cuss he was, he refilled his and filled one more. He pulled two plates out of his war bag and dropped a baking powder biscuit and two strips of jerky on each. He had to feed the hellion. He had to keep her alive.

The marshal would likely agree.

Stringbean pondered on this.

Wouldn't he agree?

Stringbean didn't know for sure, but he went over and uncuffed one of her wrists, ready for another onslaught but not too worried about it. He could handle her just fine. That shiner on her eye was proof of that.

He led her over to the fire and cuffed one wrist to the horn of her saddle, leaving the other one free. She wouldn't get far dragging the saddle. He gave her the coffee and plate of food, then went back and sat down on a rock across the fire from her where he could keep an eye on her.

They ate without saying anything, but she glared at him plenty.

Inwardly, he grinned. He'd earned her respect. And that was saying something...

When they finished the coffee and jerky, he stowed the pot, plates, and cups in his big canvas war bag, cuffed her hands behind her back, saddled their mounts, and lifted her into the saddle. He kept her hands cuffed behind her back as he tied her feet to her stirrups. He did this all as Bloody Joe would have done—purposefully, carefully, and taking no chances.

Last, he cuffed her hands to the saddle horn.

She sat grimly staring at him, looking none too happy. No, not one bit happy, her tangled, dirty hair in her face, partly concealing the rising shiner.

Again, inwardly grinning, Stringbean climbed onto his dun's back and booted the mount, tugging La Stiletta's sorrel along behind, back out to the old Spanish freight trail and swung south.

They rode for a couple more hours, up and down one pine-clad ridge after another, the massive Black Range quartering ahead and on their left. As the day wore on, shadows grew long until the sun started to teeter on the point of a steeple-like ridge in the west.

Time to make camp.

Stringbean found a good, low spot surrounded by rocks and boulders and backed by a granite wall. A little stream trickled along the western edge and around the base of the wall and down the ridge and into the thick fir forest beyond, which was turning darker by the minute.

La Stiletta hadn't said anything to him since lunch and she said nothing to him now while he got her and the horses situated and set up camp complete with a growing cook fire ringed with stones, his dented black coffee pot hanging from the tripod.

He'd poured himself and the sullen hellion, who'd had her fangs filed, for sure, coffee and had beans and bacon cooking over the fire, when a loud, eerie screech sounded distantly. Both Stringbean and the girl started and looked around.

So did the horses, both of which Stringbean had picketed in a notch in boulders down a rise to his right.

"Mierda," said La Stiletta, letting her fork drop to her plate with a loud *ping!* Stringbean had released her right hand so she could eat. "That's a jaguar or I don't know my cats!"

Stringbean looked around. He had to admit his heart was beating a little faster than before, but then he chuckled as he gave the beans a stir. He gave a casual shrug. "Long ways away."

"Now, maybe," said La Stiletta.

The sun had gone down and out beyond the sphere of guttering firelight, it was nearly pitch-black.

"The fire'll keep it away."

"Uncuff me." She jerked her left hand cuffed to the horn of her saddle. "I don't want to die cuffed to this damn saddle!"

Stringbean laughed and considered what the marshal would say. "If wishes had wings, pigs would fly!"

"Please!"

He looked at her. She appeared genuinely afraid though of course she might be faking it. Stringbean was taking no chances.

"Like I said—don't worry. The fire'll keep it away. If not, I got my rifle right here and I'm right handy with it." Stringbean patted the Winchester leaning against a rock to his left.

He gave the beans and bacon another stir then spooned up a plate for him and La Stiletta. He gave her a plate of beans and a cup of coffee then went back and sat on the rock, washing the succulent beans and bacon—if he may say so himself—down with the rich, black mud.

Again, the cat gave its angry cry.

The girl gasped and jerked her head in the direction from which the cry had come. Stringbean thought the beast must be up in those dark rocks to the west, beyond the rocky course of an ancient riverbed, high above the camp.

Yeah, long ways away. Nothing to worry about.

La Stiletta set her plate aside, no longer hungry, and turned to Stringbean. "Por favor. You have to release me. I won't go anywhere. Where would I go?"

Stringbean pointed his fork at her and smiled knowingly. "Now, that's just what I'd figure you'd say."

"Don't be an idiot! That cat is coming closer!"

"The fire will keep it away," Stringbean said again, casually, and went back to forking the beans and bacon into his mouth.

Again, the screeching cry came from the west. Louder. Closer this time. From down lower on the rocky ridge.

Maybe the girl was right. Maybe it was heading this way.

Again, Stringbean shrugged. The fire would keep it away from the camp.

His heart was beating faster and his palms were slick, but he ignored both and continued to eat though the beans didn't taste nearly as good as they had a few minutes ago.

The cat continued to issue its angry cry every minute or so, each cry a little louder than before as it moved down that dark ridge. The horses were really whickering now, their hooves stomping the stony ground as they tugged at their halter ropes tied to tough roots webbing out from cracks in the rocks.

The girl glared at Stringbean. She put her head down and flared her nostrils at him. "You are going to get me killed, you fool!"

Another cry, louder than the previous ones.

Stringbean jerked with such a start that he dropped his plate and fork and spilled his coffee. The cry had come from much lower on the ridge than before. He turned to stare down through the boulders but could see nothing but darkness.

The cat had come down the ridge and was in the hollow below the camp.

"Mierda!" the girl cried.

"Easy," Stringbean said, slowly rising.

He grabbed his Winchester and pumped a cartridge into the chamber.

"Release me! I demand it!"

"Shh!" Stringbean moved out away from the camp, saying with an assurance he didn't totally feel, "I'll get him. Don't you worry..."

"Don't leave me here alone!"

"Shh!"

"Pendejo!"

Stringbean stepped between two boulders as he made his way down the declivity, moving slowly. When he moved out from between the boulders, he stopped on a low shelf and stared out across the hollow between himself and the forested ridge beyond. There were stars and a thumbnail moon, revealing the hollow as a giant dinosaur mouth of pale, shadowy rocks jutting this way and that. Through the middle of the mouth ran an ancient riverbed sheathed in cottonwoods and willows. It was a pale rectangle in the darkness beneath him, fifty yards down and beyond him.

Another roar sounded, echoing off the surrounding ridges and confirming his suspicion that the cat was on the prowl in that riverbed.

Above and behind Stringbean, the horses whickered

and whinnied anxiously. They might be what the cat was after. Fresh horse flesh. Or señorita flesh...

Stringbean couldn't let the beast climb up out of that riverbed and get into the camp. It seemed to be getting brave enough that the fire might not ward it off.

Another roar vaulted up out of the hollow. Stringbean had been expecting it. Still, it was so loud and savage and filled with such preternatural fury that the deputy's spine momentarily turned to stone.

He peered down the rocky declivity to his right. There was a narrow corridor in the rocks that way, rising from the riverbed. That was the route by which Stringbean and the girl had ridden up from the bed. The cat was likely taking that route as well.

Stringbean drew a breath against his fast-beating heart. Time to find out.

He moved down through the rocks, angling to his left, moving slowly, stepping from one stone to another. He didn't try to stay behind cover. The cat knew he was here; it had winded him already, probably some time ago, in fact. Hell, it likely knew just how many humans and horses were in the camp up and behind the deputy, whose slick hands squeezed the Winchester tightly, his right index finger curled against the trigger.

He stepped down through the shelving rocks into the winding gap that angled down toward the riverbed. He stopped and squatted on his heels, resting the rifle across his knees.

A sickly-sweet smell filled his nostrils. The feral smell of the cat hung heavy in the air, like the rotten stench of powder smoke after a gun battle. It was so thick it made Stringbean's eyes water.

The cat was close.

Very close.

Stringbean rose. His knees were trembling, his heart racing.

Damn, he was scared, and make no mistake!

He chuckled dryly to himself. The old fear. He hadn't conquered it yet. Would he ever? Would the marshal be scared in such a situation?

Sure, he would. Any man would, Stringbean told himself, hopefully.

He moved through the corridor, jagged rock walls rising on each side of him, limned by moonlight.

He followed a bend in the corridor then stopped suddenly.

The stench was thicker than before. Stringbean's heart hammered. Cold sweat bathed him.

The cat was here, within a few feet. He was sure of it!

He raised the rifle to his shoulder, waved it around, ready to shoot at the first moving shadow.

"Where are you, blastit?" he yelled. "I know you're here, goddamn your—!"

A shrill screech rose from nearly straight above him.

Stringbean yelled and raised the Winchester's barrel and his heart hiccupped when he saw the giant beast silhouetted against the starry sky, hunkered low atop a flat-topped boulder maybe thirty feet above. Two red eyes flashed in the large, square head. The cat scuttled forward and dropped over the edge of its perch, flinging itself toward its hunter with a ferocious snarl.

Stringbean screamed as he fired, heard the agonized wail as the cat dropped toward him. Stringbean flung himself straight back as the cat struck the ground before him with a heavy thud then rose in a blur of fast motion and swung to Stringbean's right—a large, cat-shaped shadow in the darkness.

The beast's wild stench burning his nose and eyes,

Stringbean rolled onto his belly, pumping another cartridge into the rifle's action, and sent two more shots howling toward the cat's shadow just as it disappeared in a notch on the corridor's far side, pulling its angrily curling tail after it.

Stringbean felt the warm, oily wetness of blood under his right arm.

He'd wounded the cougar, but it was heading up the ridge toward the easier prey of the girl and the horses!

He rose and, ejecting the spent casing and pumping a live round into the Winchester's action, took off running up the corridor. Despite his logy hip, he ran hard, breath raking in and out of his lungs, heart banging against his breastbone.

Above and ahead of him, the horses' cries grew shriller. The cat was closing on the camp.

"No, dammit!" Stringbean said. "I got you—*slow down!*"

His spurs jangled raucously as he ran toward the fire-light flickering between the two boulders.

The girl screamed.

Stringbean ran out from between the two boulders, dropped to a knee, and fired just as the big cat hurled itself toward La Stiletta.

The cat gave another loud, shrill, agonized wail and stuck the ground at the girl's feet. It tried to lift itself, clawing the ground. Stringbean put two more rounds into it. It leaned forward and collapsed on the girl's legs with one more groan then shook and wagged its head as though in defiance of the life leaving it.

Stringbean peered through the powder smoke wafting over the fire.

The girl's left hand was still cuffed to the saddle horn. Her right was flung out to her side. She was half sitting up, her hair partly covering her face but not those hate-filled eyes.

Her chest rose and fell sharply as she breathed, making a face against the stench of the beast that had come within a foot of turning her into a meal.

"*Pendejo!*" she screamed.

CHAPTER 15

"FELLAS," BLOODY JOE SHOUTED ON MAIN STREET OF Del Norte, "throw those damn shovels down—we're takin' you in for drunk an' disorderly! I'm plum sick of this shit!"

"Go to hell, Mannion!" shouted one of the four drunk miners trying to beat each other's heads in at high noon between the Wooden Nickel on one side of the street and the San Juan Hotel & Saloon on the other.

The man—bald and wearing a thick, black walrus mustache—swung around toward Joe, swinging his shovel toward Mannion as well, and threw it with a loud, angry grunt.

Mannion ducked.

The shovel made an eerie *whooshing* sound as it spun through the air where Joe's head had just been and smashed into the side panel of the wagon behind him and on which THE HIGH & MIGHTY MINE was painted in large, green letters. All four miners were from the High & Mighty, and they'd gotten into a kerfuffle over a half-breed whore while having beers in the Wooden Nickel—or so had said the young, towheaded odd-job boy, Harmon Haufenthistle, who'd reported the foofaraw to Joe just a few minutes earlier.

The blonde nine-year-old, tan as a Mexican and in patched overalls with a U.S. Mail pouch hooked over one shoulder, stood nearby now, cheeks flushed and eyes wide with excitement. No one enjoyed a fight like the hardworking young Harmon. He needed a diversion now and then, Harmon did. And Del Norte was not short on them.

"Look out, Joe!" the younker shouted, jumping up and down in his worn half boots.

The brigand who'd thrown the shovel ran toward Joe now, bellowing like a poleaxed bull, crouching and throwing his head and broad shoulders into Joe's chest and lifting him up off the ground and throwing him back against the High & Mighty supply wagon. The man's attack had happened so fast that Joe had had no time to wield the hide-wrapped bung starter he'd brought to the fight, along with his two deputies, Cletus Booker and Rio Waite, both armed with bung starters instead of rifles or shotguns so's not to bloody up Del Norte's main drag and get Mayor Charlie McQueen's under frillies in any more of a twist than they already were.

As he struck the back of the wagon, Joe saw the other three miners swing their own shovels at Rio and Cletus, who also ducked to avoid the would-be brain-crushing blows. The walrus-mustached man's blow rattled Joe's own brains but just as the big brigand attacking him tried to wrap his big hands around Mannion's throat, Joe headbutted him with a bellowing wail of his own.

That sent the man stumbling backward, hands to his forehead.

Joe stepped forward and buried his right boot in the man's balls.

As the man jackknifed with a wail, Joe brought his right knee up and felt the man's nose turn sideways as it exploded, sending blood spewing in all directions around Joe's black denim-clad knee.

That pretty much took care of the walrus-mustached man, who dropped to his knees wailing.

As he did, one of the other three High & Mighty miners swung his own shovel at Joe's head, stretching his lips back from gritted teeth, cobalt blue Norwegian eyes as large and round as silver dollars. The shovel raked across the side of Joe's left temple, infuriating him.

With another enraged wail, Joe picked up the bung starter he'd dropped during the walrus-mustached man's assault, stepped forward, and swung it back behind his right shoulder and then forward until it smashed against the temple of his current attacker's big, blond head with a resounding, crunching thud. That spun the man full around, staggering and wailing.

Joe stepped forward just as the blonde man swung back toward him, and Joe smashed his right fist into the blonde gent's lantern jaw. He smashed his left fist into the lantern jaw and kept punching as the man staggered back toward the yelling and excitedly jumping young Harmon Haufenthistle.

The blond-headed man dropped to the street. Joe crouched over him, jerking his head up by the collar of his blue work shirt and went to work on the man's face with his right fist, delivering jab after jab to the man's mouth until his lips looked like chopped liver.

"Dang, Joe," Harmon warned. "You're gonna *kill* the son of a buck!"

"Intend to!" Joe bellowed, fury a wild stallion inside him. Indeed, he was sick of this crap. He'd put the lid on

Del Norte once and he damned well intended to do it again, by God!

"Joe!" a familiar voice yelled behind him.

"Go to hell, Rio!" Joe shouted and delivered to the Norwegian another jaw-crunching punch.

Mannion pulled his fist back to his shoulder and was about to let it fly once more when two hands wrapped around it and a familiar voice as though from the mists of the past said, *"Joe!"*

The voice stopped Mannion cold. He turned to see Jane crouched to his right, holding his big, brown hand in both of her delicate, beringed, long-fingered ones. Her amber eyes were haunted, repelled, and commanding. "Enough."

He stared at her.

She stared back at him.

Joe slackened the muscles in his right arm and slowly relaxed his fist.

He nodded, glancing at young Harmon Haufen-thistle staring over Jane's left shoulder at him, then returned his chagrined gaze to that of his estranged wife.

"For God sakes," Jane said and, straightening, released his hand.

Mannion felt the coals of rage in his head lose their heat and looked down at the Norwegian's ruined mouth. The man stared up at him, fjord-blue eyes glazed in agony. Mannion rose and turned to see both Rio and Cletus Booker kneeling on the backs of two miners, both of whom had their hands cuffed behind them, docile as sheep for the shearing. Both deputies regarded Joe skeptically, deep lines carved into their foreheads beneath the brims of their hats.

Rio shuttled his gaze from Joe to Jane then back to

Joe, and his expression softened, a faint smile tugging at the corners of his mouth.

Mannion turned to see the walrus-mustached man still down on all fours behind him, shaking his head as though to clear it.

"Get them back to the jail," Joe said. "The judge is gonna have a busy day tomorrow."

Mannion hauled the Norwegian to his feet by his shirt collar and gave him a shove down the street toward the jail. Rio hauled the walrus-mustached man to his feet and Booker grabbed the Norwegian by his arm, gave him another shove, and both deputies and their four suddenly meek, bloody charges headed off down the street toward Hotel de Mannion, the traffic having come to a standstill during the bloody fight that had broken out in the middle of it.

Mannion felt all eyes on him. Again. They eyed him like a circus lion that had broken out of its cage.

Again.

Harmon Haufenthistle stared up at him, lower jaw hanging.

Feeling a sheepish flush in his cheeks, Mannion turned to see Jane still standing nearby, gazing up at him, eternally confounded.

"You sure gave 'im the what for, Bloody Joe," young Harmon said.

Jane placed a hand on the boy's shoulder. "Harmon, you run along now. I'm sure you have plenty of work to do. This was nothing for you to see"—she turned to Joe, her eyes disgusted and incriminating—"or to learn from, I might add."

Mannion flinched at that.

When the crowed that had gathered around the dustup had dispersed and young Harmon had jogged off down the street to the north, likely headed for one of his many and sundry daily chores—few men worked as hard as young Harmon—Jane turned to Mannion, staring up at him. "Let me get you cleaned up."

She turned and walked toward her elegant, sprawling hotel and saloon on the street's west side, the broad front verandah filled with men and working girls who'd gathered to watch the midday entertainment. Jane lifted the hem of her long, burnt-orange skirt, which matched the thick tresses of her hair piled atop her head, sausage curls dangling down along her freckled cheeks, and started up the steps. The crowd above parted for her, the eyes of both men and her own working girls regarding her with characteristic warmth and admiration before returning to Mannion, their expressions then stretching from skepticism to downright disdain.

That was all right, Mannion thought, looking at the scraped, bloody knuckles of his right hand. He wasn't here to be loved.

At least, not by them.

What about by Jane?

Suddenly, he didn't know.

Who was he kidding?

Feeling self-conscious with all eyes on him but staring back at them with customary defiance, he crossed the street and mounted the veranda steps. No one said anything. In fact, the entire street was still unnaturally quiet, the wagon traffic only just then beginning to move again. His boots thudded on the steps, spurs ringing.

The crowd parted for him. As he made his way to the saloon's front door a short man shouldered up to him on his left and the grocer, Sam Carlisle, said, "Should've given that Norski one more, Joe. He's nothin' but a brute!"

Mannion continued into the San Juan, holding his fist up against his chest, his left hand wrapped around it so he wouldn't drip blood on Jane's carpeted floors. She ran a tight ship, Jane did. Most of the clientele was on the veranda, it appeared; there were only three or four diners and/or drinkers seated at tables, three men with the looks of drifters standing at the bar, nursing beers and whiskey shots. They regarded Mannion dully in the back bar mirrors.

He crossed the room to the broad, carpeted stairs running up the room's right wall. He climbed the steps heavily, apprehension touching him, distracting him from the burn in his bloody knuckles.

What did Jane have in store for him?

He climbed the steps to the third floor, where Jane kept her suite of rooms along with her dozen or so doxies. As he moved along the hall, a door opened farther down on the left. A girl poked her head out. Eyes found Mannion, widened, and then the girl, a blonde named Sissy, pulled her head back into the room, and the door clicked closed.

Joe knocked on Jane's door. He didn't use to have to knock. After his and Vangie's house had been burned, he'd lived here with Jane. Vangie had lived down the hall, in a room of her own.

"Come," Jane said on the other side of the door.

Mannion walked into the lavish suite.

Jane was just then removing a pan of steaming water from the chrome-faced Porter stove that stood against the far wall, to the right of a round, oak table on which account books and tablets were neatly piled. A porcelain washbasin stood on the table.

Jane glanced at Mannion, who was just then closing the door, and poured the water from the steaming pan into the basin. She moved through a door to the left of the table—a large closet, Mannion knew; he knew the suite intimately—and came out with several soft, cotton cloths, a roll of bandages, and scissors.

She moved to the table, slid a chair out with her foot, and glanced at Joe. "Have a seat," she said with a sigh.

She set the cloths, scissors, and bandages on the table then sat in a chair facing her unruly charge, only a few feet from the chair she'd slid out from the table.

Mannion stood in front of the door, staring at her.

She stared back at him. She sat sideways to the table, resting one arm on it. She raised her hand, splayed her fingers, then set the hand back down on the table.

"Come on, Joe. We're not exactly strangers, you know." She paused, wrinkling the skin above the bridge of her nose. "Are we?"

CHAPTER 16

"OF COURSE, WE'RE NOT STRANGERS." MANNION SAT IN the chair Jane had indicated. "That's why I'm here. I don't let just anybody fix my knuckles."

"I was wondering what it was going to take to get you here. Now, I know."

Joe shrugged. "Been busy. A lot has happened since you left so unexpectedly. Under the circumstances, I sort of figured you'd have come to see me."

"Been busy." Jane rose and slid a lock of his salt-and-pepper hair back to reveal his left temple, which the miner's shovel had tattooed. She made a face. "That's going to need a stitch or two. Or three or four."

"It's fine."

Jane sighed and walked into the closet again. She returned with a small leather kit in which, Joe knew, resided a needle and catgut thread she kept to sew up her girls when they were knocked around by drunk jakes. The only bona fide medico in town, Bohannon, was often busy.

Mannion winced. "Jane, I'm fine."

She set the kit on the table then walked over to the

liquor cabinet abutting the wall to the right of the front door. She opened the cabinet, produced a bottle and two cut glass goblets, and set the bottle and the goblets on the table.

"Four Oaks?" Joe said, incredulous. "You know I prefer rotgut to the finest bourbon on the market."

"You know I don't stock rotgut." Jane pulled the cork from the bottle, filled each glass, returned the cork to the bottle, and started to sit down. Mannion grabbed her wrist, turning her back around to face him.

"Why did you leave? Why did you come back?"

Jane looked at his hand wrapped around hers, met his gaze without expression, and shrugged a shoulder. "When you were gone, my father—"

"Vangie told me all about that," Mannion said. "Your father came. He and your mother needed your help up in Glenwood Springs. Still, you could have waited until I got back, told me of your plans, Jane. Told me when and if you were coming back. Instead, you rode on out of town on that infernal stage just as I was riding into town. You saw me. You knew I was back. You kept going anyway, without so much as a wave."

"I'd made my plans, Joe. Besides, I didn't know if you ever *would* be back. I regretted leaving Vangie, but I knew how independent she is. The apple doesn't fall far from the tree there."

"It was a hellish job I was on, Jane. A gang killed a good friend of mine."

"And you needed to hunt them down."

"Of course, I did."

"Without letting your wife know anything about it."

"Jane, there was no time."

"I find it hard to believe you couldn't have sent someone to Del Norte with the information, Joe. But even if you couldn't have, the nature of your work...your own personal nature...is a big problem for me. Even when you were here, with me, you weren't always with me. This town, your job meant more to you than I did. It always has. I should have known better than to marry you. We should have kept it the way it was. Lovers only. No ties."

She pulled her hand free of his, sat down in the chair, scooted up closer to him, taking his right hand in hers, and lowered her head to scrutinize the bloody knuckles.

"Don't call it a mistake, Jane," he said. "You loved me. I loved you."

She lifted her gaze from his knuckles to stare into his eyes, brows arched. "Past tense?"

"You first."

Jane laughed, shook her head. She soaked one of the soft cotton cloths in the basin and wrung it out. She took Joe's right hand and held it over the basin, picked up the bottle, and poured the bourbon over his knuckles. Mannion drew a sharp breath through gritted teeth and clenched his fist.

Jane gave a devilish little smile.

"I'll be damned if you're not enjoying this," he said in a pain-pinched voice.

"I'll be damned if I'm not," Jane admitted.

She dabbed the cloth at the knuckles, a couple of which were scraped nearly to the bone. The blood had semi-dried, resembling cherry jam. They burned like hell.

"Now, to your second question," she said as she dabbed at the cuts, occasionally resoaking the cloth in the water, "I came back to check in on the San Juan. Mister Lillegard is a reliable manager, but I still need to return to check on the books from time to time." She glanced up at him as she soaked the cloth once more. "Don't look so glum, Joe. I had you in mind as well."

She continued dabbing at the knuckles, gradually cleaning them, being none too gentle. Joe kept his teeth clenched against the burn. "I've brought a divorce decree. I had it written up by an attorney in Glenwood Springs. All you have to do is sign it and have it witnessed by an attorney. May I suggest our good mayor, Mister McQueen?"

Mannion scowled at her in astonishment. "So, that's it? You want a divorce?"

"Don't you?"

He studied her, keeping his teeth gritted as she more and more brusquely cleaned his wounds. "I don't...I don't know. I guess if you do, I do." His scowl turned more severe. "Is that really what you want, Jane?"

"If it's not what you want, Joe, tell me," she said, testily.

He looked down at the knuckles she was cleaning.

What did he want?

Could their marriage work? It sure as hell wasn't working now.

Could it ever? Was there any point in them trying again? Wouldn't the same thing happen once more?

With Vangie trapped in the middle...

Jane was probably right. They should have remained lovers only. At least, they'd had that. Now what did they have?

Pain. Accusations. Competition. Challenge.

He sighed with relief when she finished cleaning his knuckles. She dropped the cloth back into the basin and sat back in her chair, regarding him with brows raised again, waiting.

"Jane," Joe said, anguish twisting his guts in a knot, "honey...I honestly don't know..."

Jane pursed her lips. She nodded slowly.

She reached for the sewing kit and produced needle and thread. "Now for that cut on your temple..."

Mannion groaned.

HE GROANED AGAIN AS HE LEFT JANE'S SUITE AND, walking down the hall toward the stairs, brushed a finger across the sutures bristling at his temple.

"Don't think I needed those last two," he mused aloud. "Those were for Jane."

He chuckled as he started down the stairs.

God, he loved that woman. He probably should have admitted it to her. He hadn't been able to lest she'd confessed her love first. That would have been a sign of weakness in Bloody Joe's eyes. He had many faults, but weakness was not one of them. Besides, she'd probably go ahead and divorce him anyway, adding insult to the injury of his revealing himself. A good gambler didn't show his cards.

Wasn't life one big poker game, after all?

He gave another dry chuckle as he descended the stairs, aching and drunk, marveling at his own contrary character.

No one was more an enemy of Bloody Joe than Bloody Joe himself.

He just wanted to go home and take a long nap, maybe chew on a bullet against his frustration at the complications of life and love. But he needed to relieve Cletus, who'd pulled the night shift, and help Rio keep a lid on the town. If that were possible anymore with the two railroads converging on it, and drunk miners thick as thieves.

Mannion was too old for this shit. Long rides.

Getting shot off his horse. Fighting square heads armed with shovels on Main Street.

Falling in love with headstrong redheads. Marrying them, no less!

If it wasn't for Vangie, he'd go home, pack his bags, saddle Red, and ride up into the mountains. He'd find some remote, abandoned trapper's cabin and settle in for the rest of his life. Maybe get a pet skunk like his friend Theo O'Flanagan had done. Thomas, the Irishman had called the surly beast. Build himself a still, stay drunk till his Maker called him home.

But he had Vangie and a town to keep the lid on, so here he was...

He was striding along the boardwalks in the direction of Hotel de Mannion. He noticed a man staring at him from across the busy street.

The man snapped his head back forward and continued walking nearly stride for stride with Joe. He was a little man dressed in black broadcloth trousers, white shirt and suspenders, black broadcloth coat, and a black derby hat set far back on his dark-haired head. He was angular faced with close-set eyes and a thin, black beard. He strode with a silver-capped walking stick in his left hand. A silver-chased Colt was holstered on his right thigh.

The man's eyes, in the brief second or two Joe's had locked on them, had appeared dark with a cunning sort of menace. Now the man continued striding with a casual air, rolling his head from side to side as though stretching out the kinks. He dipped a hand into a pocket of his broadcloth coat, pulled out a long, black cheroot, and stopped to touch flame to it.

Mannion stopped as well. He regarded the derby-hatted gent dubiously.

Blue tobacco smoke billowed around the man's head, he waved his match out and tossed it into the street. He pulled the cheroot out of his mouth and looked at Mannion over his right shoulder. He grinned, teeth the color of old ivory showing inside his beard.

Joe's guts tightened. His heart thudded.

"Hello, Joe."

Mannion snapped his head forward to see another man step out of the grocery store to his right.

"Nice day, eh?" said Cal Taggart, owner of the White Horse Saloon, as he stepped in front of Joe on his way to the street, a bag of groceries in his arms.

Mannion got a whiff of pickled eggs and ham hocks, which Taggart served with his free lunch in the White Horse, an eye wink before yet another man stepped out from the break between the grocery store and the ladies hat shop just beyond it. The third man—garbed in worn trail gear, tall, thin, ruddy-skinned, blue-eyed and wearing a gray-blond mustache—turned toward Mannion, who saw the gun in the man's hand just before it *popped!* and orange flames lapped from the barrel.

Taggart had not yet stepped past Joe.

The saloon owner gave a yelp and tumbled forward onto the boardwalk, dropping his groceries.

The man who'd fired the revolver snapped his eyes wide in shock before swinging around and running up the street, away from Mannion.

"Cal!"

Joe crouched over the saloon owner and saw the big, bloody exit wound in nearly the dead center of his chest. The man was shaking, and thick, red blood was pooling on the boardwalk beneath him.

"Shit!"

Mannion looked up to see the shooter, clad in a cream

Stetson, blue work shirt, pinto vest, and black denims, running up the street.

Mannion palmed one of his Russians and broke into a run of his own, yelling, "Come back here, coward!"

He stopped in the middle of the next cross street when he saw the man who'd just lit his cheroot toss it away, drop his walking stick, palm his silver-chased hog leg, crouch, and extend the popper toward Joe.

Mannion threw himself forward as bullets hurled toward him, caroming through the air where he'd just been standing.

Mannion rolled onto his left shoulder, extended the Russian, and snapped off a shot. The bullet puffed dust from a hitchrack support post, causing a saddled horse tied there to pitch and whinny shrilly, pulling at its reins. Mannion was about to snap off another shot but stopped when the derby-hatted gent wheeled and ran into a break between two buildings, his shadowy figure dwindling quickly.

Folks on that side of the street were yelling and scattering. Traffic on the street had once again stopped.

"Outta the way, folks," one man bellowed, dropping his reins and hurling himself back into the box of the wagon he'd been driving. "Bloody Joe's at it agin!"

CHAPTER 17

STRINGBEAN GRABBED THE CAT'S HIND LEGS AND
dragged it off the girl, who sat shivering, staring at the
shaggy, gray puma, her dark eyes glazed with tears. She
had her free arm crossed beneath her breasts, which
trembled behind her blouse. Her left hand was still cuffed
to the saddle horn, shaking, the light from the dying fire
glinting off the quivering silver bracelet.

The horses were still kicking and whinnying. The
smell of the cat, dead as it now was, was fresh in their
nostrils. Horses feared nothing as much as they did wildcats. Apparently, judging by La Stiletta's reaction to the
beast, women didn't much care for them either.

Neither did Stringbean. He'd had a few run-ins over
the years. But nothing like this.

Revulsion clawed at him as he dragged the heavy
beast, which had to weigh a good hundred and twenty
pounds, down the slope to the west of the camp, then
rolled it into a deep hollow. The stench of the cat caused
tears of his own to dribble down his cheeks from his
burning eyes.

He looked down at the cat piled up in the hollow, gave another shiver of revulsion then walked up into the camp. He dropped to a knee in front of La Stiletta, who'd drawn her legs up beneath her now and stood staring into the darkness beyond the camp as though in shock, tears still glistening like gold in the firelight on her olive cheeks. Stringbean fished the key from his jeans pocket and released the cuff from her left wrist.

He looked at her. She looked back at him, lips trembling, eyes opaque with terror.

She flared a nostril and slapped him hard across the face with the hand he'd just released from the cuff.

Stringbean winced against the burn of the assault and nodded. "Yep, I had that one comin'." He drew a deep breath.

He looked the girl over. She didn't appear to have any blood on her. Her legs, however, were foamy with the cat's drool. The stench of the beast lingered over her and Stringbean and the rest of the camp.

"Why don't you go over to the creek yonder, get yourself cleaned up?" he said, canting his head in the direction of the narrow stream making faint sucking sounds as it dribbled over rocks only a few yards away and down a slight rise.

Stiffly, La Stiletta rose and walked down the rise to the water.

Stringbean drew another heavy breath and then added some wood from the small pile he'd gathered to the fire, building up the flames. The night had grown chill. He brewed a fresh pot of coffee and was sipping a cup when she returned to the camp, moving as stiffly as before. She crouched to grab a blanket from her bedroll and wrap it around her shoulders. She sat down on her saddle and turned to Stringbean, her expression vaguely curious.

"You're not going to cuff me?"

"Nah." Stringbean leaned back against his own saddle. "I reckon if you want to brain me with a rock and ride on out of here, I have it comin'."

He meant it. For some odd reason, he no longer cared what Marshal Mannion would think about that.

He finished his coffee, checked on the horses, which had gradually settled down now on the leeside of the cat attack then returned to the camp. La Stiletta lay curled up by the fire, wrapped in her soogan, head resting against the woolly underside of her saddle. She stared into the flames that had burned low again, the umber light flickering in her dark eyes.

Stringbean curled up in his own blankets. His nerves were still singing, so it took him a long time to fall asleep but before he did, he heard his charge breathing deeply, slowly, asleep on the other side of the fire. She moaned as she slept, likely enduring the attack all over again.

Stringbean woke to the gray wash of dawn in the east. He cast away his blankets and rose and fed and watered the horses then, walking past La Stiletta, who was still asleep in her blankets, lying as he'd last seen her, facing the fire, he walked down to the stream and bathed his face and drank deeply of the cold mountain snowmelt.

He went back and built up the fire to warm the coffee and grub from the previous night. As he did, the girl stirred, moaned softly, then sat up quickly with a gasp, breasts rising and falling sharply as she awaited the panther to pounce all over again. She looked around as though trying to get her bearings.

She turned to Stringbean and blinked and wrinkled the skin above the bridge of her nose, incredulous.

"I did not kill you in your sleep," she said, as though surprised at her own inaction.

"I reckon not." He grinned as he poured them each a cup of coffee. "I reckon there's always tomorrow night."

"You won't cuff me?"

"Nope. I reckon it's time I started makin' some of my own decisions, bad as they might be. If I fail"—he shrugged as he set the pot on a flat stone—"I fail. But I reckon it'll be on my own terms, not the marshal's." He narrowed an eye at her and dipped his chin resolutely. "I do aim to get you to Tucson, though. There ain't no ifs, ands, or buts about that. I just intend to do it while keepin' you in one piece. No, I won't cuff you, but I will watch you like a hawk, and I'll be leading your horse. Oh, and I'll be shooting you if you try anything."

"Fair enough. But I will try to escape. If I testify in front of that jury, I will be carved into very tiny pieces by the men of a very violent man."

"Fair enough."

They ate the leftover beans and bacon from the night before and drank their coffee watching the sky grow lighter in the east until the sun blossomed behind the tall eastern crags like an enormous yellow flower casting bayonets of rose between the peaks and stretching quick, long shadows over the rocky, sage- and cedar-stippled terrain before it. La Stiletta cleaned their plates and silverware in the stream while Stringbean led the mounts into the camp and saddled them.

Fifteen minutes after sunrise they were both mounted and once again following the ancient riverbed southwest, edging to the right of the Black Range looming on their left. Stringbean thought they should make Arizona by sundown. Once they crossed the territorial border, they'd head straight south toward the

Gilas and the Superstitions, threading the gap between them.

Following the landmarks on the maps folded in his saddlebags, that's what they did, the land changing from grassy prairie peppered with cedars to low desert with mesquites, creosote, and barrel cactus. Skinny coyotes darted off through gaps in the surrounding rocks. The occasional roadrunner dashed across the trail in a flash of red. Diamondbacks sunned themselves here and there about the trail, occasionally giving a menacing warning rattle that spooked the horses as well as their riders.

Stringbean and his prisoner camped that night in the shadow of the Gilas south and on their left, close enough that they could see the crenelations in their bastion-like stone walls glowing copper in the late light. The bald crags of the Superstitions made a stark, tan lump farther to the south and on their right, the highest peaks turning rose as the sun dropped into the undulating western desert.

As they'd traveled via the remotest route possible out here—at least, according to Marshal Mannion—the only people they'd seen were two men in floppy hats and canvas coats driving a dilapidated wagon pulled by a skinny mule toward a stark, red stone mesa through catclaw and prickly pear, picks and shovels jostling in the wagon box. Prospectors likely heading back to camp after a long day of picking and shoveling for their own personal El Dorados.

Stringbean spied three more men hazing a small herd of cattle between the cones of small, stark, ancient volcanoes. Stringbean didn't think the men had seen him and his charge, as they were heading off to the west, angling south. He'd seen them throwing loops at herd quitters and heard their whistles on the hot afternoon breeze, the mooing of the anxious cattle likely being moved from one pasture to another.

As stark as the land was out here, with only thin tufts of blond needlegrass growing in sparse patches amid the rocks and cactus and among the mesquites bristling around seeps and springs, it was hard to believe this was ranch country. But the next day, a little after noon, they saw more evidence of that when five men clad in range gear rode toward them, three from the south and off the left side of the trail, two more coming down the steep side of a high mesa to the south and off the right side of the trail.

Stringbean gave a rare curse. The riders had seen him and his charge and were riding toward them, which very well could mean trouble. He just hoped they weren't Diego Hidalgo's men, or his goose was cooked. No, these five looked like range-riding gringos.

Still...

"Well, well, well," said La Stiletta, amusedly but with a tremor of fear in her voice as well. "What do we have here? So much for avoiding people—eh, deputy?" She paused to study the men as they came within a hundred yards and loped their horses through the bristling desert brush, rising and falling over the low, rocky swells. "I don't like the looks on their faces. I might need a gun, uh? Do you have an extra one?"

"Don't push your luck, señorita," Stringbean said, tension drawing his voice taut.

The five riders converged on the trail roughly fifty yards ahead of Stringbean and the girl and came on, reining up ten feet away. The lead rider was a big man in a black Stetson trimmed with a band of silver conchos, and a thick, brushy, black mustache. His skin was burned a deep red brown and a mole bristled on his chin.

"Who in the hell are you?" he asked in a none too friendly tone, holding the reins of his frisky gelding up high beneath his chin.

"The name's Henry McCallister," Stringbean said, peeling his vest open to reveal the silver star pinned to his shirt. "Deputy town marshal, Del Norte, Colorado Territory."

"A little out of your jurisdiction—aren't you, Deputy?"

"No, not really," Stringbean said, feeling miffed. Who in the hell was this hombre to question his jurisdiction?

"You're on Powderhorn graze, Deputy McCallister," the big man said. "Strictly off-limits. Didn't you see the sign?"

"I didn't see any sign. I figured I was on open range." Which he no doubt was. Some ranchers, however, enjoyed calling open range their own, hanging any and all trespassers. It was a problem all over the west including around Del Norte. Trespassers and so-called "nesters" got their necks stretched all the time. "Just passin' through," he added.

"You come up though that old riverbed?"

"Yes, I did."

A short, thick-set man with one green and one blue eye flanking the big man off his calico's right hip canted his head to one side and said, "Rustlers come up that way, boss. Go back that way, too, on account it's hard to track 'em in them rocks."

"I know it," the boss said, scowling at Stringbean with dark suspicion.

He switched his gaze to La Stiletta and booted his horse up beside hers—so close his left leg pressed against her right one. He reached out and savagely cupped her face in his gloved left hand, scrunching up her cheeks and causing her lips to pooch out. "Who in the hell is this?" he said.

"Go to hell!" the girl said, pulling her face back from the man's brusque hand. She spit in his face.

"Why, you little dev—" The boss pulled his right hand back behind his shoulder and was about to thrust it forward but stopped when he heard the ratcheting click of a revolver.

He left his right hand in the air in front of his shoulder as he turned his incredulous gaze toward String-bean, the man's brown eyes dropping toward the old Remington Stringbean had slid across his belly and was aiming at the man from under his left arm.

Stringbean said, "That ain't polite."

The boss's cheeks turned darker, his eyes fiery. "You're pulling a gun on me on *my own range?*"

"It ain't your range just 'cause you say it is," String-bean said, keeping his voice tight and low.

He heard several clicks and slid his eyes slightly right to see all four other riders aiming cocked hoglegs at him. He kept the brunt of his gaze on the big man and said, "Tell 'em to throw them smoke wagons down and then their saddle guns."

The big man's eyes blazed. His chest rose and fell heavily.

"You're outnumbered, amigo," said one of the other men, who appeared to have some Mexican blood.

"I may be outnumbered but that don't mean I can't give Boss here a mighty big bellyache," Stringbean said, keeping his voice low and calm though inside he was anything but. The hand holding his walnut-gripped Remy was slick with sweat.

La Stiletta looked from Stringbean to the big man

then back again, lips slightly parted, eyes frightened. For once, she said nothing.

Stringbean narrowed one eye at the big man and shaped a wry half smile, waiting.

The man stared back at him, apprehension growing in his fury-bright gaze. He wanted to call Stringbean's bluff, but maybe he wasn't bluffing.

With deep reluctance, he said, "Toss 'em down, boys."

"*What?*" said the man with one green and one blue eye, his red neckerchief with white polka dots bowing in the breeze.

"You heard me," said Boss. "Throw 'em down!"

He kept his gaze on Stringbean.

Guns clicked as hammers were depressed. In the right periphery of his vision, Stringbean watched all four men toss their guns to the ground. They struck with resolute thuds.

They slid their rifles from their saddle sheaths and dropped them to the ground as well.

"Now you, Boss," Stringbean said, keeping that wry smile in place.

"Badge or no badge, you're a dead man."

"We'll see."

Boss slid the Schofield from the holster positioned for the cross-draw on his left hip and tossed it into the brush. He followed with the saddle-ring carbine, sliding it out of its cracked leather scabbard and tossing it into the brush with the Schofield.

"Tell 'em to give us the trail," Stringbean ordered Boss.

Boss glared at Stringbean, chest and broad shoulders rising and falling heavily as he breathed. He looked as though he were ready to exhale pure fire.

"Make way, boys," he said out of the side of his mouth.

When the others had moved off to both sides of the trail Stringbean and his charge had been following, Stringbean tossed La Stiletta the sorrel's reins and said, "*Let's ride!*"

He ground spurs into the dun's flanks.

CHAPTER 18

STRINGBEAN HUNKERED LOW IN THE SADDLE AS HIS DUN shot up the trail.

He glanced over his shoulder to see La Stiletta's sorrel stretching its stride just behind him. The girl, too, was crouched low, the brim of her hat wind-basted against her forehead. She glanced behind at where the Powder-horn men were quickly gathering their guns and fairly leaping into their saddles.

She turned her head forward and said, "Nice play, amigo, but you should have shot them. All you've done is make them mad!"

"I know, I know," Stringbean muttered, knowing she was right.

Knowing that Marshal Mannion would have killed them.

But Stringbean hadn't been able to do it.

Guns popped behind him and the girl, several buzzing like hornets way too close for comfort, ripping into the ground to both sides of Stringbean and La Stiletta, who cursed again, shrilly. Stringbean glanced behind again to see all five men mounted and galloping after them, whipping their rein ends against their mounts' flanks.

He'd just turned forward again when the sorrel gave a shrill whinny.

Again, La Stiletta cursed.

Stringbean heard a heavy thud and turned to see both the sorrel and the girl down and rolling, La Stiletta's hair flying around her head, skirt buffeting. The mount had tripped.

It was Stringbean's turn to curse as he slowed the dun, turned it around and booted it up close to where La Stiletta was just then gaining her feet, reaching for her hat. The sorrel was also gaining its feet, anxiously shaking its head and rolling its eyes.

"What the hell happened?"

"I think the clumsy cayuse stepped in a gopher hole!"

Facing the men now gaining on them way too quickly, Stringbean shucked his Winchester from his saddle boot and racked a round into the action. "Get mounted!"

"I'm *trying*!" She'd grabbed the reins and was trying to thrust her left foot into the left stirrup, but the anxious sorrel was curveting and sidestepping, making the girl hop on her right foot, clinging to the horn.

Smoke and flames lapped from the guns of the riders galloping toward them, bullets caroming through the air and pluming sand and gravel dangerously close to both Stringbean and his charge. One tore a hot line across the outside of Stringbean's left shoulder, causing him to suck sharply through his teeth.

"You hit?" La Stiletta said, jerking her concerned gaze toward the deputy just as she got seated in her saddle.

"I'm all right—ride!"

The riders were fifty yards and closing. Stringbean snapped his Winchester to his shoulder and returned fire once, twice, three times, spent cartridge casings arcing over his right shoulder.

The Powderhorn riders yelled and jerked back on their horses' reins, curveting the mounts sharply. One of the riders jerked back in his saddle, clutching his left shoulder. One of Stringbean's shots had hit its mark.

"*Hy-yahhh!*" La Stiletta shouted.

The sorrel, apparently unhurt after its fall, lunged off its rear hooves and shot up the trail. Gritting his teeth against the burn in his right shoulder, Stringbean reined his dun around and put the steel to it, the horse whinnying shrilly and then bounding hell-for-leather after La Stiletta and the sorrel. As it did, guns resumed popping behind Stringbean and he could hear the pounding of the Powderhorn horses as the five riders, possibly four, continued their pursuit.

Ahead, lay a low ridge stippled with rocks and creosote.

Stringbean had a feeling he and La Stiletta were not going to outrun their pursuers. As he and the girl, galloping abreast now, started up the ridge, Stringbean glanced at her and yelled, "Keep ridin'! I'm gonna try to discourage those ringtails!"

She didn't say anything. She just cast a quick glance over her shoulder at their determined stalkers fanned out in a ragged line as they continued galloping and shooting. As she and Stringbean gained the crest of the ridge, the sorrel shot down the other side and kept running. Stringbean drew the dun to a skidding halt a few feet down the far side of the ridge and leaped out of the saddle, ramming his Winchester's butt against the mount's left hip, sending it galloping off after his fast-fleeing prisoner.

He ran back to the ridge crest, dropped to his knees, cocked a live round into the action, and rested the

Winchester's barrel on a rock, taking careful aim at the riders again drawing to within fifty yards and galloping hard, crouched low in their saddles. He lined up his sights on Boss's broad chest, riding second from right in the ragged line of five—the man he'd shot remaining in his saddle and gritting his teeth just above his galloping horse's pinned back ears.

Stringbean squeezed the trigger and smiled devilishly when Boss dropped the carbine in his hands and rolled back over the arched tail of his galloping calico, his hat tumbling off his shoulder to be swept away on the wind.

Stringbean gave a wild rebel yell as he ejected the spent cartridge and jacked a live one into his Winchester's action. The four remaining riders hauled back hard on their bridle reins, all four horses skidding to halts, curveting, tan dust licking up around them. Stringbean pumped three rounds into the caliche near their horses' skitter-hopping feet before all four wide-eyed riders reined their mounts sharply and galloped back in the direction from which they'd come.

As they did, Boss climbed heavily to his feet, turning his hatless head toward Stringbean, his eyes as wide as the others', his jaws hard and his teeth gritted with fury. He held his right hand over the top of his left, bullet-burned shoulder and yelled, "Hold up—wait for me, dammit!" as the four other Powderhorn riders galloped past him, spurring their horses, whipping their rein ends over their mounts' flanks, and casting wary looks over their shoulders and up the ridge to where Stringbean raised the Winchester, holding his fire and grinning his satisfaction at having filed the Powderhorn riders' horns.

At least for now.

Boss's calico had whipped around to follow the others back across the cactus-stippled desert. The foreman whipped around, as well, and was running after them, limping, occasionally removing his right hand from his wounded left shoulder to pump his fist angrily in the air at the men abandoning him.

Stringbean's glee drained out of him quickly when he felt the hard, thudding burn in his upper left arm. He groaned and rolled onto his back, dropping the Winchester and closing his gloved, right hand over the bloody wound from which dark-red blood issued profusely.

It was more than a burn.

Hooves thudded, growing louder.

He reached for the Winchester but staid the movement when he opened his eyes to see none other than his prisoner herself trotting back toward him from fifty yards away, hair bouncing on her shoulders, the sorrel chewing the bit and anxiously shaking its head.

La Stiletta reined up before him, pulling the reins up high against her chest and scowling down with concern. "How bad you hit, pendejo?"

Stringbean looked up at her in surprise. "Thought fer sure I was gonna have to run you down before you got to Mexico."

She swung down from the saddle, walked up the ridge, and knelt beside him. "How bad?" She peeled his hand off his wounded arm and stretched her lips back from her teeth. She sucked a sharp breath. "Not good."

"As the good marshal would say, I've cut myself worse shavin'."

"You and I both know you don't shave."

Stringbean winced. "You're awful good at cuttin' a man to the quick, La Stiletta."

"I've had a lot of practice."

"Don't doubt it a bit."

She removed his neckerchief, wrapped it around the wound, and knotted it. She hooked an arm under his. "Come on. We need to get you mounted, find shelter. That wound needs to be cauterized before you bleed out."

Stringbean frowned. "Where's my...where's my...?"

He let the question trail off and grinned when he saw his dun walking toward him, through La Stiletta's and the sorrel's still-sifting dust, dragging the reins along behind, occasionally lifting its head and snorting. "Well, I'll be hanged...Skeeter, if you ain't the loyalist dang horse I ever owned..."

"Be quiet. Save your strength, Deputy." La Stiletta gave a grunt as she helped haul him to his feet. "Let's get you on your loyal horse."

"Let's...get me on my hoss," Stringbean said, feeling light-headed likely from blood loss and pain.

With his prisoner's help, he walked, occasionally tripping over his boot toes, to where Skeeter had stopped beside the girl's sorrel, who nuzzled the dun's snout with his own. Stringbean grabbed the reins and La Stiletta steadied him as he toed a stirrup then swung up into the leather. He thumbed his hat brim up off his forehead and glowered down at her. "How come you ain't headed fer Mexico?"

"Be quiet or I will!" she said as she marched over to the sorrel and swung up into the leather.

Still regarding her curiously, he reined the dun around and booted him on up the trail, looking for a place to light for a spell and tend the wound. The girl was right. If he didn't get the bleeding stopped, he likely wouldn't have much left by nightfall. He wasn't really minding the idea, however. This trip had looked bad from the start, and it was only looking worse.

He wasn't up to it. No, sir. He just wasn't up to it, and make no mistake.

If it wasn't for his bad hip, he'd go back to horse gentling. Maybe saloon swamping was more in his realm of capabilities. Of course, Molly Hurdstrom wouldn't marry a saloon swamper, but then, he'd likely lost her anyway.

"Ah, look at this."

Stringbean hadn't realized he'd dozed off. He jerked his head up now, blinking and looking around incredulously. Off the right side of the old horse trail they'd been following—likely an old Indian hunting or trading trail—lay a cave in a stone wall up a slight rise from a rocky, runout seep. Casting his gaze around more broadly, he saw that he and his prisoner—or was he suddenly hers?—were in a narrow, stone-walled canyon. Shadows were growing long, and the sky was tufted with dirty, gray clouds.

Distant thunder rumbled.

Stringbean smelled rain on the chill breeze liberally perfumed with the smell of pinyon pine.

"It will rain soon," said La Stiletta. "We'd best hole up there."

She swung down from her saddle and walked over to Stringbean, gazing up at him impatiently, angrily, placing a hand on his arm. "Can you make it?"

"I can make it, I can make it." But when he swung his right leg over his dun's rump, weakness overcame him. He wasn't able to pull his left foot out of its stirrup before the right one came down. He gave a grunt as he struck the ground on his head and shoulders before his left foot slid free of the stirrup.

He lay there, looking up at La Stiletta gazing down at

him disdainfully. He gulped air like a landed fish and winced against the bells tolling in his ears.

She rolled her eyes. "Ah, si, si. You can make it, all right." She crouched, gave his good hand a tug, and with her help he hauled himself heavily, groaning, to his feet.

"I can make it, I can make it. You take care of the hosses, and I'll go and sit down in the cave yonder. I do believe I need to take a load off."

"Si, si. Go!"

He moved around the seep and climbed rocks to the cave, which was low and roughly egg-shaped. No beasts appeared to currently call the cavern home though scattered bones with tufts of fur clinging to them told him at least one had in the not too distant past. Crouching beneath the low ceiling, he moved into the cave and sat down against the back wall.

He saw his prisoner jerking on the horses' reins, leading them off to shelter in some boulders off to String-bean's right and out of sight. The growing wind was blowing her hair and nipping at the wide brim of her brown hat.

Distant thunder rumbled. Cool air blew into the cave, the smell of rain stronger than before.

A large, tender heart thumped in Stringbean's arm, and, despite the pain, he was suddenly so sleepy he could hardly hold his eyes open. He heard himself snore and then he heard nothing and felt nothing but the ache in his arm until a wave of warm air pushing against him roused him suddenly.

He lifted his head to see his prisoner kneeling to his left and feeding sticks to a fire she'd built in a ring of stones. He saw the handle of a skinning knife—his own skinning knife from his war bag—resting on one of the stones, the blade resting in the flames, smoldering.

Ah, Jesus, he thought, staring at the smoking blade.

What the hell is she gonna do with that?

Then he vaguely wondered why she hadn't dragged the blade across his throat by now.

She set another stick in the fire and glanced at him. She gave a devilish half smile, as though reading his mind.

Outside the cave, lightning flashed.

Thunder crashed, making the cave floor leap beneath him.

The cool wind made the flames dance. He felt it against his left arm. Looking down at it, he saw that his sleeve had been cut away. The wound had been cleaned but was still oozing blood.

He looked at La Stiletta again. She tossed her hair back behind her left shoulder and picked up the knife. It was glowing red. She held it up as if to show him.

Yep, glowing red, all right.

She crawled over to him. He looked at her skeptically.

"That looks," he said, slurring his words as though drunk, "mighty hot."

"It's very hot." She picked up a bottle—the bottle he carried in his war bag for medicinal purposes only. He did not imbibe. That was the only thing he hadn't picked up from the marshal. Oh, he'd have a beer now and then just to be sociable, but never hard liquor. He got his legs tangled up well enough on his own, sober.

He saw that a good third of the liquor was gone.

Either she'd drunk it or...

Oh, that was why he was slurring his words. She'd poured it down his throat!

"Oh, you're sneaky," he heard himself mutter, and chuckled. "Me, I abstain."

"I'll make a drinker out of you yet, Deputy." La Stiletta held up the bottle and gave another devilish grin.

"You're going to want to take another drink. Believe me."

Stringbean looked at the smoking, glowing blade of the knife in her hand. His guts coiled like snakes in his belly.

"Ah, jeepers..."

"Si, jeepers."

She slid the bottle closer to him.

He looked at the blade again and winced when he imagined what was coming. He raised his right hand, which felt as heavy as lead, and took the bottle from her. He tipped it back and gasped when the toxic liquid burned down his throat, setting his chest and belly on fire.

"Ah, Lordy, don't know how the marshal can drink so much of that—"

He stopped when something as cold as fresh January snow ensconced his scrotum and spread a penetrating chill all through his loins, all the way up to this heart, which thudded. He smelled the stench of burning skin and blood and realized that she'd just laid the blade across the wound.

He'd only just begun to feel the burn when the cave floor pitched like a bucking bronco, and everything went black.

CHAPTER 19

BLOODY JOE TURNED AWAY FROM WHERE HE'D SEEN THE little man with the neat beard, walking stick, and smoking, silver-chased hogleg disappear down a break between buildings on the opposite side of the street.

He turned toward where the man who'd drilled a bullet into the owner of the White Horse Saloon—a bullet meant for Mannion—darted into a break between buildings on Bloody Joe's side of the street, a block beyond Joe's position.

Joe heaved himself to his feet, yelling, "Get back here, you murdering coward!"

Rage was a wild stallion galloping inside him.

A good man was dead with a bullet meant for him!

Joe ran despite the kicked-up pain in his left arm, which he'd removed from its sling that morning. A town marshal could not function one-armed. At least, not the town marshal of Del Norte in the Colorado Territory. Mannion leaped up onto the boardwalk fronting a drug store on the other side of the cross street and kept running along one boardwalk after another until he stopped at the north front corner of a Chinese medicine shop, which sold mostly opium and the charms of several deferring Chinese doxies.

Joe could smell the cloying odor of the midnight oil now as he pressed his shoulder against the building's front corner and edged a look down the alley where his second stalker had disappeared.

Joe drew his head back as the assassin in the blue work shirt and pinto vest slid his own head and revolver out from the rear corner of the building on the other side of the alley.

Bang! Bang-Bang!

The bullets clipped the corner of the building behind where Joe had taken cover, blowing chunks of wood in all directions.

As the echo of the last shot continued to resonate over the town, which was still under the held-breath hush that had fallen when Cal Taggart had taken the bullet meant for Mannion, Joe stepped around the corner of the Chinese place and, extending both big Russians straight out in front of him, shouted, "*Get back here and face me like a man, you son of a bitch!*"

He strode quickly toward the rear corner of the building on the opposite side of the trash-strewn alley behind which his would-be assassin had disappeared.

He swung around the rear corner of that building and stopped, drawing his index fingers taut against the triggers of both cocked Russians.

Nothing back here but sage, old lumber, and trash, which the breeze was nipping at. Beyond lay connected pens shaded by big oaks; the air was foul with pig stench.

Kicking a can, Joe hurried forward and swung around the building's opposite rear corner, casting his gaze as well as his aimed Russians up toward the front of the building owned by a tarot card reader who called herself

Madame Chervenak and who'd come to town and bought the building from a game butcher after hearing about the two competing railroads heading for Del Norte.

Progress—crap!

Mannion triggered both Russians once, his bullets chewing into the lip of the shake-shingled roof onto which his stalker was just then pulling his booted feet. Split logs were still tumbling off the top of the wood pile the man had climbed to make his leap onto the roof of Madame Chervenak's place.

Joe hurried forward then stepped to his left when he saw his assailant rise to a crouch on the roof and swing his gun toward him.

The man fired three times quickly, the bullets thudding into the ground to Mannion's right.

Mannion stepped out away from the building and aimed both Russians toward where the murdering son of a bitch had fired from but held his own fire when he saw the man run up to the peak of the roof and then down the other side and out of sight.

Cursing, Joe hurried to the wood pile, shoving both Russians into their holsters. He leaped onto the woodpile. He leaped again, thrusting his forearms onto the edge of the roof of Madame Chervenak's place. Digging his fingers into the shakes, he hoisted himself up with a grunt, pulling his legs up and over the lip.

Gaining his feet, he unsheathed one of his Russians and ran, crouching, to within a few feet of the roof's peak and edged a cautious look over it. His quarry stood crouching on the peak of the Chinaman's place, extending his cocked Colt toward Joe, teeth gritted beneath his gray-blond mustache which contrasted the tanned leather of his sunburned face.

Mannion pulled his head down as the man fired.

The bullet tore into the peak just above him, sending a wooden shingle flying over his head and into the alley behind him. Mannion edged another look over the peak, bringing the Russian to bear. He held fire when he saw the cream hat of his quarry drop down beneath the peak of the building just beyond.

"Cowardly damn devil!" Mannion bellowed as he ran up and over the roof peak of Madame Chervenak's place.

He ran down to the edge of the roof, judged the distance between this roof and the roof of the building just beyond and over the peak of which his quarry had just disappeared.

Roughly ten feet.

He could make it.

Couldn't he?

Only one way to find out.

He backed up then ran forward and, holding his breath, made the leap. The narrow gap of the alley passed beneath him. His feet thudded onto the edge of the next roof. He dropped to his hands and knees, the Russian still clenched in his right fist.

"Damn," Joe said, feet and knees aching, breathing hard. "I'm getting too old for this shit!"

He gave a grunt as he pushed to his feet and ran up to the peak of the roof. He edged another cautious look over it. His assailant's cream Stetson appeared as the man lifted his head to cast a glance over the peak of the roof just beyond Joe's. Hardening his jaws, Mannion extended the Russian and fired.

His assailant's eyes had just cleared the peak of the roof he crouched behind. They widened when they saw Mannion and the extended Russian. The man drew his head down but not before Mannion's bullet tore through the crown and ripped the Stetson off his head, sending it sailing off to the south.

The man's sandy-haired, hatless head appeared again. So did his Colt.

Mannion pulled his own head down behind the peak of the roof he was on an eye wink before his assailant's bullet screeched through the air, nicking the edge of the peak above Joe.

Joe jerked his head and Russian up once more but held fire.

His target had disappeared.

Mannion rose, leaped over the peak, and ran down the other side. He ran to the roof's edge and, not wanting to give himself too much time to consider his next move and possibly pee down his leg, he kept running and made the leap across the trash-strewn alley passing in a blur beneath him. He vaguely noted a drunk sitting passed out against the base of the wall of the building Joe had just left, head down, arms crossed on his chest.

Mannion bent his knees to absorb the blow as his feet struck the edge of the next roof. He straightened and hurried to within a few feet of the peak and edged a look over the top and beyond.

Nothing but the roof of the next building beyond the one Mannion was on. Three blackbirds were perched on the peak, spaced evenly apart. They stared dubiously, black eyes toward Joe.

He saw movement in the corner of his right eye.

Mannion pulled his head down quickly.

Bang! Bang!

Two bullets caromed through the air where Joe's head had just been and thudded into the roof behind his left shoulder.

Mannion jerked his head up. His hatless assailant

stood to the left of the high false façade at the front of the building, which Mannion thought was probably the Wooden Nickel Saloon though with all the commotion, he'd lost track of where he was.

Joe jerked his head and Russian back up.

He fired one second after his hatless assailant gave him his back, looked down, then, spreading his elbows as though they were wings, dropped down over the front of the building, out of sight. Mannion's bullet sailed through the air where his target's hatless head had just been.

Joe straightened and ran up to the front of the building and stopped just left of the high false façade. He looked down. His assailant was running, limping badly on his right leg, into the street where traffic was once again moving. He was clutching his right leg with the hand holding the Colt, dragging that foot.

Mannion extended the Russian, aimed carefully, and fired.

His bullet tore a hole in the back of his target's left leg.

The man lunged forward as his left leg bent inward and screamed. He glanced over his shoulder at Mannion, his lips stretched back from gritted teeth. His sandy hair hung over his right eye. When he saw the big log dray caroming toward him from the north, from both his and Mannion's right, he jerked his head around to face it and gave a shrill scream half a second before the first two mules of the six-mule hitch smashed into him.

"Outta the way, ya blasted fool!" bellowed the driver sitting in the wagon's high driver's box, a weathered sugarloaf sombrero on his bearded head.

The wagon was loaded with long, unskinned pine logs likely headed to a weaver's mill south of Del Norte.

Mannion's assailant threw his arms up, dropping the

Colt, as the team hammered him flat and plowed him over. Mannion could see him being hammered mercilessly beneath the mules' scissoring hooves as the wagon continued forward. Joe winced, watching the body, which now resembled nothing so much as a ragdoll being kicked, torn, and pummeled beneath the mules' pounding hooves. The wagon rolled over him, spitting him out behind, leaving him twisted in a dusty, bloody heap in the middle of the street.

The man lay belly up, one arm pinned beneath him, the other thrown up above his head. One leg was bent awkwardly, broken. He lay still in death.

As the driver of the log dray bellowed to his team, trying to get it stopped, Mannion cursed. He'd wanted to take his would-be assassin alive. He'd wanted to find out what beef he'd had with Mannion.

Or who'd sent him.

Yeah, someone had probably sent him.

Who?

As the log dray drew to a stop fifty feet beyond the man it had just churned out behind it, and a crowd gathered on the street around Mannion's would-be assassin, Joe swung around and walked back to the rear of the building he was on. After some searching, he discovered another wood pile, onto which he dropped. He dropped from the wood pile to the ground, again cursing his age, then walked around, limping slightly, both knees aching, to the front of the Wooden Nickel and out into the street.

He pushed through the small crowd of men standing around and staring down at Mannion's would-be assassin.

As he did, the bearded driver of the wagon that had cleaned the man's clock ambled up on his bowlegs, the mule ears of his time-worn boots flapping around his shins.

"Christalmighty, he ran right out in front of me, Marshal!" the driver said. "I can't stop a six-mule hitch on a *dime*!"

"Don't worry about it, Jed," Mannion said, staring down at the dead man. "He had other things besides negotiating wagon traffic on his mind." The man's lips were still stretched back from his teeth in a grimace, as though he'd taken the agony of his unceremonious demise to the hereafter. His thin, sandy hair was graying and his well-sun-seasoned face appeared that of a man in his mid-thirties, possibly forty.

Mannion didn't recognize him.

He glanced at the other men—miners, prospectors, track layers, woodcutters, and muleskinners, mostly, as well as two men in range gear and who were likely in town for ranch supplies. One was rolling a sharpened matchstick around between his lips and slowly shaking his head as he grimly regarded the dead mean.

Mannion recognized only a couple of the men around him. A few years ago, he'd known the names of most of the folks in and around Del Norte. Not anymore; the town was growing too fast for him to keep up.

"Any of you fellas recognize this son of a bitch?"

They glanced around at each other, shrugging and shaking their heads.

One man with an enormous paunch bulging out of his striped shirt, a thick, gray-brown walrus mustache, and a hat with its brim pancaked down on his head, took a step forward and said, "Alvin Castle. Killer from Wyoming. Started out huntin' wolves for ranchers up thataway. Said he got talked into huntin' men for the same ranchers— rustlers and nesters an' such. Couldn't turn down the money and wouldn't you know he turned out good at it? Leastways, I think it's Castle. Played cards with him a few times in Laramie. Several years ago, now. Cold-blooded devil. Talk about a poker face!"

"Hired killer," Mannion muttered, raking a thumbnail back and forth across his chin as he pondered the information confirming what he'd suspected.

His next question was: Who'd hired him? He kept that one to himself. Lots of men had beefs with Bloody Joe. One in particular he could think of right off hand...

He'd be paying the superintendent of the Rio Grande Southern Railroad a visit soon.

And he'd be keeping an eye out for that second shooter—the little man with the walking stick and silver-chased Colt...

A woman's wail made him jerk with a start.

He turned to stare up the street toward the grocery store out front of which another crowd had gathered—this one larger than the one gathered around the dead man on the street. The larger crowd was gathered on the boardwalk where Mannion had watched Cal Taggart take the bullet that had been mean for him.

His guts churned when he saw through the men and some women standing around the dead man on the boardwalk out front of the grocery store a stout woman in a gingham dress kneeling over Taggart's body. She was sobbing loudly.

Again, the street had gone quiet, only a few wagons passing slowly, drivers turning their heads to investigate the carnage on the street and in front of the grocery store.

One of the wagons belonged to the undertaker, Mortimer Bellringer, who had obviously already been summoned. The undertaker's small, brown dog rode next to the tall, thin, sharp-featured man on the driver's seat, looking appropriately solemn. Bellringer angled the wagon toward the grocery store.

"Oh, Cal," Mannion heard Taggart's wife cry. *"No! No! No!"*

Joe couldn't see Maggie Taggart clearly because of the crowd around her. But he recognized her voice. Who else would be wailing like that, like some injured animal, than the wife of the man who'd been so suddenly and brutally taken from her? Maggie Taggart worked in the White Horse with Cal, mostly cooking steaks and chili in the kitchen.

A good couple. The White Horse was one of the few respectable eateries and watering holes in Del Norte. Mostly, men minded their p's and q's in the place because of Maggie.

Mannion looked down at the dead man before him. Rage rose in him, swelling his face and bulging his eyes.

"Goddamn murdering son of Satan!" Mannion bellowed as he drew his right foot back and thrust it forward, slamming the toe of that boot into the dead man's side, rolling him onto his belly.

Feeling sick and heavy-footed, still fuming, he crossed the street at an angle and pushed through the crowd gathered around Cal Taggart's unmoving body.

"Make way, make way," he said, shouldering men and a few women—doxies from the Wooden Nickel—aside.

He stepped up to where Taggart lay on his side on the boardwalk, surrounded by groceries including two broken jars, one each of pickled ham hocks and pickled eggs. The brine mixed with the thick pool of blood on the boardwalk. The front and back of Taggart's white shirt was soaked with dark-red blood.

Maggie Taggart, a stout woman in her sixties, knelt with her head on her dead husband's shoulder, sobbing.

"What the hell happened?" asked Roy Cleary, bartender from the Wooden Nickel. He looked around. "Who'd want to shoot Cal? Never knew him to have an enemy in the world!"

"No one wanted to shoot Cal," Mannion heard himself say, his voice low and stricken. "That bullet was meant for me. Cal stepped in the way at the last sec—"

"What happened? What happened?" rose a voice on the other side of the crowd from Mannion.

Joe looked up to see the diminutive, nattily suited, bearded mayor, Charlie McQueen, hurrying toward the grocery store with Mannion's middle-aged, potbellied deputy, Rio Waite.

"What on earth happened here?" asked the mayor.

Before Mannion could speak, another man said, "Cal Taggart took a bullet meant for Bloody Joe!"

He'd practically shouted it.

All heads swiveled toward Mannion.

Mrs. Taggart lifted her head from her dead husband's shoulder to regard Mannion with exasperation in her tear-bright eyes, more tears streaking her plump cheeks. She stared at him for a long time. She didn't say anything. She didn't need to. She just stared. Then she lowered her head again to Taggart's shoulder and continued bawling.

A cold stone dropped in Mannion's belly.

He peered over the sobbing woman to see McQueen standing beside Rio. Both men's eyes were on him. Rio's gaze was hard to read. The mayor's wasn't. The mayor's eyes behind his glinting spectacles showed only cold and accusing disgust.

Mannion glanced at Rio, meaningfully. Rio nodded.

"All right, folks," Rio said, raising his hands palms out.

"Time to break it up, go about your business. We have to get Mister Taggart over to the undertaker's. Go on, now!"

As the crowd began to scatter, Mannion stepped around the woman sobbing over her husband's body and headed back in the direction of the jailhouse. Rio would stay and make sure both bodies were loaded up and hauled away and that the town's only sawbones would be fetched to tend to the grief-stricken Mrs. Taggart. Doc Bohannon would give the woman something to sooth her nerves. A friend of Mrs. Taggart would be summoned to take her home.

At the moment, Mannion needed something to sooth his own nerves.

He'd taken a half-dozen strides back in the direction of the jailhouse when he stopped suddenly. He'd glimpsed a familiar shade of red in the corner of his left eye. Now he turned to see Jane standing on the balcony outside her second-floor office, French doors standing open behind her, lace curtain billowing in the breeze.

As usual, she was immaculately dressed and coifed. Her purple dress fairly glowed in the high-country sunshine. So did the pearl necklace she wore. So did her pearl earrings as did her cherry-red lips and rich, copper-red hair pinned in a large, loose roll atop her lovely head.

She stared toward Joe, beringed hands closed around the wrought iron rail of the balcony before her. Her gaze told him that if she'd questioned her decision to leave him, all doubt was gone now.

Joe continued walking. When he reached the jailhouse, he climbed the steps of the front porch. Buster sat on the rail to his right, looking up at him, tail curled around himself. Buster gave the tip of his tail a flip.

"Not you, too, Buster," Joe said.

He stepped into the jailhouse. He pegged his hat,

swept his hand through his hair, tugging on it, making it hurt and grunting with the effort. He sat heavily down in the chair behind his desk. Guilt and self-disgust were a lead weight in his belly.

He opened the bottommost drawer on the desk's right side and pulled out an unlabeled bottle of Theo O'Flanagan's Who-Hit-John. He set the bottle on the desk, reached into the drawer once more, and pulled out a water glass.

He set the glass on the desk beside the bottle, popped the cork on the bottle, and filled the glass to the brim.

CHAPTER 20

MATHILDA CALDERON OPENED HER EYES WITH A START.

She'd heard something.

She lifted her head from the woolly underside of her saddle to gaze across the cold ashes of the dead fire toward where Mannion's young deputy, Stringbean, aka pendejo, lay in his blankets, head resting back against his own saddle.

He chuckled softly and shifted his legs around beneath his soogan.

"Stop that," he said, chuckling again, wriggling around beneath the blankets. He waved a hand in front of his nose. "That tickles, you shyster!"

He turned onto his side, away from La Stiletta, and gave a deep sigh.

She rolled her eyes. He'd only been dreaming.

Good.

She studied the canyon outside the cave. It was false dawn, a milky light casting long, dense shadows. Birds were piping and flitting around in the canyon. There wasn't much light yet, but it would have to do.

She flipped back her own blankets then, casting a

cautious look toward where the deputy was snoring softly, quickly rolled her bedroll together with her yellow oil slicker, and tied each end with rawhide. She shrugged into her leather jacket against the desert's morning chill, grabbed her tack, and hauled it out to the floor of the canyon.

Quietly, she walked into the boulders where she'd tied the horses. She untied the sorrel and led it slowly and quietly back into the canyon below the cave.

Quickly but quietly, casting several anxious glances back over her shoulder at where the deputy slumbered in the cave, she saddled and bridled the sorrel, and slung her saddlebags over its rump. She returned to the cave for the rest of her gear and again regarded the sleeping deputy.

She'd poured enough whiskey down his throat that he'd likely sleep for a few more hours. Enough time for her to get a good way up the trail to the south—toward the border. She intended to lose herself deep in the bowels of her home country, which she realized now she should have done from the start though she'd thought the army or U.S. marshals would have suspected she'd head in that direction and overtake her before she could reach the border.

She'd managed to slip away from her rancho when the soldiers and federals were arresting Diego; she'd been outside gathering berries to have with cream for breakfast—a favorite of Diego's, who'd grown up as poor as she had. She'd dropped her basket, run to the barn, saddled the fastest of her two horses, and lit a shuck, as the gringos say, while the soldiers and the federals were in the cabin with Diego.

She'd felt bad about abandoning her man. He had broken her out of *Mission de St. Agnes Para Niñas Rebeles*,

St. Agnes's Mission for Wayward Girls, after all. He'd gotten her away from those evil nuns, whose scars she still bore. But she didn't see how her being arrested would help Diego, so she'd run. If he truly loved her, he'd have wanted her to save herself.

But he would not want her to testify against him and give the whereabouts of the stolen Gatling guns. He'd wanted the guns to rob gold from American banks which he'd use in a revolution.

Now in the cave she looked around at her remaining gear—her war bag and the deputy's six-shooter resting in its holster near where she'd slept against her saddle, within an easy reach if she would have needed it. Now she picked it up, wrapped the belt around her waist and cinched it. She reached for his Winchester carbine leaning against the cave wall.

She paused, fingers brushing the barrel.

She chewed her lip, pensive, as she turned her pondering gaze to the slumbering young man.

She drew her hand back from the rifle. Like his horse, she'd leave it for him. He'd need both on the way back to Del Norte. Of course, she owed him nothing. Especially after he'd nearly made her a wildcat's supper! Still, she'd unlikely, improbably, found herself harboring a soft spot for the guileless young man, who'd only been doing the job he'd been ordered to do, after all. By a man he unjustifiably respected and was unduly influenced by.

Besides, she was better with her stiletto, which she did not have, and a six-shooter than she was with a rifle. She was not a big woman, and rifles were often too heavy for her to shoot accurately.

Now she wedged the deputy's wooden-handled knife behind the cartridge belt, over her belly. The knife and pistol would be enough. They would get her to Mexico if she avoided the main trails.

She left the cave, hung her war bag packed with food-stuffs from her saddle horn, grabbed the sorrel's reins, and had just started to toe a stirrup when she heard the deputy groan, mutter, and sigh.

She set her foot back down and scowled into the oval-shaped, black opening of the cave. She sighed, muttered a Spanish curse, and returned to the cave. The deputy rolled onto his back and moved his lips, muttering in his sleep. He blinked several times and stared up at La Stiletta.

"You, uh...you ain't...Molly..."

"No, and you ain't Diego Hidalgo." She knelt beside the stirring young man, raised him to a sitting position, sort of cradled him with one arm, then picked up the bottle and emptied it down his throat. There was a good third of the stuff left. He gurgled and shook his head, but she kept the bottle held fast to his lips, over the top of one he was growing a ridiculous-looking mustache.

"There," she said, pulling the bottle away when it was empty, some of it dribbling down his lips and throat, dampening his shirt collar. But she got enough into him. She let him drop down to his saddle, out like a blown lamp.

She dropped the bottle and stared down at him. "Don't try to stop me, pendejo. I ride fast and I know how to cover my trail. Go back home to your girl."

She turned and went back out to her horse, mounted up and rode away, leaving Stringbean snoring behind her.

Once she'd ridden up out of the canyon, she paused on a rocky knoll studded with cactus and looked around, getting her bearings. When she figured out where south was, she booted the sorrel in that direction, heading for a low pass between mountains just then turning pale in the first light.

She put the mount into a fast gallop, occasionally looking behind her to make sure the deputy was not on her trail. She'd gotten him good and drunk, but he was a determined young man. She'd give him that.

She chose hard, rocky terrain so as to leave as little spoor as possible. She followed a rocky canyon between large, slanting outcroppings of solid, white rock and drew rein on the saddle above.

She curveted horse to gaze back behind her.

No sign of anyone on her back trail.

Good.

She'd started the saddle's south side when she reined up suddenly with a gasp.

Four men sat upon four horses at the bottom of the saddle.

The same four who'd attacked her and Stringbean the day before! The big man the deputy had shot off his mount, dressed nearly all in black, had a red cloth suspending his right arm across his vest.

He sat with a devious smile, his head canted to one side.

The others wore similar expressions. Their horses blew and switched their tails.

La Stiletta's heart thudded.

"Mierda!" she screeched as she whipped the sorrel around and batted her heels against its flanks, taking off like a freshly branded horse leaping from a holding pen.

Immediately she heard the whoops and yells of the human coyotes behind her as they booted their mounts up the pass, their horses' hooves clacking on the rocks, occasionally making a ringing sound when a shod hoof clipped a stone.

At the bottom of the pass, La Stiletta glanced behind her to her five assailants bounding down the pass, still whooping and hollering and closing on her fast. Their mounts were likely fresher than her sorrel, dammit!

She looked around for somewhere she could turn off the trail and possibly lose them but could find none. Her pursuers' horses were pounding louder behind her. There was a *whooshing* sound. The lasso dropped cleanly down around her shoulders.

She screamed as the noose grew tight and then she was tumbling nearly straight back over the sorrel's tail. The ground came up in a blur of fast motion to slam hard against her back. She lost her hat and she lay staring up at the grinning men gathered around her, dust wafting, horses snorting, blowing, and stomping.

"Lyle, throw her over your hoss! We're takin' her with us to the line shack." Boss grinned coldly. "Have a little fun before we cut her purty throat!"

"You got it, Boss!" said Lyle, a thick-set blonde with mismatched eyes and a missing front tooth.

He scrambled down from his saddle, reached down for La Stiletta and before she knew what had happened—that tumble from the saddle had scrambled her brains—she was lying belly down across Lyle's saddle, wedged between the big man and the horn.

She tried to fight him, but he held a large, strong hand down hard against her back. Then they were galloping up and over the pass and down the other side. They switched onto a side trail and out into flat chaparral country until they pulled up in front of a low-roofed, mud brick cabin flanked by a mud brick barn and a corral of woven mesquite branches.

A humble place shrouded in spindly tufts of buckbrush and greasewood. A few scraggly cows milled in the corral.

These sons of gringo bitches did not ride for any Powderhorn Ranch. They were rustlers...

Lyle stopped his horse, dismounted, and pulled the girl down from his horse—none too politely. She hit the ground again on her back. Again, she was dazed but just then felt Stringbean's knife wedged behind her belt. These men were so lust-crazed they hadn't seen it on her yet, partly hidden by the frilly front of her blouse and her wide, black, gold-buckled belt.

Now she pulled the knife and gave an angry wail as she skidded around on her butt and swung the knife toward Lyle's leg. Big as he was, Lyle leaped from her arm then kicked the knife out of her hand.

He reached down, pulled her to her feet and gave her a shove toward the cabin while others followed, Boss saying, "I get her first!"

"Pigs!" she intoned as Lyle gave her another kick toward the door.

There were four moldy cots in the cabin, army blankets draped over them. The table was littered with bottles, glasses, and meal scraps. Boss stepped up, grabbed her by a handful of hair at the back of her hair and threw her onto a cot.

"Pig!" she cried rolling onto her back as he began unbuttoning his shirt while the others milled around him, goatish lust in their eyes. One kicked the door closed and removed his gun and cartridge belt and pegged it on the wall by the door.

"Where's that skinny deputy you were ridin' with?" Lyle wanted to know.

"Right here!" said a familiar voice as the door was suddenly kicked open with a *bang*!

CHAPTER 21

MANNION BACK-AND-BELLIED HIS DEAD WOULD-BE assassin over a horse from the livery barn.

It was early morning, but the sun was up, and the usual raucous crowd was toiling on the streets of Del Norte, kicking up roiling dust clouds despite the morning dew.

"Want me ride out there with you, Joe?" Rio Waite asked from the front porch where he sat with Buster on his lap. He had a steaming cup of coffee on his chair arm. "Them railroad crews can get a might colicky...and I know you're not gonna be none too polite about Mister Alvin Castle there."

"You're needed here, Rio. I won't stir up too much trouble but do want Mister H. Jerome Libby to know that I got his message. I'm just sending one back to him." Mannion finished lashing Castle to his saddle then tightened Red's cinch and climbed heavily into the leather.

He was feeling the weight of his years.

"Keep the lid on, Rio," Joe said then pinched his hat brim to the older deputy and turned Red out into the street.

"Will do, Joe," Rio said with a nod.

"Oh, and keep an eye out for that second assassin, will you? Little guy, sort of a dandy with a silver-chased Colt and walking stick. He might be keeping an eye on the jailhouse, waiting to make a play on me. I want him. I want him real bad."

"Will do, Joe. I'll try to lasso him for you."

Mannion put Red north along the street, negotiating his way among the buckboards and ore drays and every other blasted contraption known to the frontier. They were all here—in spades. As he rode, he felt more than a few woolly eyeballs on him. Cal Taggart had been a respected man in the community and Joe knew most of Del Norte blamed him for the man's death.

Despite the fact he hadn't pulled the trigger.

Hell, Joe blamed himself. His own colicky nature brought trouble upon himself and thus upon the town. It was just his way, and this zebra just seemed unable to change its stripes.

When he'd ridden north along the old freight and stage road for two miles he swung east, the Sawatch Range shouldering high on his left, glorious in its magisterial splendor this early in the morning. He rode through the forested valley up which the railroad tracks were being laid. It was a pretty valley, bisected by the Cimarron River running to the left of the tracks. Few rivers prettier. Mannion hated that a railroad was spoiling the view.

Damn progress, anyway!

He didn't have to ride long before he could hear the hammering of picks and shovels and the whinnies of the mules pulling the pie-shaped graders driven by big, bearded men in watch caps, beards, suspenders, and flannel shirts. He rode past the hubbub. Just beyond, the track layers were hard at work, toiling in the sun, some with their shirts off, spiking in ties and laying track.

Some were giants of men—even the Chinese—with large, rippling muscles.

Tent shacks around which men of all races milled lay on both sides of the tracks. Beyond the newly laid tracks, a tony looking parlor car outfitted with brass lights and trim around the windows. It was a pretty car, spruce green with RIO GRANDE SOUTHERN LINE written in ornate gold letters through a swath of red. Below that, in another swatch of red, H. JEROME LIBBY, SUPER-INTENDANT was written in just as ornate but slightly smaller letters.

Two beefy men in three-piece suits were smoking cigars on the front vestibule, leaning on the brass rails, one on each side. Each was armed with a holstered pistol. They regarded Mannion with flat expressions as he reined up outside the rail car and swung down from the saddle.

"Boss in?" Joe asked.

"Who's asking?" asked the man on the left. He had a full, ginger beard and one crossed eye. Libby's bodyguards.

"You know who's asking," Mannion said, cutting the ropes lashing Alvin Castle to his horse.

The cross-eyed gent looked through the coach's door open behind him. "Boss, Mannion's here."

"Tell him I'm busy," came H. Jerome Libby's voice from inside the car.

The other bodyguard, short but broad and swarthy, turned to Mannion. "Boss is busy."

Mannion pulled the dead man off his horse and draped him over his shoulder.

"He's come with a surprise, boss," the cross-eyed bodyguard called into the coach.

"What is it?"

"You might have to see it."

"Oh, all right, all right. But I only have a minute."

"It'll only take a minute," Mannion said, mounting the vestibule steps with the dead man draped over his shoulder.

He stepped between the bodyguards and into the car. It was lushly appointed with velvet drapes over the windows, a brocade sofa with scrolled wooden arms and several brocade armchairs. The head of a snarling grizzly was mounted above Libby's ornate, leather-covered desk outfitted with a green-shaded Tiffany lamp at the back of the car.

On one wall was a large, framed map of the proposed line of his railroad.

He had his gray head down and was busily scribbling with a pen on a notepad, too busy apparently to look up until Mannion was halfway across the car. He frowned at the grisly cargo on the lawman's shoulder and leaped to his feet, dropping his pen. His face turned ashen.

"Good God, man—have you gone *mad*!"

"Long time ago."

Joe dropped the dead man on the desk, knocking over the lamp and scattering ash trays, tipping over Libby's drink, and knocking account ledgers and papers to the floor.

Mannion hardened his jaws as he glared across the desk at the man. "I got a feelin'—mind you just a feelin' but a feelin' just the same—that you sicced this killer on me and another one just like him, except shorter and better dressed. This one here shot a good man in town with a bullet meant for me. This because I sent your ramrod, Marvin O'Bannion, to the territorial pen and still have nearly a dozen of your men locked up in my jail. This piss-burns me to the quick, Libby! If I find out it's you, I'm gonna put a bullet right there!"

Joe pressed a gloved thumb to the man's forehead, hard.

Libby stepped back, fear in his eyes, and stumbled up against the liquor cabinet behind him, below the grizzly head. A tintype tumbled from the cabinet to the floor.

Libby looked around to his two bodyguards standing near the front of the coach, facing his boss and the lawman. "Get this crazy son of a bitch out of here!"

Joe swung around and began walking toward the front of the coach. "I was just leaving."

"You'll be helped," the one with the crossed eye said and grabbed Joe's arm.

Joe punched him. Cross-Eye gave a yelp and fell into one of the chairs.

The other one lunged at Joe. Joe punched him, too. He went spinning onto the sofa clutching his bloody nose. When they both started to heave themselves to their feet, Joe drew both Russians and clicked the hammers back.

That stayed the two bruins.

Mannion grinned and backed out of the car.

He mounted Red and rode back in the direction from which he'd come.

HE'D RIDDEN AN HOUR, TAKING HIS TIME, ENJOYING the cool countryside scented with pine pitch and sage and with the lack of roiling dust and squawking wheels and barking dogs of Del Norte, when he spied movement atop a sandstone escarpment ahead and on his left. The scarp was aproned by fir and pine forest, and more firs and pines grew out of cracks in the facing steep side of the scarp itself.

What had drawn his attention were several crows cawing over there, among the trees. At first he wondered if he was having another deranged vision of Sarah, but then he saw the hatted head of a man lying prone against the flat top of the escarpment, aiming a rifle at him.

Before Mannion had time to maneuver, smoke puffed from the maw of the man's rifle. The bullet screeched in, followed by the hiccupping rifle crack. The bullet tore into the ground inches from Red's left hoof, making the horse whinny shrilly and pitch, nearly bucking off its rider. Joe cursed and, holding Red's reins taut in his left hand, shucked his Yellowboy with his right hand and racked a round into the chamber.

"Hy-*yahhh!*" he said, spurring the horse into an instant, lunging gallop.

As he did, more smoke billowed from the barrel of the rifle of the son of a bitch hunkered atop the scarp. A bullet screeched in again and curled the air off Mannion's right ear before spanging off a rock behind him. He'd zigzagged Red just in time to avoid a third eye.

Now as he galloped toward the scarp, holding the reins up against his rifle as he aimed toward the hatted head atop the formation, he cut loose with three quick shots, rocketing reports that echoed off the near ridges and sent the crows winging off over the top of the scarp and beyond, giving their cawing complaints.

Mannion's bullets plumed rocks and gravel atop the scarp and the bushwhacker drew his head and rifle back quickly.

Joe continued toward the scarp at a dead gallop,

keeping two sharp eyes on the crest of the ridge, ready to fling lead again if he saw that hatted head. He did not see it, however, so when he approached the base of the formation, he spurred Red hard left. He'd been out here before and thought he remembered a cut through the side of the rock that led around to the back. He rode up the shoulder of the apron slope, weaving around pines and firs and skirting a pile of scattered, bleached bones— likely the remains of an elk killed by a grizzly—and found the cut through the scarp.

It was narrow and rocky, with sloping sides, so he had to put Red through it slowly.

The cut was roughly fifty yards long.

He put Red cautiously up to the cut's back door and peered first to his left and then to his right. He smiled. The shooter had been coming down the backside of the scarp and now he stopped suddenly, one foot on a rock two feet lower than his position.

His eyes widened in surprise.

It was the little dandy with the walking stick and silver-chased Colt. He held that awkward position, one boot up, one boot down, a Henry repeating rifle in his right hand. He was sweating and red-faced from the descent. He had dark features and a dark-brown beard, small, dark eyes that were suddenly filled with both caution and cunning. His long nose was sunburned and peeling.

At the moment, in his awkward position, he was no real threat.

Mannion set the rifle across his saddle horn.

"Who are you and who sent you?"

"If I tell you that, I'm a dead man."

"You're a dead man either way. Was it the Rio Grande Southern?"

"If I tell you that, I'm a dead man."

"Like I said, you're dead either way."

"We'll see!" The bushwhacker pulled his left foot down from the rock and twisted around toward Mannion, pressing the Henry up against his shoulder, aiming down the barrel.

Bang! Bang!

Mannion's two shots barked out shrilly against the backdrop of the scarp, blowing the man off his perch and down the rest of the way to the ground, where he struck with a dull thud beyond where Joe could see him.

Joe lowered the Yellowboy and put Red around a thumb of rock and stared down at the dead man staring up at him with sightless eyes.

The lawman saw something in the corner of his left eye and rode over to another, smaller escarpment to see yet another man slumped back against the rock as though only taking a nap. But a man didn't nap with two bloody holes in his chest. He was dressed in common trail gear and his battered hat lay on the ground beside him.

"Well, I'll be damned," Joe said, raking a thumbnail down his cheek. "Now who in holy hell are *you*?"

Just then there was the loud, angry rasp of a rifle being cocked behind him. A sharp female voice said, "Hold it right there, Mister. One fast move and I'll feed you a pill you won't digest!"

CHAPTER 22

"ALL RIGHT, ALL RIGHT—EASY, NOW, MISS," JOE SAID, tensing in the saddle.

"Who are you and what are you doing out here?" the angry voice inquired.

"Can I turn around?"

"No! Throw your guns down!"

"I'm Joe Mannion—Del Norte town marshal."

"I said throw your guns down!"

Mannion sighed.

He leaned down as gently as possible to drop his prized Yellowboy to the ground. He unsheathed both Russians and dropped those to the ground as well.

"Now can I turn around?" he asked.

"First step down from the saddle. I have a Spencer repeating rifle here, and I know how to use it!"

She sounded as though she did, Mannion thought.

"All right—I'm stepping down."

"Slow!" Her voice trembled with emotion. Not only anger, Joe thought, but sadness...bitterness...as well.

He swung his right leg slowly over the cantle of his saddle and, turning slowly, stepped to the ground. She

206 / PETER BRANDVOLD

faced him now about eight feet behind Red, who had turned his head to see what all the fuss was about and was giving his tail a few angry switches. He wanted no more lead hurled in his vicinity. Joe didn't blame him. He didn't either.

Mannion brushed his thumb across the badge that peeked out from behind his black vest over his dark-brown corduroy shirt. "Joe Mannion—Del Norte town marshal," he repeated.

That didn't seem to impress his assailant overmuch. She was a large, fleshy gal somewhere in her twenties with fair, doughy cheeks and a recent sunburn. She wore a print dress that, while cut conservatively and appeared hand-sewn around a kitchen table in the guttering light of a hurricane lamp, did little to hide her broad hips and heavy breasts. Her hair was long and brown, her eyes cornflower blue, her hat bullet-crowned and black.

The rifle in her gloved hands was an old-model Spencer.

"What're you doing out here?" she demanded.

"My job."

"Does your job include killing my Roy?"

Mannion glanced at the dead man sitting up against the rock, head turned to one side, arms hanging straight down to the ground. He wore gloves and chaps over denim jeans, and the holster on his hip was empty. He was big and blond, broad-shouldered, and appeared to have been dead several days.

"That's your Roy?" Joe asked her. "Husband, I take it?"

She switched her gaze to the dead man, and tears filled her eyes and dribbled down her cheeks. Turning back to Mannion, her nostrils flared in anger. "Did you kill him for Park?"

"For who?"

"James Park. Owner of the Pueblo, Colorado Springs, and Del Norte Line. You did—didn't you? I don't trust the law. Park has the money to buy and sell the law!"

"Why would Park want your Roy dead?"

"Because Roy wouldn't sell our land to him. I've been trying to track him for three days, Roy. He went out looking for stray cows. When he didn't come home, I was worried one of Park's assassins had shot him. His horse came home without him. When I heard your shooting, I came and...found Roy."

Again, her eyes filled. Tears rolled down her fleshy cheeks. Her shoulders quivered with fresh heartbreak.

"I didn't kill your Roy," Joe told her. "I came out here to find out who's been trying to kill *me*. That fella over there was one of 'em. Do you recognize him?"

She turned to the dead man and shook her head. "The men who came to our cabin a week ago wore masks."

Mannion sighed. Maybe he'd had it wrong. Maybe it wasn't H. Jerome Libby who'd tried to have him killed, after all. Maybe it was Park, owner of the Del Norte Line. God knew Mannion had locked up enough of Park's men over the past few weeks, stemming his own progress toward reaching Del Norte before Libby did.

Apparently forgetting about Mannion now, the woman lowered her rifle. She walked over to where Roy slumped back against the rock, leaned the rifle against the rock, and ran her hand through Roy's thick, yellow-blond hair with deep affection and sorrow.

Joe gave her some time while he loaded the man who'd tried to snuff his wick over the saddle of the man's horse he found tethered nearby, near the woman's beefy dun mare, who stood with its reins drooping. When he'd tied the would-be assassin over his saddle, he walked over to the woman, who knelt beside her husband, quietly sobbing.

"What's your name?" Joe asked her gently.

She looked up at him through tear-filled eyes. "Alva," she said, sniffing. "Alva Peterson."

"You have a ranch near here, Mrs. Peterson?"

"Just a little one...and a mine. It became in the path of the Del Norte Line when Park realized he had to make a turn around some deep limestone he couldn't blast through. Roy wouldn't sell. Park didn't offer us nearly enough for it. Five hundred dollars! We worked hard to keep up that homestead and claim. We were planning on raising a family there." Her voice broke on that last.

"Why don't I help you get Roy home?"

She shook her head as she turned back to her dead husband. "I can do it."

"I'd like to help." Not only did he genuinely want to help—he didn't think she could get the big man home alone—he wanted to know more about this James Park, whom he'd never met. Just his toughs in town including a big, nasty Scot named Max McGillicuddy, who'd had his own room at Hotel de Mannion for nearly two weeks three weeks ago. A supervisor had come and bailed him out.

The woman frowned up at Joe. She ran her eyes up and down his big frame and granite face with skin the color of a Colorado sunset, and a droopy, gray-brown mustache. She seemed genuinely surprised by the offer from such a hard-looking man.

"You'd do that?"

"I'd like to. If you'd let me. It sounds like under the circumstances now, you're gonna need all the help you can get in keeping your place...if that's what you still want."

"You may be big, Marshal, but you're only one man. Park has many riders. Most people don't know that, but he does. Roy and I have seen them."

Joe smiled. "Don't underestimate this old mossyhorn, Miss Alva. I still have a trick or two up my sleeves."

He had no idea what those tricks might be, but he liked the sound of his bravado.

She smiled then, too. "Okay. I guess I can let you help me get Roy home, at least."

"It's a deal."

———

MANNION GOT ROY PETERSON STRAPPED OVER THE back of his wife's horse and then he and Alva and the dead assassin started riding north, Alva leading the way to her and her husband's ranch and mine. Mannion didn't pester the grieving, young widow with questions. He'd wait till later.

Their place was small and humble, just a small cabin and stable and a privy and keeper shed behind the shack, with a milk can on the sagging front porch, under a pair of snowshoes hanging from spikes in the cabin's front wall. This was snowshoe country in the wintertime.

Mannion took the man inside and laid him out on the table so Alva could prepare him for burial while Joe dug the grave on a knoll on the other side of a creek that meandered in front of their place, and which was flanked by a pristine, green beaver meadow where the elk and moose probably came down to drink in the mornings and early evenings.

Another beautiful free and wild place threatened by another railroad.

The worse thing to come to this country was the iron horse.

When Mannion went back into the house, having finished the grave, Alva had bathed and washed Roy and somehow all by herself had gotten him into a threadbare suit that was too small for him, fitting too tightly across his shoulders and leaving too much white shirt cuff exposed, and combed his hair. He didn't look half bad, Mannion thought, for a man who'd taken two bullets to his chest and had been dead three days.

They wordlessly agreed there was no time for a coffin. Alva knew Mannion didn't have time to build one and while she probably could—she seemed right capable of many things—there was no time. Roy had already been dead three days. She and Mannion wrapped the body in an old buffalo robe then Joe carried it outside, rested it across Red's back, and led it to the grave.

Alva followed in a dress she probably wore for special occasions though it, too, showed signs of age and being cooped up too long in a steamer trunk. There were likely few special occasions out here. Mannion didn't think there were any nearby neighbors and Del Norte was a good twelve miles to the southwest. That's likely why he'd never heard of the couple till now. A black shawl draped her head and shoulders. She carried a Bible in her work-roughed hands.

She was a widow in grieving.

She read a few passages from the Good Book, tearing up only a few times, lips fluttering, then nodded at Joe to lay the body in the grave. When he'd finished that task, he hadn't even climbed up out of the grave before she'd turned and headed back to the house relieved in the late saffron light of the west-falling sun and deep shadows stretching long from the San Juan Mountains in the west.

By the time Mannion had filled in the grave, it was almost dark. Rather than start back to Del Norte tonight, he'd sleep in the barn if Alva didn't mind. She'd probably enjoy the company since she likely wouldn't have much from now on.

The house's two front windows were lit behind flour sack curtains. Joe was halfway back to it when a smell in the air stopped him dead in his tracks. He hadn't realized he was hungry until he detected the rich, spicy, succulent aromas of pot roast emanating from the shack's tin chimney pipe.

He had a feeling she was going to invite him for supper. The notion made his stomach groan and his mouth water.

She'd filled a wash bucket on a wooden stand on the front porch with warm, soapy water, and provided a brush, a rag, and a towel. He took full advantage, first stripping off his shirt and pulling his long handle top down for a good, thorough wash, making him feel like a new man. He noted that his shotgun-pellet-torn left arm was not so sore anymore, as it had been several weeks now since La Stiletta had peppered it.

He wondered briefly how Stringbean's and the girl's trek was going then knocked on the door and entered the house.

"Thanks for the wash," he said to the woman standing with her back to him.

"The least I can do, Marshal," she said without looking at him. She was dishing food onto a platter as she faced the small, potbelly stove standing with a dry sink and cupboards hammered together out of packing crates at the rear of the small cabin, which was only ten feet from the door. Sausages and webbed baskets of vegetables hung from a ceiling beam over her head. The table lay between the door and the rear wall. It was now covered in oilcloth and fully outfitted for a meal.

There were two plates and two glasses of rich, white milk.

"I take it I've been invited to stay for supper," Mannion said, hopefully. The smell in the tiny cabin was almost overpowering.

This time she looked at him over her shoulder and gave him a wan smile. "The least I can do, Marshal. I couldn't have you ride back to Del Norte after all the work you've done for me."

"I'll spend the night in the barn," he told her.

She carried a platter filled with steaming vittles—nicely browned beef, wild onions and potatoes and turnips likely from a cellar—drowning in rich, brown gravy to the table. "That will be just fine."

He waited until they were finished with the meal, and she was spooning canned peaches into two small, tin bowls to ask, "Miss Alva, where does this James Park reside, anyway? Is he with his work crew or in Denver, maybe Colorado Springs?"

A superintendent, like Libby for the Rio Grande Southern, would likely stay with the crew at the Pueblo, Colorado Springs, and Del Norte Line's end-of-track. An owner might be many miles or even states away.

"Oh, no," Alva said, setting a bowl of the sugary fruit down in front of Joe. "He lives in Del Norte. I heard from a traveling tinker that he lives in the San Juan Hotel. Has his own private room where he's seeing—I shouldn't say this, gossip is beneath me—the female owner of the place. A pretty redhead. What's her name...?"

Mannion's heart thudded. He scowled across the table at the woman in shock. "*Jane Ford?*"

He'd heard she'd gone back to using her maiden name.

Had she gone back to seeing other men already as well?

"Yes, that's it. I don't get much gossip out here, but the tinker loves to talk and he's just full of—"

The night exploded in sudden gunfire, and bullets blew out the windows and hammered through the rickety door.

CHAPTER 23

STRINGBEAN HAD TO LEAN AGAINST THE DOORFRAME TO steady himself against the whiskey fogging his brain and which his pretty charge had poured down his throat.

By sheer force of will he'd roused himself in the cave and followed her. He wasn't a half-bad tracker. He and the marshal had tracked many rustlers. Of course, hearing the whooping and hollering of the men attacking the girl had helped. He'd seen them from a distance and booted his dun into a hard gallop that had almost unseated its drunken rider more than a few times.

By sheer force of will, he stood in the cabin doorway now, bleary-eyed, seeing double, but knowing he had no choice but to start shooting...cocking...shooting...cocking...shooting again, vaguely seeing through his own powder smoke La Stiletta scream and roll over on the bed, burying her head in her arms. One of the men fell on top of her. The others were punched back deeper into the cabin, piling up on a table in one case, over a rocking chair in another, and out a back window in a screech of breaking glass in another.

Outside, the would-be rapists' horses whinnied and ran.

The effort had so drained Stringbean that with every shot he felt himself sagging farther and farther down against the frame. When the fourth man had been blown out the window, he dropped to his knees, letting the smoking barrel of the rifle sag to the floor.

He banged his head against the frame to keep from passing out.

Closing one eye, he saw only one girl just now turning over on the bed to regard him in wide-eyed fury. He said, "Now...that there...weren't nice. You kn-know I c-can't hold my...liquor." He chuckled and shook his head. "I wasn't gonna...wasn't...wasn't gonna let you l-lick me, though."

He had to bang his head against the doorframe again to keep from passing out.

"Mierda!" She rose from the bed like a chocolate-haired, black-eyed cyclone and charged over to him. "You almost shot me you crazy pendejo!"

She punched him on one temple with the end of one fist.

She punched him in the other temple with the other fist.

He was so weak he fell flat on his back. Then she was straddling him on her knees, punching and slapping him until he could taste the metallic taste of blood on his lips. He chuckled under the onslaught, making sure he squeezed the neck of his Winchester hard in his right hand.

"That's all right," he said. "You just...you j-just keep at it." Her onslaught and string of Spanish epithets was keeping him from passing out.

When she was done, still furious and frustrated, she

pulled his head up by his shirt collar, frowning. "How did you *find* me?"

He chuckled, blinking his eyes, trying to merge the two images of his lovely attacker. "Th-that's the thank... thanks I get?"

"Don't worry, I was holding my own. They were about to get their just desserts!" She gave a loud, agonized groan and reached for the rifle. She grunted, trying to pull it from his grip.

Stringbean chuckled again. "Oh, no. No...no you...d-don't." He told her in his drunken, slurred fashion that he'd been arm-wrestling Del Norte's new deputy, Cletus Booker, and that while he'd never once beat the bruin of a man and had lost considerable nickels and dimes to him, in fact, the game had given him a vice-like grip.

"Give it here...give it here, damn you!" she cried, tugging on the rifle.

Stringbean chuckled and maintained his grip on the rifle.

"All right, then, pendejo! There's another way to skin this cat!"

She lifted herself off the deputy and walked over to the bed where Boss had been about to rape her. The man lay belly down, six-shooter jutting from the holster on his right hip. She pulled the Schofield from the holster and swung back around to Stringbean, clicking the revolver's hammer back.

He'd managed to push up on one elbow, taking the rifle in both hands. He cocked it and aimed it at her, grinning, as she aimed Boss's six-shooter straight out from her right shoulder at him.

Her eyes were ablaze, lips pursed.

"So, what?" Stringbean said, again trying to make the

two images of her merge in his vision, "We're gonna shoot each other now?"

"Why not?"

"Wh-what'd be the point of that?" he asked, feeling his drunken, shit-eating grin on his face. "Besides, y-you could have sho...sho...shot me back in the cave."

"That was under different circumstances, pendejo. I thought I'd left you *near* death!"

"I'm still near death." Stringbean lowered the rifle to the floor and closed his eyes. "Go ahead and shoot."

That caused the skin to wrinkle above the bridge of her nose. "¿Qué?"

"Go ahead." Stringbean lay back, half in and half out of the cabin. "Me—I'm gonna...gonna...have a little nap. I really can't hold my..."

And then everything went black until the smell of frying meat woke him. He opened his eyes and blinked at the crudely beamed ceiling above him. For an entire minute he strained to remember where he was and what he was doing there.

His head was an exposed nerve, and a giant with a sledgehammer was whacking it repeatedly and without mercy. His mouth tasted as though a mouse had crawled in and died days ago.

He heard the sputtering of a fry pan.

He pushed up on his elbows. He lay on a bed against the front wall. How in heck had he gotten here? Had she *carried* him? She was stronger than she looked. He knew that. He licked his cracked and busted lips.

Along the back wall, La Stiletta was working at a sheet-iron monkey range, forking meat around in a skillet.

Stringbean cleared his throat.

She heard him and glanced over her shoulder at him.

She arched one pretty brow as she continued forking the meat around in the skillet. "Hungry?"

Stringbean winced at the merciless gent going at his head with that sledgehammer and thought about it. "Yeah." Come to think of it, his belly felt like a hollowed-out log. He was even more thirsty than hungry, though. "Got any water?"

"Si."

She pulled a tin cup off a shelf, walked out the door and came back in. He'd followed her with his eyes and saw three of her dead attackers lined up neatly just off the front porch, sage and sallow sunlight of late afternoon striping them. Birds piped. Stringbean could see them flitting around in the furry, deep-green pines beyond the cabin.

She sat on the edge of his bed and said, "Sit up."

He sat up against the wall and accepted the cup. He drank thirstily, deeply as she returned to the stove and the popping, sputtering meat.

Stringbean sniffed and frowned. "Venison?"

"Si. I found a keeper shed out back. A freshly shot deer is hanging in it. I carved out some steaks. Those vermin weren't *entirely* worthless." She scowled over her shoulder at Stringbean. "You might have killed me, barging in here like a drunken sailor, shooting from the hip."

She started to smile but turned her head quickly forward as though to hide it, hair flopping across her cheek.

"I figured you were as good as dead, anyway. Worth the risk." Stringbean took another drink of the water. "I was thinkin' what the marshal would have done. Of course, he would never have let his prisoner get him drunk and steal his six-gun, but even if he had, that's what he'd have done, all right."

"You admire him too much," she said, pulling two plates down off a shelf and forking a big, greasy steak onto each.

"You can't admire a man like him too much."

"Oh, yes you can." La Stiletta brought two steaming plates over to the bed. They each had a three-tined, wooden-handled fork and a serrated knife resting across them, over the dark brown, nicely charred meat. "You're nothing like him, and you should be grateful."

Stringbean set his empty water cup down between his legs and rested his plate on his right thigh. God, he was hungry, and the meat smelled so good. Forking the first bite into his mouth, he looked at her, frowning where she sat on the edge of the bed, eating her own steak.

"How come you didn't shoot me?"

Chewing, she glanced over her shoulder at him. "Because you're nothing like him."

"I'm not, am I?" he said with some disappointment.

"Hah! No." She looked at him again. "You wouldn't have that girl if you were. She might be kind of bossy and mousy and wears her drawers a little tight, but she's the right one for you."

"Well..." Stringbean didn't want to go into the subject of Molly Hurdstrom. He had enough trouble. He chewed another mouthful and glanced around, seeing his rifle leaning against the wall to his right. He turned back to La Stiletta still working on her steak and said, "I'm still gonna get you to Tucson, you know. We got us another two days till you have to be in court."

She grinned at him over her shoulder. "You'll try."

Stringbean chuckled. "Dang, this good!" He aimed his fork at her. "You'd make a fine wife, I'm thinkin'."

She glared at him. "Don't insult me after I cook you a steak, pendejo!"

————

WITH HIS BELLY FULL, STRINGBEAN MANAGED TO RALLY his inner forces. Still hungover, he rose from the cot, drank some more water, then saddled his dun and rode off to find La Stiletta's horse, which he didn't run down till an hour later. By the time he got the sorrel back to the cabin, it was too late for reasonable travel through the rugged terrain of southern Arizona.

Besides, he didn't even know where he was. He'd get his bearings tonight with the use of the marshal's maps.

So they stayed in the cabin and ate more venison and drank coffee and enjoyed the beds of the dead men so much, having not slept in beds in several days themselves, that they slept like the dead.

Stringbean rose early the next morning. He freed the stolen beeves from the rustlers' corral, saddled both horses, and led them around to the cabin. La Stiletta was ready to ride. He saw no use to cuff her or tie her to her saddle. He knew she still had a few tricks up her sleeve, but they seemed to have come to an unspoken truce. He wouldn't cuff her, and she wouldn't try to kill him in his sleep.

Those terms were good enough for Stringbean.

He'd keep a close eye on her, though. He still needed to get her to Tucson. She'd try to escape him again, all right, but he'd proven himself more than good enough at running her down.

Drunk as a gandy dancer on a Saturday night in Del Norte, no less!

They had one day to get to Tucson and they were still

a good hundred miles out. They'd have to push hard. Stringbean didn't know how they were going to do it, but they'd do it, by God.

The answer came to him when, heading southwest through low mountains stippled in saguaro cactus, catclaw, and cholla, the heat blazing, the thunder of many hooves and the crack of a bullwhip rose behind them. He turned to see a stagecoach just then mounting a hill behind them and hauling ass down the near side, dust roiling behind it, the jehu and shotgun messenger seated in the box, bandannas drawn up over their noses.

Stringbean grinned at his charge.

"Señorita Stiletta, I think we just caught us a whirlwind ride to Tucson!"

She scowled at him, incredulous. "No, no, no. I don't ride in stagecoaches. Not after the last one!"

"You sure change your tune right quick. Just a few days back you didn't understand why we wasn't catching the stage or train. Well, now we are!"

The coach held up long enough for Stringbean and the girl to climb aboard. The deputy didn't want to leave either his own horse or the girl's rented sorrel, which he was responsible for getting back to Del Norte, but he saw little choice in the matter. The only way to cover that hundred mile stretch to Tucson as fast as they needed to was to take the coach.

The driver had no problem with it, as he and his messenger were only carrying the mail and an old cowboy from Payson named Ike. Stringbean paid the jehu cold, hard cash, too, and that put a smile on the man's weathered face. He shared a cunning glance with the shotgun guard. Stringbean knew that money would never make its way to the stage line.

After they set out, Stringbean and his charge seated

facing the front of the carriage and the little, ancient cowboy named Ike, who looked the girl over carefully. Fear shone in his eyes above his gray patch beard.

"La Stiletta," he whispered, awfully.

"Pleased to make your acquaintance señor," the girl said with a prideful, cordial dip of her chin.

"You're on the way to Tucson!"

La Stiletta drew her mouth corners down then glanced snidely at Stringbean. "We'll see."

"Yes, yes," said the old man, deeply, ominously. "You will see. I have news for you."

She scowled at Ike curiously.

Fear grew in the old man's frosty eyes that matched the gray in his beard.

"Diego Hidalgo broke out of the Tucson jail two days ago. He is haunting the trail for you. In fact, he and nearly a dozen of his men were at the stage relay station we just came through!"

"*Diego?*" the girl said, leaning forward hopefully in her seat. "He's looking for me?"

"Si, si, La Stiletta," Ike said. He was so wizened he resembled the desert itself, probably worked with as many Mexicans as gringos over the years. "He said he and you have a sixth sense about each other. He also said he intends to cut out that 'disloyal little backstabbing puta of a bandita's black tongue so she'll never be able to testify against him about anything again!"

Stringbean and La Stiletta shared a dark look.

"Ah, hell!" came the cry of one of the men in the driver's boot. "I just knew they were trailin' us. Here they come!"

La Stiletta reached up to pound her fist against the roof. "Who's coming?"

"*Diego Hidalgo, his own kill-looney self!*"

La Stiletta turned to Stringbean, eyes ablaze. She punched his shoulder hard and said, "You were bound to do it eventually, weren't you?"

"Do *what*?" Stringbean asked, indignant, rubbing his shoulder. He hadn't quite wrapped his mind around what he'd just learned.

"Get me *killed*. At least I won't be going alone, though." She threw her head back and gave a savage laugh. "You can bet the love of your beloved Bloody Joe on that!"

CHAPTER 24

"*Alva, down!*" Joe shouted as he threw himself across the table at the woman, knocking her backward in her chair and throwing her to the floor, feeling the bite of a bullet nip his right calf.

The din continued relentlessly, bullets plowing into the table, sending the fruit bowls and spoons flying. One slug nipped the oil tank on the hurricane lamp, making the flame gutter and smoke. They spanged off the potbelly stove, ricocheting around the tight confines.

Mannion looked down at the terrified woman beneath him staring up at him in shock, and said, "Stay down!"

He rolled off her to his left and crawled around the table to the front wall where he'd leaned his Yellowboy. He grabbed the rifle and his hat off the peg above it— somehow it seemed as necessary as the long gun—and set it on his head. He jacked a round into the action, rose to a knee, and returned fire through the window right of the door, aiming at the gun flashes he could see in the darkness maybe two hundred feet away from the cabin, out in the brush along the stream.

More rounds were coming through the two windows in the cabin's rear wall, so that bullets hammered the log walls at both front and rear, screeching with tooth-gnashing menace just over Joe's head. They busted pictures off the walls—the few that were there—and shredded tack that hung from pegs in the sitting area of the cabin, left of the kitchen. The harnesses, hames, and traces had likely been in the process of being mended by night by Roy while sitting in the rocking chair on the hemp rug in the cabin's far corner.

Judging by the gunfire, Joe thought there were at least ten men surrounding the cabin.

During a brief lull, he rose and quickly snatched the lamp off the table, blew it out, casting darkness around him, and set the lamp on the floor. He didn't want it to get hit and burn them out. Their attackers would likely do that soon enough themselves. They certainly seemed determined to trim the wicks of those inside, which had Mannion believing they knew there was someone else here besides the woman.

They might have been on the lurk around the place and seen Mannion ride in with Alva and had waited for dark to make their play.

If Joe had a dollar for every man who wanted him dead, he'd could retire in San Francisco and live off the fat of the bay.

As the gunfire resumed in earnest, he crawled back over to Alva who'd rolled onto her side, drawn her knees to her chest, and had closed her arms over her head.

"Is there anyway besides the front door out of this place?" he asked her, raising his voice to be heard above the din.

She shook her head.

Then she raised it and looked at him. "Yes! The cellar!

Roy put a trapdoor in here so we could get to it in the winter when the snow was too deep outside!"

"Where is it?"

She turned over and pointed while bullets continued to whistle and thud. "Under his rocking chair!"

"Let's go! Stay down!"

They rose to hands and knees and crawled side by side, Mannion clutching the Yellowboy in his right hand, to the cabin's far corner. Mannion grabbed a leg of the rocking chair and pulled it off the rug. Then he slid the rug away from the four-by-four-foot trap door embedded in the floor.

It's a chance, he thought. *Probably not much of one, but it's a chance...*

He rose to his knees and pulled on the steel handle.

Stuck!

Bullets shrieked and thumped into walls and sparked off the stove. One tore the Peterson's wedding tintype from the wall above Mannion and Alva, and it fell to the floor with a crash of breaking glass.

"Oh, no!" Alva cried, picking up the photo and brushing the broken glass from it.

Gritting his teeth, Mannion pulled at the trap door again. It didn't come free, but he did feel some give in it. He pulled even harder, and it came free so suddenly he was knocked back on his heels. He shoved the door up against the wall and smelled the loamy smell, tinged with the smell of potatoes and other root vegetables, rise from below. Wooden rungs dropped away into darkness.

He held his hand out to Alva who lay holding the picture before her, staring at it, sobbing.

"Come on—we have to move fast!"

Holding onto the tintype with one hand, she accepted

his hand in the other. He dropped down the rungs into the cellar as she followed in his wake. At the bottom of the hole, which was roughly ten feet deep, he could see the outside door angling over the rear half of the cellar. Releasing Alva's hand, he climbed more wooden rungs and gave the door a hard shove with his head and shoulders...and was surprised when it gave so easily. He grabbed the latch quickly so the door didn't open all the way and slam against the ground with what would no doubt have been a loud *bang!*

He lifted the door a few inches to peer out into the Peterson's backyard.

Suddenly, the shooting ceased.

"Close on the cabin!" a man yelled from the front. "They gotta be shot to ribbons by now!"

"Damn!" Joe rasped out, closing the door.

They'd be on him in a minute.

He thought it over, then grinned. The woman stood beside him. It was almost pitch-black in the cellar, but ambient light glinted off something she clutched to her breasts. Hers and Roy's wedding picture.

"What is it?" she whispered.

"Get ready to climb up out of here and run fast straight out toward the stable when I start shooting. Do you understand me, Alva? Fast! Get the door open. I'll be right behind you!"

"All right," she said softly, voice trembling with anxiousness.

He shoved the door up a few inches and peered into the darkness behind the cabin. He could hear crunching footsteps and presently saw the silhouettes of five men take shape in the darkness, approaching the cabin from the brush and rocks flanking it. They were roughly fifty to a hundred feet from Joe, ahead and to the left of the stable and corral, moving around the privy and keeper shed, closing on the cabin.

"They're not here!" a man shouted from inside the cabin. "Look out—we could be caught in a whipsaw!"

"You got that right," Joe said through gritted teeth as, nostrils flared, he pushed up hard on the door and climbed the steps.

He surfaced from the cellar just as the heavy wooden door gave a loud *bang!* on the ground to his left.

The five silhouettes stopped suddenly in the darkness and whipped toward him, starlight glinting off the rifles in their hands.

Joe cut loose with the Yellowboy, firing straight out from his right hip, the rifle bucking and roaring, flames lapping from the barrel. As he did, Alva ran up the steps behind him, gasping, and ran toward the stable, still clutching the tintype in her arms.

Two of Mannion's targets snapped off shots, but the bullets whined wide, thudding into the cabin wall behind Joe. All five men screamed and danced and dropped their rifles, losing their hats, and went down hard.

The echoes of his shots were still chasing each other skyward when Joe ran to the stable. Alva was waiting inside, cowering against the wall beside the open door. Joe wasted no time in backing Red out of his stall and leading him to the open door.

He'd no sooner lifted Alva onto that bay than running footsteps sounded from the direction of the cabin, which he could now see through the broken rear windows was on fire, flames glowing inside. Three men were just now running along the side toward the rear.

Mannion dropped to a knee and started flinging lead.

He killed the first man outright, blowing him back against the end of the cabin, head wobbling as though his neck were broken. He flung more lead at the other two, but they wheeled, cursing, and ran back around the cabin's front corner.

Joe leaped onto Red's back behind Alva and ground his spurs into the mount's flanks. He'd have stayed and fought these bastards to the death, but he had to get Alva out of here. The bay whinnied, pitched up off its front hooves, and galloped out of the stable and took a hard left, into the brush behind it. The way was partly lit by flames licking up out of the broken windows.

"Our beautiful cabin!" Alva cried behind Joe.

"Don't worry," Joe growled as the bay picked its own way through the brush, following what appeared a narrow, meandering game trail, "they'll pay. Park will get his head blown off soon as I get to town!"

Alva was still clutching the tintype she'd taken from the cabin.

Behind Joe, she sobbed.

Behind her, the bushwhackers shouted in momentary chaos over the unexpected predicament of their quarry having slithered out from under them. Glancing over his shoulder, Joe now saw flames lighting up the sky as the flames consumed the cabin.

They dropped into a wash and Joe leaned forward, clutching the horn in front of Alva keeping them both in the saddle as the big bay lunged up the opposite bank through willows and evergreen shrubs perfuming the cool mountain air.

Then they were climbing a steep, forested ridge, the bay again making his own way, lunging and blowing, the bit rattling in his teeth.

"Keep going, Red," Joe said, leaning forward to pat the stalwart mount's left wither. "Keep going...that's the way, boy."

They topped the ridge and dropped into a canyon on the other side. Tree-studded dikes rose around them and Joe looked around, wanting a place to cold camp for the rest of the night. As tough as Red was, he couldn't keep climbing ridges all night with two on his back. And that's all there was out here—one ridge after another between narrow ravines. He wasn't sure where they were, just somewhere southeast of the burning cabin, the fire's glow now hidden behind the ridges they'd crossed.

They came to a rock-studded hollow, the rocks rising ghostly in the starlight around them. A nighthawk screeched and coyotes sang their bizarre chorus on a distant ridge to Mannion's right. Nearby, a creek murmured and glittered like the skin of a black snake. He pulled Red to a halt, dropped the reins, and eased Alva out of the saddle, ushering her into the hollow under a concave boulder jutting up like some giant's tongue from the earth's bowels.

She sat stiffly, clutching the broken tintype, making no sounds now, just staring as though in shock.

Of course, she was in shock. Roy was dead, her cabin burned. Life ruined.

Also, she wore only the dress she'd worn at the so-called funeral. It looked ridiculously out of place out here, on the run from killers. And it wasn't enough to fend off the mountain chill. Before leaving the Peterson stable, Mannion had thought to grab his bedroll and had ridden with it sandwiched between himself and Alva. He'd also draped his canteen over his shoulder.

He untied the soogan now and draped it over the woman's shoulders then led Red over to the stream so the sweat-silvered bay could draw water and crop the thick tufts of nourishing green grass growing along its edges.

He let the halter rope dangle. Red wasn't going anywhere.

Joe drank from the stream himself then emptied the old water from his canteen and filled it with fresh. He took it over to Alva and handed it to her. She didn't seem to see it or even him at first, staring in shock as she was. Then she looked up at him and frowned as though seeing him for the first time. Sluggishly, she accepted the canteen and merely set it in her lap with the tintype.

She looked up at Mannion again and, clearer-eyed, said in a thin, trembling voice, "What will I do now?"

Mannion sat down beside her and drew his arm around her shoulders. He wasn't usually a man given to much empathy or sympathy, but he felt both for her now. He gave her a squeeze and said through gritted teeth, "Find out what you're made of."

She looked up at him.

She gasped when hoof thumps sounded on the ridge above them.

CHAPTER 25

"SHH!" JOE SAID.

They both sat listening.

Mannion looked over at Red who'd been cropping grass along the creek but who now stood craning his neck to peer toward the ridge behind him. Joe thought the bay was about as well concealed in the boulders as he could be, hidden from the ridge by a cabin-sized one about thirty feet out from where Joe sat with Alva.

Up on the ridge, a man's voice came soft but crystal clear in the cool, quiet mountain night. "Think they're down there?"

"Hard to say," came the voice of another man. "Can't see shit in the dark. Hard to know where they are. But I know the boss is gonna want an accounting."

Silence.

The second man who'd spoken said, "I'll ride down and take a look around. You three spread out, try to pick up their trail. Like Dave said, the boss is gonna want an accounting."

Who's your boss? Mannion silently called up the ridge.

He curled one-half of his upper lip. He knew. Oh, he knew...

His knowing had nothing to do with Jane stepping out on him with James Park. Did it?

Nah.

"All right," said the first man who'd spoken. "You check out that canyon down there, Anders. We'll check out this one. You see anything, give a coyote yip."

"All right."

Hooves thudded. Brush crackled.

The thudding and crackling of only one horse grew gradually louder as Anders descended the ridge toward Mannion and Alva.

Red switched his gaze to Mannion, twitching first one ear and then the other. He was about to whinny.

Joe pressed two fingers to his lips and wagged his head, heart thudding.

Don't do it, Red. Don't do it!

The horse studied him.

Mannion silently pleaded with him.

Finally, Red gave his tail an incredulous switch then turned his head forward and resumed cropping grass along the creek.

Mannion sighed. Alva glanced at him.

"I owe him an extra bait of oats for that bit of self-restraint," he whispered very softly as the hoof thumps and brush crackling grew louder.

The approaching horse kicked a stone, sent it tumbling...*thump-thump-thump-thump* till it piled up at the bottom of the canyon maybe forty feet to Joe's left.

The hoof thuds stopped when the man pulled up at the bottom of the canyon. Silence.

Then the horse came ahead slowly.

Anders said in quiet, sing-song mocking, "Mannion... Missus Peterson...y'all down here...?"

Again, Red turned his head to look behind him though all he could see was the boulder that concealed him from Anders. The horse had gotten its master's orders and obeyed though it kept looking over its right wither as Anders came slowly along the canyon floor, twenty feet away from Mannion and Alva now and closing very slowly—*clomp...clomp...clomp...*

Beside Mannion, Alva gave a soft gasp and closed her hand over her mouth.

Quietly into her ear, Joe said, "Stay very quiet, all right? Apache quiet." Pressed up against her, he could feel her heart hammering through her shoulder.

Holding a hand over her mouth, she gave her head a single nod.

To their left, *clomp...clomp...clomp...*

Anders said, "Mannion...Missus Peterson...?"

"Stay here," Joe whispered into Alva's left ear.

As Anders continued toward them, Mannion leaned the Yellowboy against the rock beside him then shoved up onto his knees, crouching, hearing the hoof clomps grow gradually louder until he could see the horse's head with the bit in its teeth. Then he saw the horse's wither and the leg of the man in the saddle...and then the man in the saddle himself.

Anders wore a butternut canvas jacket and a high-crowned cream hat. He appeared tall.

Straight out away from Mannion's and Alva's hiding place, Anders stopped his horse. The rider looked straight ahead. If he turned his head toward Mannion and Alva, he'd have a hard time seeing them in the dark recess of the boulder.

Or so Joe hoped...

If he kept moving forward, however, he'd see Red, who kept his neck craned to peer back over his right wither.

Tension had Joe's guts in a tight knot...growing tighter as Anders sat straight out before him, eight feet away, staring straight ahead. His horse stomped its right front hoof, lowered its head, and shook it, rattling the bit in its teeth.

It had scented Anders's quarry. Probably all three—Mannion, Alva, and Red.

Soon, it would sound the alarm.

Mannion rose slowly from his knees. Walking quickly on the balls of his feet, he hurried forward, crouching, gritting his teeth and hardening his jaws. He closed the gap between himself and Anders. When he was two feet away, Anders jerked his head toward him. Mannion saw him widen his eyes in shock beneath the brim of the cream hat.

"Hey!" he said just before Joe reached up, grabbed his right arm, and jerked him down the right side of the horse, which lurched forward and curveted, whickering.

Mannion placed a knee on the groaning Anders's back then pulled one of his Russians and smashed the butt against the back of the man's skull, hard. Deadly hard. The body slackened beneath his knee. Anders lay belly down, unmoving.

"One way to skin a cat," Joe muttered, taking a deep inhale of the chill night air, relieved but knowing his job wasn't over.

When Anders didn't ride up to meet the others, the others would ride down here.

He couldn't let them do that.

Besides, they'd killed Roy and burned his and Alva's

home, leaving her with only a tintype to her name. They had to pay for that.

They had a reckoning coming.

Joe knew that he and the woman should mount Red and just ride away, but that, God forgive him, was not the man he was. He had more blood to extract and his heart fairly thudded with eagerness at the prospect.

Quickly, he pulled off Anders's butternut jacket and shrugged into it. He picked up the man's hat and donned that, too. The man's horse stood a few yards away, whickering softly as it regarded Mannion dubiously. Joe grabbed the reins then led it over to where Alva remained as before, clutching the tintype to her chest.

"Wait here," he said quietly as he swung up onto the nervously sidestepping chestnut's back. "I'll be back soon."

"Please don't leave me!" she rasped out from the dark recess in the rock.

"I'll be back!" Joe rasped back at her and booted the chestnut back along the canyon in the direction from which it and its now-deceased rider had come.

When he saw the large rock that the chestnut had kicked down the slope, lying in front of him in a patch of otherwise clear ground, Mannion swung the mount to the left and put it up the slope. He rode slowly, head down, swaying leisurely in the saddle, making sure the broad brim of the cream Stetson concealed his face.

He rode through some trees that started about three-quarters of the way up the ridge and when he gained the ridgetop, the three remaining riders—killers, arsons—sat their own mounts facing him, waiting for Anders. One of them was smoking a cigarette, the coal glowing in the darkness when he raised it to his lips and drew on it.

He turned his head to one side to send a plume of

smoke into the darkness. Then he turned back to Mannion.

"Nothin'?" he said.

"Oh, there's somethin', all right." Mannion stopped the chestnut and pulled both Russians, clicking the hammers back as he extended both revolvers at the men facing him. "Sudden death if you don't tell me who the hell you're working for!"

All three jerked back in their saddles with fierce starts.

They were so startled they reacted instead of thought.

All three reached for iron.

Joe blew all three out of their saddles, his Russians flashing red in the darkness.

"Dammit," he said, looking down at all three inert bodies as their horses galloped off.

He'd hoped to leave at least one alive.

But he hadn't.

That was all right. He knew who had sent them, all right. He'd just wanted to hear it from them.

He'd see that man as soon as he got back to Del Norte and paid a visit to his two-timing wife's San Juan Hotel and Saloon.

———

WITH THE WOMAN RIDING BEHIND HIS SADDLE, Mannion pulled Red up to one of the three wrought iron hitchracks fronting the San Juan a few hours later, well after sunup. The unlikely pair couldn't have looked more trail weary. The woman looked anxious and deeply haunted—reasonable given what she'd been through. Bloody Joe looked like he had one hell of an especially large chip on his shoulder.

Nothing new there but this was especially vexing, given Jane's apparent involvement with James Park.

"I'll get you a room here and have water hauled up for a bath," Joe told Alva. "I'll have one of the girls go out and get you some fresh clothes."

Alva looked at the large, sprawling, tony structure before her, and shook her head. "I don't need any such fancy a place as this, Marshal."

"After what you've been through, I disagree. Don't worry—I'll buy. We'll figure out something more permanent later. Right now, I have business to tend."

He led her up the broad wooden steps, across the veranda, and through the stout oak doors. Mannion looked around and saw one of Jane's girls standing at the bar, sipping a cup of morning coffee. It was only around nine, but she was all gaudied up and ready to start the workday. With Del Norte booming the way it was, most of the businesses were ready for business at the crack of dawn—if they'd ever closed their door at all, that was.

Joe led Alva over to the whore.

"Sissy, this is Alva Peterson. She's been through holy hell. Would you see her to a room and have water brought up for a bath? Then maybe you could go out and set her up with a fresh set of clothes? Charge it all to my accounts." Mannion flipped the pretty blonde a silver cartwheel. "That's for you."

The whore looked at the coin in her hand and smiled winningly. "You got it, Marshal." She dropped the coin into her low-cut bodice then took Alva by the arm. "Right this way, Mrs. Peterson. We'll get you freshened up in no time."

The woman ambled along beside the spry doxie uncertainly, looking around in bewilderment at the San Juan's fancy furnishings. Mannion lifted his dusty Stetson from his head, ran a hand through his sweat-damp hair, and looked around himself.

Even for so early, Jane had a pretty good crowd. There were several card games being played, and cigarette and cigar smoke webbed around the large, crystal chandeliers strategically placed about the carpeted, cave-like drinking hall. Some customers were eating breakfast. Some were drinking and smoking as though it were after five. It wasn't hard to spot Jane. Her beauty and rust-red hair stuck out in any crowd, not to mention the fine cut of her gowns and sparkling jewelry.

She was seated on the other side of the room, near the Bear Den gambling parlor, with a tall, handsome, dark-haired man with a thick, black mustache lightly flecked with gray. He was dressed in a three-piece suit with a gray coat, paisley vest, and string tie.

James Park. Had to be.

Joe puffed his chest up, drawing a deep, calming breath. He tried to calm himself. There was something about having killers sicced on you and then finding the man who'd most likely sicced them on you having what appeared a most friendly conversation with your wife that made it damned hard to remain calm.

Mannion made his way through the tables and stopped at Jane's. She and her gentleman friend were just then laughing at some quip. Jane raised her cup of coffee to her lips but before she could take a sip, she glanced up and saw Mannion.

"Joe!" she said, frowning in surprise, a light flush rising in her pretty, lightly freckled cheeks.

"Yes, it's Joe." Mannion pulled out a chair and slacked into it, saying, "Mind if I sit down?" He didn't wait for an invitation. He doffed his hat and set it on the table.

"Of course, of course," Jane said, frowning at his

brusque demeanor. "Joe Mannion, I'd like you to meet a friend of mine. Joe this is—"

"James Park. Owner of the Pueblo, Colorado Springs, and Del Norte Line," Joe finished for her.

"Marshal Mannion, the pleasure is mine," Park said, removing a fat stogie from between his lips and extending a hand with a warm smile.

"Sorry, Park. I don't shake the hand of cold-blooded killers."

"Joe!" Jane intoned.

"What?" Park said, deeply incredulous. "What're you talking—"

"Your men shot Roy Peterson in cold blood, and then you sent them to burn out Mrs. Peterson and assassinate me. They must have picked up my trail after I left your competitor, Libby. It was one helluva night, Park, and I don't appreciate it one bit!"

"That's a mighty big accusation, Marshal," Park said, riled now himself. "I suggest you take it back."

By now the rest of the room had gone quiet and all eyes were on Mannion and the railroad owner.

"The hell I will. Mrs. Peterson said you offered to buy her and her husband out, but they weren't going for it. You threatened them. Sent masked riders."

"I offered to buy them out but be that as it may, I threatened no one. And I certainly didn't send masked riders."

"And then I ride to town and see you making calf eyes at my wife. We are still married, you know, Jane. An unseemly display—you and this popinjay in his forty-dollar suit!"

Park leaped to his feet, red-faced. "I don't have to take that from you. I don't care who you are! As for Roy Peterson—"

He stopped when Mannion rose to his own feet, rage seething through him like a wildfire fueled on late season grass after a summer without rain. "Yes, you do." He tried to stop himself, but he just couldn't do it. Before he knew what he was doing, his right fist flew across the table and into his opponent's mustached mouth.

"Joe, for God sakes!" Jane fairly screamed, rising from her chair.

Park stumbled back, shaking his head and brushing a fist across his cracked lower lip. "How *dare* you strike me, you cheap tin star!"

His own right fist came flying across the table and smashed Joe's right cheek. Park was big and strong, and the blow sent Mannion stumbling into Jane, almost knocking her over. She gave an enraged wail as she righted herself, using her chair.

Totally out of his head now with fury, Mannion hurried around the table, tossing chairs out of his way, jaws hard, teeth gritted. Park stepped back, preparing for another assault, but before Mannion could raise his right fist again, a man behind him shouted, "Got him, boss!"

The man behind him was also big and strong. A big, potbellied bull of a man. He drove Joe straight down to the floor and then took Joe by the hair and smashed his face against the floor. Right away, Mannion knew who his assailant was.

The loud-mouthed, bearish Max McGillicuddy—Park's own personal bodyguard.

Joe rolled over and tried to fight, but the big man smashed his fist into Joe's face twice, making his eyes dim and his ears ring.

"Keith! Waylon!" Mannion heard Jane bellow for her two big, thuggish bouncers. "Out with him. Throw him in the street like the rabid cur he is!"

Keith and Waylon were mighty effective at their work. Mannion had seen them at work before. With the help of McGillicuddy, they got Joe to his feet pronto and before he could resist, they were rushing him toward the doors so fast that Mannion's feet could hardly keep up. He dragged his boot toes drunkenly. He had no more fight in him. McGillicuddy's punches had left him reeling. Suddenly he was out the door and hurled straight out into the street.

He hit the dirt like a one-hundred-pound sack of cracked corn.

"Oh," he groaned, raising his head and spitting dirt from his lips.

"What the hell's goin' on?"

Joe turned his head slightly left to see Rio Waite walking toward him in his bandy-legged fashion, a look of deep incredulity on his craggy face. He was accompanied by young Harmon Haufenthistle, the towheaded odd-job boy.

Behind Joe, Jane said, "Rio, get him out of here. He assaulted a customer of mine for no good reason! I want him arrested. Hold him overnight then fine him just like *he'd* fine any other man who did what he's done!" She tossed Mannion's hat into the street beside him. She fairly screamed, "My place is off-limits to you, *Marshal Mannion*—for the rest of your life!"

She wheeled around and, lifting her skirts above her ankles, climbed the porch steps and went back inside.

"Marshal Mannion," young Harmon said. "What in holy blazes..."

Mannion flushed with humiliation, shook his head and groaned.

The boy stared down at him, wide-eyed and in shock. Here lay the great mighty Joe like a drunk in the street.

"Ah, hell." Those were the only words he could find though he normally did not swear in front of children.

Everybody within a block had stopped to stare at their notorious town marshal lying on the street with his bloody mouth full of dirt. Getting his hat handed to him by his wife, no less.

"Ah, hell," he said again as Rio and young Harmon moved in to help him to his feet. "Just hell."

Mannion heard footsteps on the veranda behind him once more and then Jane's voice again. "I will be expecting that signed divorce decree posthaste!"

"Ah, hell," Mannion said again.

CHAPTER 26

"AH, HECK."

Stringbean had just stuck his head out the coach window and saw the riders galloping along the trail behind them. They wore brightly colored clothing and sombreros, and they were coming hell-for-leather. As Stringbean watched, holding his hat on his lap, several of the riders—there appeared a good eight or so—pulled six-shooters and started shooting, smoke and flames lapping from the barrels.

"Not again," the deputy said. He'd had his fill of stagecoaches.

The driver hoorahed his team and popped the black-snake over their backs. The coach lurched forward, gaining more speed.

Stringbean looked out the window, and a cold stone dropped in his belly. Diego Hidalgo's bunch was still gaining on the coach.

"Oh, Lordy, Lordy, Lordy!" said the little, ancient cowboy named Ike. "Just what I need at this late date—after fightin' Injuns and banditos of every stripe! Now it's none other than Diego Hidalgo!" He cackled ironically. "Oh well, young feller—better get to it!"

He pulled his six-shooter, the grips held together with rusted wire. He doffed his hat and poked his head and six-shooter out the window and commenced cutting loose with his old Schofield.

Stringbean pulled his own gun, poked it out the window on the opposite side of the coach from Ike, and started shooting. He and Ike's bullets caused their pursuers to waver slightly, but they kept coming...and shooting.

The carriage pounded over chuckholes, making accurate shooting nearly impossible. As they began to trace a broad curve in the trail, their pursuers suddenly swung off the trail's left side.

"Ah, damn," Ike said. "They're gonna try to cut us off at the pass!"

Stringbean saw it was true. The gang was crossing the broad horseshoe in the trail, the shortest route to a distant, low pass among pines and rock outcroppings and up which the stage trail climbed. La Stiletta was staring out the window as well, and she and Stringbean shared a dark look.

"Save one of those bullets for me, pendejo," the girl told him in a hopeless tone. "If Diego gets his hands on me, it will not go well. Not well at all! I skinned out on him and he's not very happy with me. No, not at all."

"You got it," Stringbean said, feeling dread pool in his belly.

They'd almost made it to Tucson. Now it wasn't to be.

He wouldn't be heading back to Del Norte. He'd never see the marshal and his girl, Molly, again, though of course whether she was still his girl was debatable.

The thought had no sooner passed over his mind than the driver bellowed, "Ah, hell—hold on, folks!"

The coach fishtailed violently, throwing all occupants toward the right side of the coach. Stringbean glanced out the window on his side of the coach and saw them heading nearly sideways to a massive, black boulder on the trail's right side. The driver was taking the turn too quickly.

Stringbean stared awestruck as the big boulder grew closer and closer and larger and larger so that he could see the cracks and dimples in it. Somehow, the jehu managed to pull the coach back onto the trail just in time to avoid a full-on collision. However, the back rear wheel on Stringbean's side of the coach struck the rock.

Immediately, the coach dropped down on its rear right side as the wheel went spinning off into the cacti along the trail.

The jehu bellowed another curse and then Stringbean saw them caroming toward another boulder on the trail's left side.

"Get right with your Maker, folks, an' do it quick," yelled Ike, clinging to a ceiling strap.

"Mierda!" screamed La Stiletta.

The coach's left rear side struck the rock and then the jehu and shotgun messenger were both yelling as the coach plunged onto its right side with a violent *crash*! And then they were suddenly rolling down the trail, Stringbean, Ike, and La Stiletta, flying around inside the contraption like dice in a cup. On one such roll, Stringbean saw Ike fly out one of the doors to disappear in a cloud of roiling dust, eyes big as 'dobe dollars, reaching both hands for the coach in total futility.

The coach rolled one more time and then it broke up

and Stringbean felt himself hurled out of the right side, through a sudden break. He hit the ground and rolled... rolled...and rolled.

He didn't think he would ever stop rolling until he did, coming to rest on his back, staring up at the cobalt desert sky obscured by billowing dust.

The world pitched around him.

Lying there, the wind knocked out of him, he took silent inventory, coming to the conclusion that he might have some cracked ribs but the rest of him, despite many scrapes and bruises, felt relatively intact. He sat up, shook his head to clear it, and looked around.

The coach resembled a pile of giant matchsticks strewn along the trail through the rocky corridor. The team was galloping into the distance, toward the pass. The jehu and shotgun messenger lay among the wreckage in twisted heaps, unmoving.

Beyond them, Diego Hidalgo's group was just then gaining the pass.

Stringbean turned to his right.

The girl lay belly down roughly twenty feet away from him. She wasn't moving except he thought he could see her breathing, back rising and falling quickly. Stringbean's rifle lay between him and her.

He rose with a grunt and spat grit from his lips. He picked up his rifle and went over and dropped to one knee beside La Stiletta, placing a hand on her back. "If you can get up, you'd best." He glanced toward the pass. The gang of Mexico lobos had swung their horses down the pass and were spurring them into gallops. "Your boyfriend's headed this way, and I don't think it's gonna be a happy reunion."

That seemed to startle her out of her stupor.

She lifted her head abruptly. Her hair was as dusty as an old mop. She turned toward the pass and gasped. She thrust her hand out at Stringbean, and he pulled her to her feet. He kept hold of her hand and began climbing a rise toward an outcropping of red sandstone rocks capping the rise a hundred yards away.

They'd fort up there, try to make a stand though they were outnumbered at least ten to one. Maybe a dozen to one. Hard to tell.

Meanwhile, Stringbean could hear the rataplan of their hunters' horses' hooves growing louder on the hot, dry desert air.

Halfway up the rise, Stringbean turned to see the gang roughly seventy yards away and closing fast, angling toward their quarry.

"Come on, Chiquita!" yelled Diego Hidalgo, riding at the head of the pack. He wore a red, Spanish-style shirt with a ruffled front and black chaps, two silver pistols bristling from black holsters on his hips. He held a rifle in his right hand. "Why are you running from your beloved Diego? I have been long awaiting our reunion!"

"Mierda," the girl said. "I can tell from his tone, he's really mad. Thinks I pulled out on him, leaving him to the federals, which I guess I did, but..."

"No time for regrets, I don't think," Stringbean said as guns popped behind them and bullets screeched through the air around them, spanging off rocks. He stopped and gave her a shove. "You run and fort up in them rocks to the left. I'm gonna try to hold 'em off, buy us a little time!"

He didn't have to tell her twice. She cast another horrified look toward her seething lover and took off running, limping on her right ankle, weaving among the rocks that grew thick now near the top of the rise.

As she fled, Stringbean stopped and dropped to both knees behind a rock, jacked a round into the chamber, picked out one of the riders galloping toward him up the rise and fired.

The man's horse whinnied and dropped, the man rolling clear in a swelter of red dust.

Stringbean cursed. He'd aimed at the man's chest but somehow hit the horse. That's because he was nervous. Bad nervous. His hands were trembling and so were his knees. He supposed he could be forgiven. It was obvious now he'd never be the stalwart soul his boss was. Looking death in the eye, he had all he could do to keep from turning and running as he'd done once before.

"Nah, nah," Stringbean said, hunkered behind the rock when three more bullets caromed in to smash its face. "Keep your nerve and go out in style, not like a whimpering dog. You might be able to get enough of these lobos, buy enough time for the girl to get away.

He didn't know why that seemed important at the moment, but it did. Maybe he'd taken a fancy to her?

He squeezed off three more shots and gave a victorious whoop when one of his targets went turning a near perfect backward somersault over the arched tail of his horse. He was trampled by the horse and rider behind him, and then Stringbean shot that man off his horse as well.

Again, he gave another victorious whoop.

Two down!

That left nine or ten to go, but still...

His accurate shooting had caused Hidalgo to stop and curvet his fine buckskin stallion and give Stringbean the woolly eyeball from beneath the brim of his black, silver-stitched sombrero. He dropped down the side of his horse and scrambled for cover as two more of Stringbean's bullets plumed dust just behind the large, Mexican-style spurs on his tooled black boots.

The rest of the lobos went to the ground as well, but as they fired their pistols or rifles, they skinned out from behind their covering rocks to run up the rise toward the quarry, firing and pausing only to quickly reload from their cartridge belts.

The bullets were getting so close to Stringbean that he fired one more round then rose and ran crouching up the rise, weaving among the rocks and boulders. Several bullets curled the air off the sides of both his ears—one bullet clipping the spur on his right boot, making the rowel sing eerily.

"Not much more time now, I reckon," Stringbean said, throwing himself to the ground and rolling behind another large rock at the top of the rise, two bullets kicking dirt and gravel in his face. He thumbed fresh rounds from his cartridge belt into his Winchester's receiver then, lying prone, snaked the rifle around his covering rock's right side. "I reckon I'll be seein' just how good I been livin' here in a minute."

Saint Pete or Old Scratch? Hmm.

He vaguely opined that one of the things he was going to miss most, besides Molly, of course, was the beef pot roast and lemon pie he consumed almost daily for lunch in a local eatery in Del Norte.

And a nice, big, glass of cool, creamy milk fresh from the springhouse...

Funny the way a man's mind strays when he's looking death in the face.

And he literally was, too. He could not clearly see the ruddy faces of several of the men snaking through the rocks, heading toward him, firing as they came, yelling back and forth to each other in Spanish.

He cocked a fresh round and snaked his rifle around the left side of his covering rock. As he did, a squat, broad-shouldered man in a ragged straw sombrero rose from a table-like rock fifteen feet down the rise and ran up the rise toward Stringbean, aiming a rifle straight out from his right hip.

Stringbean fired once...twice...and watched in grim satisfaction as the Mexican screamed and went flying back over the rock he'd just risen from.

The echo of his second shot was still swirling on the wind when another Mexican—the man tall, lean, and hawk-faced and wearing a swaying mare's tail mustache—rose from behind another rock just down the rise from the man Stringbean had just killed. He took off running toward Stringbean, firing two pistols as he came. Both bullets pounded into the boulder to the left of Stringbean's face, peppering his eyes with rock dust.

Still, calmly—he had no idea where that calm came from; he sure hadn't been known for it before!—he managed to drill a round through the tall man's black-and-white calico shirt, causing him to lower his pistols and stumble backward with a bewildered expression on his face. He stopped, dropped to his knees, lifted his head to give an agonized wail in Spanish, then looked down at the blood pumping from his chest and fell straight forward to die on the ground, shivering as though deeply chilled.

Four down! Stringbean silently congratulated himself as he rose from his position and made his way deeper into the rocks.

If he could get one more—Diego Hidalgo himself—he'd die a happy man...

As he found another rock to crouch behind, deep in a nest of sandstone rocks jutting all around him, he wondered where the girl was. He fired at a thick-set Mex wearing an eyepatch weaving toward him through the rocks—an errant round, dangit!

Then he heard La Stiletta scream.

CHAPTER 27

"Go ahead—throw me in the damn hoosegow," Mannion told Rio Waite as they walked together, Joe limping badly on a knee he'd injured in his unceremonious tumble, toward the jailhouse that had—all the more ironically, it seemed now—been nicknamed after him. "It's where I belong—with all the other cork-headed fighters."

He cursed himself loudly.

Mannion had told young Harmon Haufenthistle to run along and see to his chores. The boy had complied but not without casting his hero several disbelieving looks over his shoulder. The looks on the boy's face made Mannion's normally cold heart shrivel with humiliation.

Rio looked up at him, confounded. Shoving his hat down on his forehead to scratch the back of his head, he said, "Joe...I can't...I can't arrest *you*!"

"Sure, you can." Mannion stopped walking and held his hands out, wrists together. "Cuff me. Walk me over to the jail and throw me in the basement. I don't think i' wrong about Park tryin' to blow my candle, but I was wrong to start that fight in there. Besides, you heard the woman. She's pressing charges."

Rio looked up at him again, uncertainly, then, wagging his head in great confoundment, he reached around for his handcuffs. With a great sigh, squinting one eye up at Mannion again uncertainly, as though wondering if it was all a joke, he closed the bracelets over his boss's wrists.

"All right—have it your way, Joe," Rio said. "But it ain't gonna be easy for you in the cellblock. Hell, we got a dozen prisoners down there—track layers and miners. You arrested 'em all, and they're all mighty piss-burned!"

"Be that as it may..."

All eyes were on the handcuffed Bloody Joe Mannion as Rio ushered him across the street to the jailhouse and then up the porch steps. Buster meowed incredulously when the cat saw the cuffs on Joe's wrists. Rio opened the door and Mannion walked inside and over to the cellblock door. He stopped and looked at Rio, who stood hesitating, looking deeply pained, in the doorway.

Mannion canted his head toward the door. "Open it."

"Ah, hell, Joe."

"Open it," Mannion said more firmly.

Rio sighed and pulled the keys off the spike in the ceiling support post. He gave another sigh as he ambled over to the cellblock door, stuck the key in the lock, and opened the door.

"Have it your way, Joe," he said. "Have it your way."

He stopped and looked up at his boss. "You and Miss Jane—you, uh, really gonna get a *divorce*?"

"You heard the woman," Mannion said, grimly.

Besides, it appeared she'd already found another man.

He had a hard time believing that about her. But

there it was. Sometimes you just never know about women.

Rio wagged his head as he stepped aside to let Joe go first down the cellblock steps. "My, my, my...I can't wrap my head around none of this atall. Not atall! I do believe the world's gone crazy!"

"Nah, just me."

Mannion started down the cellblock steps. When he came in view of the half-dozen prisoners occupying six of the block's eight cells, all eyes turned to him. Men who'd been standing at the bars, conversing with each other, or lounging on their cots, some sleeping—all big, bearded men in rough work clothes, some Americans as well as two Mexicans, two Chinese, two Blacks, an Indian, a few Scandinavians, and a big Irishman with a blond, upswept mustache named Charlie O'Donovan—gazed toward Mannion at first with silent incredulity, scowling.

Then O'Donovan said, "Say, what's the deal, Deputy? Why you got Bloody Joe in cuffs? This some kind of joke?"

"Wish it was," Rio said, following Joe to one of the two empty cells. "Sure wish it was..."

"Disorderly conduct," Mannion said as he passed cells with men staring out at him through the cell door bars, deeply curious. He licked his bloody lips. One eye was swelling. "I'm one of you now, fellas."

"Hell, Joe, you always been one of us!" bellowed a big Chinaman in a thick Chinese accent, grinning between the bars of his cell.

The others roared in delight at seeing their jailor all beaten up and being led down the cellblock corridor.

Mannion gave a lunatic laugh as he stepped through the door Rio had just opened for him. He couldn't help delighting in his enemies' delight.

"Mannion, you bloody bastard," said one of the men staring out through the bars of the cell right across the stone-paved corridor from Joe's, "couldn't have happened to a more deserving son of a bitch!"

They kicked up a roar of great mirth then as Rio removed Mannion's cuffs and locked the door on him. Before Rio walked away, Joe told him to keep Vangie away. She'd no doubt hear soon about her father's humiliation, and she'd want to visit, but he didn't want her down here with these animals. He'd see her tomorrow.

"All right, Joe," Rio said with another ragged sigh and a pained look on his craggy face.

He walked away and up the stairs to Mannion's office. As he did, Joe's fellow prisoners laughed and joked and said they'd seen it all now. They jeered the marshal who'd put them all in there. They raked coffee cups against their cell bars. One tossed the contents of a slop bucket at Mannion, the smelly crap reaching Mannion's boots and jeans cuffs and soiling the floor of his cell.

Several spit at him.

Someone threw an apple core at him. It struck him in the head and bounced to the floor.

They kept up the racket for a good, long time.

Mannion grinned back at them.

He deserved the treatment he was getting. Oh, he deserved it, all right.

Still, he wasn't going to give them the satisfaction of believing they'd gotten to him. He might have been deeply humiliated—a laughingstock of the entire town including his own jail—but he was stubborn that way. He'd give them no reaction but a grin, delight in their delight. He sank down on his cot, stretched his legs out before him, crossed them at the ankles, pulled his makings sack out of his shirt, and slowly rolled and fired a quirley.

Maybe he was more like his fellow prisoners than he'd thought he was. Oddly, he didn't feel all that out of place here.

A man in the cell abutting Joe's stuck his face up close to the bars and howled his mocking laughter. Mannion flung the end of his fist at the man, connecting soundly with the big, bearded German's nose, breaking it.

"Oh, you bastard, Mannion!" the big German cried, holding his nose and backing away from the cell wall.

"Yep," Joe said, drawing on the quirley. "That'll go on my tombstone."

———

"VANGIE'S BEEN HERE THREE TIMES," RIO TOLD Mannion early the next morning, when the middle-aged deputy came down to let Joe out of his own jail. "She begged me to let her see you, but I told her Hotel de Mannion just wasn't fit for polite company. Especially female company. Especially with a dozen miners and track layers down here, waiting for the judge."

Most of the other prisoners were still asleep or just rising—yawning and coughing and stretching and cursing and otherwise grumbling. They'd become accustomed to the presence of their jailer in his very own cell to the point that, once they'd exhausted themselves with insulting him and otherwise mocking him, taking total delight in his predicament, they'd piped down and resumed their own private conversations and/or resumed insulting each other rather than their new jail mate. They smoked and played various games of poker.

"She's awful broken up," Rio added as he opened the

cell door. "I really wish you hadn't done this to yourself, Joe."

"I didn't," Mannion said. "My wife did." He yawned and worked the kinks out of his neck as he stepped into the corridor. "But I had it comin'."

"Did it teach you a lesson?"

"I doubt it."

Mannion walked down the corridor to the cellblock stairs. Rio followed him up into the office where Mannion opened the lower right desk drawer and plucked out the half-empty whiskey bottle.

He held the bottle up to Rio. "Join me?"

The middle-aged deputy scowled at him. "I'm on duty, Joe."

"Have a drink with me, Rio."

Rio shrugged and gave his head a single, slow wag. "All right."

Mannion pulled two semi-clean water glasses out of the drawer. He set them on the desk and filled each half full. He handed one to Rio then picked up his own and clinked it against Rio's glass. "To the new town marshal of Del Norte."

Rio frowned. "Huh?"

Mannion removed the badge pinned to his corduroy shirt. He pinned it to Rio's sweat-stained shirt badly in need of laundering then lifted his glass in salute. "That's you."

"Me?" Rio looked down at the badge as though it were a poisonous spider on his chest. "Oh no, I, uh..." He let his voice trail off then scowled at the tall lawman again and said, "You can't quit. This town needs you, Joe."

Mannion took down nearly half his whiskey and winced against the burn. "On the contrary, it doesn't need me makin' a fool of my damn self. I'm the last thing it needs anymore. I'm makin' mistakes all over the place. With Libby, with Park. Not even sure Park's the one who tried to have me killed and burned out the Petersons. I may have jumped the gun on that one. I reckon I'll never know now."

Mannion threw back the rest of his whiskey, set the glass down on the desk, and filled it half full again.

Rio still hadn't touched his whiskey. He frowned at his boss—er, former boss. "Who do you think did it, then?"

"God knows. Go on—drink up. We're celebrating here, Rio!"

He touched the glass to Rio's again. Rio took a couple of sips and then Mannion took a couple of sips of his as well.

Rio said, "What're you gonna do if you're not marshal of Del Norte anymore? Joe, marshalin' is the only thing you know how to do."

"I've saved up a little nest egg for me and Vangie. I'm gonna hightail it. Maybe Colorado Springs, maybe Denver. Find something else to do even if it's mucking out livery stalls. I hear rich folks down there need private security."

"You ain't a bodyguard, Joe!"

"Yeah, maybe too old even for that." Mannion chuckled and took another couple of sips of his busthead. "Maybe I'll take up professional gambling."

"You're just feelin' sorry for yourself. You know—after yesterday."

"I've been feelin' sorry for myself for a long, damn time. But especially after yesterday. I keep seein' that look in little Harmon's eyes as I was layin' there in the street, Jane throwin' my hat at me." Mannion finished the whiskey and set his hat on his head. "I'm gonna wander on home, break the news to Vangie that her no-good pa is out of work and at loose ends. I got a feeling she won't be all that surprised, poor girl."

He started for the door then stopped and glanced back at Rio. "I'll stop at the bank after it opens, pull out money for the disorderly fine."

Rio sucked his cheeks and nodded.

For a bout like his, it was fifty bucks. He knew because he'd set the price himself.

He left the office and in the blurry-edged dawn shadows retreating from the main drag, which was not yet busy this early, though shopkeepers were out arranging displays and sweeping off boardwalks. He began tramping in the direction of his and Vangie's home on the northeast outskirts of town. He'd have fetched Red from the livery barn, but he needed the walk to clear his head, if there was any possibility of clearing it.

There usually wasn't.

He had a busy mind, did Bloody Joe Mannion.

He also had a logy knee, but the walking seemed to loosen it a tad.

He patted his shirt pocket. The divorce decree was there. On his way back into town he'd collect money for the fine from the bank and have McQueen witness his signature on the decree.

And that would be that.

As he tramped down the lane that threaded the gap between his and Vangie's burned-out place and the smaller place Joe had bought when Jane had left him, he avoided the new place and swung left toward the older place. It was early, but he knew Vangie would be up working with her horses in the corrals. She was worried about him, and whenever she was worried or troubled about anything, she usually went straight to her horses.

He walked around the bones of the new house he and Jane had been building on the same plot of ground as the old one. The framing had been done and the roof covered the place from the weather, but that was as far as the builders Joe had hired had gotten before the big change of plans. Joe didn't look at the house directly. He thought it too symbolic of what his life had become.

The walls were up, and the roof was on, but there was nothing else to the place. It was an empty shell. He wondered if all that—the emptiness—had started after Sarah had killed herself. It shouldn't have. He'd had too much to live for. Namely, Vangie. But not having learned his lesson with Sarah, he'd neglected Vangie and had spent far too much time toting that damned badge around.

Well, that was finished now.

It hadn't ended the way he'd wanted it to. What lawman wanted to go out in disgrace? But there you had it. He was Bloody Joe, after all. How else could it have ended other than in disgrace?

Sure enough, Vangie was working the blue roan in the round breaking corral that Joe and Stringbean had built together after Joe and his junior-most deputy had caught the horse to keep it from being killed by ranchers for whom it had been causing a grave disturbance inside their remudas.

Joe walked up to the corral and watched his pretty, tomboyish daughter work the roan. Vangie performed the maneuvers splendidly. She'd gentled the roan right down and now she was teaching him to back up. Once he backed a few yards, she put him ahead at a dead run before swinging him around again, stopping him, and backing him up.

She was teaching him how to restrain himself.

Joe smiled at that. She couldn't restrain her father, but she'd managed to teach the wild-as-the-wind bronc restraint just fine. She didn't restrain him too much, though. When she ran him again just now—she hadn't yet seen her father watching admiringly from over the corral fence—she stopped him suddenly and let him pitch with a loud, heartfelt whinny. He raised his front hooves high, clawing at the air.

Vangie laughed and reached forward to pat the big horse's left wither. "Good boy, Cochise! Good boy. Enjoy yourself! There'll always be a little wild in you—won't there, boy?"

The bronc was enjoying the girl as much as the girl was enjoying the bronc.

When she turned the horse around again, she swung her head toward Mannion. Her eyes widened.

"Pa!"

She galloped over to her father, swung down from the saddle, dropped the reins—she'd already taught the roan how to stay with its ribbons—and ducked through the fence. She ran up to Mannion, wrapped her arms around his back and pressed her cheek up taut against his chest.

"Oh, Poppa—I heard!" She squeezed him tightly then looked up at him, sorrow in her eyes. She gently fingered the cuts and bruises and swellings on his big, rugged face that was looking more haggard with every passing year. "Rio wouldn't let me see you!"

"I told him not to. Bad element down in that cell-block." He gave a crooked smile. "Including your crazy old man."

She lifted her chin and sniffed. Then her face

acquired an admonishing expression. "There's already whiskey on your breath and it's barely eight o'clock!"

"Guilty as charged." Joe held up his hands. "Rio and I were celebrating."

"Celebrating what?"

Joe sighed.

How to tell her that everything had changed?

CHAPTER 28

NO POINT IN BEATING AROUND THE BUSH.

Mannion brushed his thumb across his chest where
his badge had once resided and said, "Turned in my
badge."

"What?" She pulled away and looked at his empty
shirt. "Why? Were you *fired*?"

"Nah. I wouldn't let him beat me to the punch. I
wanted it to be my idea." He meant Mayor Charlie
McQueen, of course. McQueen had been wanting his
badge for years. Joe was holding up progress, don't ya
know?

Vangie backed away a step, placed her fists on her
hips, and canted her head to one side. It was one of her
mother's poses, Joe remembered bittersweetly, when he'd
come home all bruised up, which happened often back in
his early days as it still did today.

"Why, you're just feeling sorry for yourself!"

"You and Rio," Joe said, chuckling and shaking his
head though he knew she was right. He was downright
thrilling in the feeling that the fates had done him wrong
though he'd knew he'd done it all to himself.

"You made a mistake. You went into the San Juan like a bull through a chute, lost your temper, got dumped in the street like any common thug. Instead of getting back up and getting back to work, you decided to turn in your badge...and do what? Drink your sorrows away?"

"Ah, hell, kid. That's not fair."

"I know you too well, Poppa."

"She threw me in jail, fer chrissakes! Not that I didn't deserve it, but..."

"Good for her! She was probably hoping you'd learn your lesson. Not turn tail and run!"

"I don't think so." Mannion tapped his shirt pocket. "We're divorcing, me an' Jane. She's found another man."

Vangie just stared up at him. Her breath caught a little in her throat, and he could tell she was trying desperately not to cry. She didn't say anything. She just held tightly to her emotions.

"I'm sorry, kid. I reckon things are changing."

"What will you do, Poppa? Without the badge. I mean, you've worn it most of your life."

"I thought we'd move to Colorado Springs. Maybe Denver. Don't worry—we'll take the horses. I have a nice little nest egg for you an' me." He grinned and broadened his shoulders. "Thought maybe I'd take up gambling for a living. I'm not half bad at it."

"Poppa, you do not have a poker face!"

Joe chuckled.

Then he sobered and placed his hands on his daughter's shoulders. "I'm sorry, kid. I messed up. I accused a man without hard evidence of trying to kill me. Likely blew my chance of ever finding out who really did. I lost my temper and belted him in front of half the town. Got thrown in the street. It's been bad before...but..." He shook his head. "This time it was really bad."

Vangie stepped forward and hugged him again, tightly. She looked up at him and said, "I'm sorry, Poppa. But I'm not leaving here. This is my home. I'll do what I need to do to stay. If you're leaving, you'll have to go alone."

"Vangie, please..." Joe suddenly felt desperate. Desperate and lonely and as lost as he'd ever been.

What would he do without this girl? He'd lost Sarah. He'd lost Jane. He'd lost command of the town, his self-respect. How could he live without Vangie?

"I'm sorry, Poppa. You've done this to yourself. I had no part in it. I've always tried to save you from yourself. I won't be taken down with you." Vangie rose on the toes of her boots and planted a tender kiss on his cheek. "Now, if you'll excuse me, I'm going to get back to Cochise."

She turned and ducked through the corral fence.

"Vangie, please," he said, hating the hopelessness he heard in his own voice. The pleading. He'd never pleaded before.

She didn't look at him again. Strong, this girl. Strong and wise. Too damn strong and wise for her miserable father's own good. She climbed onto the roan and began working him again as she'd been working him before. Tenderly, commandingly, methodically. In a world of her own.

He stood there, alone, watching.

He'd never felt so alone.

Finally, he pushed away from the fence and walked back into town. He walked as though in a daze, still half drunk and lost.

Feeling sorry for himself.

Oh, so lost. He felt the absence of his badge, his self-respect. All the mistakes he'd made, not the least of which was sending Stringbean down to Tucson with La Stiletta. That weighed heavy on him, too. He'd probably gotten the kid killed.

Oh, Christ—all the mistakes. He knew that if he'd continued to wear the badge, he'd only continue to keep on making them and likely get more people killed.

He went home and had a tall drink and a smoke on the porch, gathering his courage to return to town, which he did after he'd polished off half a bottle of whiskey. He hated himself for drinking like that, but it was the only thing that would assuage his nerves.

In Del Norte, his first stop was Charlie McQueen's office.

When he'd found out that Mannion had turned in his badge and that he and Jane were divorcing, McQueen tried to maintain a calm demeanor. But Joe knew by the light dancing in the little dandy's eyes he was having a devil of a time keeping himself from jumping up and down and howling like a moon-crazed coyote. His hands shook a little as he added his signature to the divorce decree.

He handed it back Mannion, manufacturing a concerned expression, thumbed his glasses up his nose, and said, "Good luck to you, Joe. I'm sorry it had to end this way, but...well, I did hear about what happened yesterday. Believe me, I'm no fan of James Park, but—good Lord man, punching him in public like that? Tsk-tsk."

"Go to hell, Charlie." Mannion plucked the decree out of the little mayor's hand, folded it, stuffed it into his pocket, and lit a shuck for the bank.

As he did, all eyes were on him, of course. By now the entire county had heard what happened. People saw the bruises on his face and gasped or wagged their heads.

268 / PETER BRANDVOLD

Predictable end of the notorious career of Bloody Joe Mannion.

Taking money out of his account to pay for a fine for disorderly conduct was not the least of his humiliations this day. He took the money over to Rio, counted it out on Rio's desk, took another slug from his bottle, then headed over to the San Juan.

The next humiliation would be returning the divorce decree to his wife.

Former wife.

His beloved Jane.

Yeah, he still loved her. But he didn't deserve her. Now, he realized he never had.

Best to make a clean break.

He tapped on her door. Having just awakened, she answered wearing a powder blue robe. She did not invite him in, only accepted the divorce decree and, like McQueen, wished him luck.

"Thanks," Joe said.

He started to turn away, but she stopped him with: "Joe?"

He turned back to her. "Another parting volley, Jane? Have at it."

"James Park is just a friend. I would never step out on you. Not while we were married. He's a good man, a good friend. His wife died recently. You're wrong to believe he burned the Petersons out and tried to kill you. He didn't need to burn the Petersons out. He'd found a route *around* their place. They're laying track now."

"He told you this?"

"Yes."

"And you believe him."

"Yes. He's a good man, Joe."

"What about Alva's husband? Someone shot him

twice in the chest and the only one with a motive was Park."

Jane laughed. "Don't be silly, Joe. You should mingle with the folks in the country more. The ranchers. Roy Peterson was a known rustler. Same with his wife."

Mannion gazed at her in mute shock.

"One of the area ranchers likely shot Roy Peterson. He'd been caught several times and warned, but he kept on steeling beef and mixing it into his own small herd."

Now Joe really felt the fool. He just stared at his now ex-wife.

"You've been drinking."

"Yup."

"Go home, Joe. Sleep it off. Tomorrow, get up and try to be a better man."

"Well, that was a hell of a parting volley. Thank you." Mannion touched two fingers to his hat brim, swung around, unsteady on his feet, and tramped back in the direction of the stairs. "Tomorrow...I'm gonna wake up... and be a better man."

But he did not go home. Instead, he went down to the main drinking hall, bought himself a bottle of the cheapest whiskey Jane stocked, and hauled it back to a table at the rear of the room. He didn't care that all eyes were on him. In defiance, he remained, sitting alone at a rear table, somewhat concealed by the stairs angling overhead. He pried the cork out of the bottle and filled his shot glass.

He leaned forward over the glass, thinking and drinking.

He tried to make sense of what Jane had told him and of all the times he'd been bushwhacked here in town and out in the country. Someone sure as hell didn't want him around. It had to be one of the two railroads.

Which one?

Both had a bone to pick with him for locking up so many of their track layers, graders, cooks, and gandy dancers. Since Libby and Park hadn't been able to keep their men on leashes, Mannion had had to do it. For the sake of the town.

Not the least of his niggling questions was why and who had burned out Alva Peterson?

Something strange was going on. The venom with which someone wanted Mannion dead was severe even for him. It was almost like a personal grudge.

Of course, given who he was, that was understandable. Had Alva Peterson been burned out merely because he'd been in the cabin?

He'd put away a good third of the bottle when Charlie McQueen entered the San Juan. McQueen stood looking around for a time, glasses glinting in the late-morning light from the windows, and then, apparently picking someone out of the crowd of early drinkers, headed to the table where two men sat, drinking beer and shoveling breakfast from large platters into their mouths.

Mannion frowned.

The two men McQueen had picked out of the crowd were a couple of misfits—Ray Dumas and Cullen Ventress. A couple of scalawags Mannion had never been able to pin any crimes on though he knew for a fact they robbed stagecoaches from time to time, rustled beef, and did general troubleshooting for businessmen with bones to pick with other businessmen though it was damned hard to prove these outlying crimes which often involved murder under cover of darkness, and arson under same.

Odd that Charlie McQueen would have anything to do with those two.

McQueen sat down and spoke to both men though not for long. He'd barely sat down before he'd left again, not staying for breakfast or a drink. After McQueen had left, looking all business, both Dumas and Ventress increased the speed with which they ate, rose from their chairs, tossed coins onto the table, doffed their hats, and left.

Odd, Mannion thought. Damned odd.

He'd never known ol' Charlie to associate with such lowlifes. Whatever he'd had to say had to have been important, though, for him, the mayor of Del Norte, to be seen with such guttersnipes.

Mannion had another drink and pondered on the unlikely association. He had one more drink and then decided to saddle Red and head up toward both rail lines and do some sniffing around. He knew it wasn't his job anymore, but maybe he could draw out some answers to all the questions he had.

He'd just finished his last drink and shoved his bottle into his coat pocket when a man sitting at a table two tables away from his—a rodent named Sonny Beech, of the same low character as Dumas and Ventress—leaped up from his chair and turned to Joe, yelling, "*Mannion, you're not so bloody much—now, are ya?*"

He stood with his broadcloth coat tucked back behind the six-shooter riding high on his right hip, his right hand near the pistol's gutta percha grips. His dung-brown eyes were glassy with drink. The three other men at the same table as Beech slid their chairs aside, wary of getting caught in a crossfire.

Mannion snorted ruefully, tucked his coat behind the Russian holstered on his right hip, and rose from his own chair, bellowing angrily, "Maybe not, Sonny, but I can still kill the hell out of you, so why don't you sit down and finish your breakfast before it's the last breakfast you'll ever see!"

"You got no badge to hide behind, now, Bloody Joe. Hah!"

The old rage burned in Mannion, exaggerated by frustration and by the whiskey. "Never did hide behind it, Sonny. Now, shut up before this former lawman snuffs your wick!"

"Go to hell! Been wantin' to kill you for years, an' now, by God, I'm gonna do it even if I hang for it!"

"Don't worry, Sonny," Mannion laughed. "You won't live to hang!"

Sonny hesitated for just a second, his eyes going dark. Then he grinned savagely and reached for his pistol.

Even drunk, Mannion was two hairs faster.

The Russian in his hand bucked and roared, buck and roared, sending Sonny Beech back to whatever demon had spawned him.

Joe spun the smoking Russian on his finger and holstered it. He headed for the front door, yelling at the bartender at the far end of the room, "Tell Jane she needs to tell her clientele to mind their manners!"

He pushed through the stout oak doors and headed for the livery barn.

CHAPTER 29

STRINGBEAN LOOKED AROUND DULLY AT THE DEAD Mexicans surrounding him.

Had he shot them all?

He...alone?

He must have. He knew he was probably in shock, but he couldn't remember having any help.

He had a fresh wound to show for it. This one in his right arm, halfway between his elbow and his shoulder. He'd knotted his green neckerchief around it. It hurt like blazes but at least it evened things out, what with his having the left arm perforated by the four rustlers that had tried to rape La Stiletta.

Some trip. He could hear the old rattler rattling atop the rock from which he'd killed the last three Mexicans.

La Stiletta.

Where in blazes was she, anyway?

As if response to his unspoken question, she screamed.

It was then he remembered through the haze of violence and pain that he'd heard her scream twice before. The screams seemed to be coming from those rocks to the north.

He stepped over the last Mex he'd killed and began walking—staggering would be a more fitting description —in that direction.

He came to a pile of rocks that had a small break in it near the ground. Through this break he could peer through the mound to the other side. As he did, his guts tightened.

La Stiletta lay stripped naked, her clothes strewn around her olive-colored body. She'd been staked out spread eagle, and a big Mexican with long hair and a thick mustache in a red shirt, black chaps, silver-capped boots, and a black and silver sombrero staggered around her, drinking from a clear, unlabeled bottle, pausing every now and then to crouch down and cut her tender skin with the upcurved tip of a big, bone-handled bowie knife!

The girl lay shouting in Spanish at the man—Diego Hidalgo, for sure—while he laughed and staggered around with his bloody knife, taking long pulls from the bottle.

Stringbean recoiled at the savagery.

Hands shaking, he cocked a round into his Winchester's chamber, intending to drill a slug through the break in the rocks and into Hidalgo's ugly head. Only, he could not seat a fresh round. The Winchester was empty.

He dropped the carbine and palmed his Remington. He flicked open the loading gate and spun the cylinder, letting the empty casings drop into his open palm. There wasn't an unspent cartridge among them.

None in his cartridge belt either. He'd popped off all his ammo!

Stringbean gave a start when La Stiletta screamed again.

"Help!" she cried. "This savage is killing me!"

She cried loudly.

Stringbean quickly sheathed his Remington. He looked at the pile of rocks. The break was too narrow for him to crawl through. There had to be a way around the break, for La Stiletta and her torturer had gotten around it, but he didn't see it. It must be much farther up the slope.

There was little time. Stringbean would crawl over it.

He fairly leaped onto the pile and began climbing, finding cracks and fissures and small ledges that aided the maneuver. He worked his way to the top and then hoped like blazes the big Mexican—who likely outweighed Stringbean by a good forty pounds—didn't see him before he could climb down to the ground and somehow work up behind the man and brain him with a rock.

He wasn't sure what he was going to do. He had no strategy. Panic overwhelmed him as did the shrill cries of La Stiletta. They'd come too far for either of them—or both!—to die now.

As the Mexican took another swig from the bottle and leaned down to carve a bloody line across the girl's left breast, evoking another tooth-gnashing scream, Stringbean began his careful descent, keeping his eyes on the big Mex and the girl below. If Hidalgo looked up just a little, shifting his attention away from his victim, he'd spy Stringbean and shoot him off the escarpment.

For that reason, Stringbean hoped that for the time being the crazed, laughing torturer kept his gaze on his victim. Slowly and carefully, Stringbean made his way down the scarp, hands and knees quivering, making the difficult maneuver all the more difficult.

He was halfway down, maybe twenty feet from the ground, when Hidalgo stopped with his back to the scarp and leaned down and hurled a long string of shouted Spanish at his victim. Stringbean didn't understand the Spanish, but he knew the big Mexican bruin was castigating her from running out on him when he was arrested.

He cut her once more, this time on her left thigh.

La Stiletta screamed shrilly—a keening, ear-rattling wail.

Then she looked up and her eyes widened when she saw Stringbean making way down the scarp toward her.

Oh, no, Stringbean thought. *Look away! Look away!*

Too late. Hidalgo must have seen the hopeful expression in her eyes. Slowly, he straightened and began to turn his head to look up at the scarp.

"*No!*" Stringbean cried...and flung himself off the rock.

He hurled himself straight down toward Hidalgo, who kept turning his head toward the scarp. Finally, the man's eyes found the young deputy hurling toward him, and his eyes widened in shock. He'd just started to raise the savage bowie in his right hand when Stringbean smashed into him.

Hidalgo gave a great wail of drunken surprise as Stringbean, light as he was, drove the man to the ground to the left of La Stiletta, who gave yet another scream when she saw the two men hurling toward her, turning her head away and squeezing her eyes closed.

Stringbean lay atop Hidalgo, who smelled like a drunken grizzly. The man grunted and writhed beneath him, trying to roll Stringbean away. Stringbean centered his weight on the man and sat up, straddling him on his knees, and, yelling his panic, punched the man's face first with his right hand then with his left.

The man's jaws were hard as anvils.

Yelling his frustration, Stringbean punched him twice again before Hidalgo gave a bear-like wail of fury and rolled onto his left side, throwing Stringbean like flotsam off of him.

Stringbean scrambled to his feet as the big man heavily and drunkenly gained his own feet. Hidalgo regarded his attacker with his black, glassy eyes. He snarled and reached for the big, ivory-handled six-shooter sheathed over his belly.

"*No!*" Stringbean ran toward him, smashing into him again just as the six-shooter cleared leather.

Hidalgo cursed loudly in Spanish as he dropped the gun and was bulled back onto the ground once more. Desperately, Stringbean again climbed to his knees, straddling the big bruin of a savage Mexican and started to hammer the man's face once more, smiling inwardly with satisfaction when he saw blood sprout on the man's lips and begin to trickle down from the man's right nostril.

Again, Hidalgo gave a savage wail and raised a stout arm to deflect another punch, then smashed his own right fist across Stringbean's left cheek. Stringbean went flying off the man, head reeling, little birds chirping in his ears. Stringbean knew he was a dead man if he didn't gain his feet quickly, but he just couldn't do it. His legs were too weak. When his vision cleared, an icy rod of dread slid up along his spine.

Hidalgo stood over him, grinning down at him, shoving the big man's bushy, black mustache up taut against his broad, pitted nose. He reached down and pulled Stringbean up off the ground by his collar and smashed his left fist against Stringbean's mouth, opening up his lips.

He dropped Stringbean back down to the ground like he would trash, laughing hysterically. He pointed at La Stiletta and said, eyes squinted devilishly, "You want her to be yours, mi gringo amigo? Then you better fight for her or I kill you slow...like I kill her!"

He tipped his big, savage, long-haired head back on his shoulders and cast a rollicking, preternatural laugh at the afternoon sky. Then he turned away and began to stagger over toward where he'd dropped the bowie.

Stringbean glanced at La Stiletta. She had her head tipped back and to one side to stare at him in bright-eyed horror, bleeding from the several cuts the savage had inflicted on her. As she did, she grunted as she pulled desperately at the ropes tying her to the stakes Hidalgo had driven into the ground.

Stringbean looked through his blurred vision at Hidalgo. He was only a few feet from the knife. Stringbean gave a savage wail of his own as he summoned all the strength left in his body to heave himself to his feet. Just as Hidalgo crouched to pick up the knife, Stringbean hurled himself onto the man's back.

Hidalgo bellowed angrily as, leaving the knife where it was, he staggered forward, Stringbean on his back, the deputy snaking his arms around the man's neck and drawing them taut against his throat, trying desperately to strangle him.

Still staggering forward, Hidalgo choked and gurgled, reaching up with his big hands to try and pry Stringbean's arms away from his throat. Stringbean grimaced as he held firm, feeling the man's throat work desperately against his arms, practically the size of ropes in comparison to the big Mex's own. As he did, he could feel the big man's legs weakening.

When Hidalgo had staggered ten feet from where La Stiletta lay struggling against her stays, he twisted sideways and fell to the ground, half on top of Stringbean, the man's bear-like body punching the wind out of the deputy's lungs.

Still, Stringbean held on, desperately trying to cut off the big man's wind.

Hidalgo wailed his fury and smashed his left elbow hard against Stringbean's ribs.

That further punched the wind out of Stringbean's lungs. Stringbean yelled with the sharp, spike-like pain of the blow and felt an icy dread as his arms came loose of the big man's neck. Hidalgo turned to him, drew his head up off the ground with one hand and smashed his other fist once, twice, three times against Stringbean's mouth, rattling his brains so that the world became a blur...the ground a pitching bronco beneath him.

"Ha, little man!" Hidalgo bellowed. "You fight good for a runt, but I got you now!"

He gained his feet and stood over Stringbean, smiling down at him. "Now I kill you both—very slowly...until you can scream no more. Apache-style, no?" He tipped his head back and sent another roaring laugh at the sky.

Somehow Stringbean summoned a few ounces of strength into his battered body.

He rose onto his elbows, tipped his chin up, closed his eyes, and wailed as he lifted his right leg and thrust that boot up hard between Hidalgo's legs, connecting solidly with the big man's oysters.

Hidalgo's face instantly became a big, brown mask of unadulterated misery. He crouched forward, closing his big, brown hands over his balls. For a moment he squeezed his eyes shut. When he opened them again, they were even more enraged than before. He hurled himself forward, throwing all two-hundred-plus pounds onto Stringbean, once again knocking the wind out of Stringbean's lungs.

Straddling his victim, he closed his hands around Stringbean's neck and pressed both thumbs against the deputy's windpipe.

Instantly, the world started to go dark as Stringbean, fighting for air, could find none.

Darker and darker the afternoon grew.

Stringbean could feel his face and eyeballs swelling as the life left him...

He closed his eyes. When he managed to slit them open once more, for one last look at the world he was leaving, sorry to see that his last image had to be of the man killing him, a strange expression flashed over his killer's face.

Hidalgo looked down at Stringbean, confused:

The man's hands slackened against Stringbean's throat, came away from his neck.

Slowly, the man straightened, lifting his head up.

As Stringbean began to suck air back down his throat and into his lungs and the world began to lighten and come back to life, Hidalgo straightened. He slowly turned around.

It was then that Stringbean saw the handle of the man's own big, savage knife protruding from his back.

La Stiletta stood over him, naked and bloody, bare feet a little more than shoulder width apart, her lips twisted savagely. She raised the pistol in her right hand, aimed at Hidalgo's head, narrowed one eye, and fired.

Blood and brains from the man's ruined skull splashed across Stringbean's face.

Hidalgo fell straight back on top of him, sort of twisted on his side, again forcing the wind out of Stringbean's battered lungs.

"Pendejo!" La Stiletta cried.

As cut up and bloody as she was, she managed to pull the big, dead Mexican off Stringbean. He drew an unrestricted breath and looked up at her.

"Damn," he said, raking her poor, cut-up body with his gaze. "You still kickin', señorita?"

She knelt beside him. She had a good dozen cuts on her, but Stringbean could tell they were shallow ones. Hidalgo had wanted to kill her for a good, long time. She'd need some doctoring, but she'd live, as would Stringbean.

"I guess I proved it, didn't I, pendejo?"

She knelt beside him and threw her arms around his neck, hugging him tight. She pulled her head up, kissed his forehead, and smiled, her eyes meeting his. "I mean...Henry."

CHAPTER 30

MANNION WAS A GOOD FIVE MILES DEEP INTO THE mountains southeast of Del Norte when he reined up suddenly on the narrow horse trail he'd been following up one forested ridge and down another.

Red had just whickered deep in the bay's chest and craned his neck to peer behind him.

Joe frowned down at the stalwart stallion. "What is it, boy?"

He whipped around in the saddle, following the bay's gaze with his own. "Someone back there?"

For the past twenty minutes or so, riding through the fragrant, sun-splashed forest, he'd had the nagging suspicion he was being shadowed. That was why he'd freed the keeper thong from over the big Russian holstered for the cross-draw on his left hip.

Peering along his back trail, he could see nothing. But then, he couldn't see that far. He'd just crossed a narrow canyon. The next ridge behind him wasn't even a hundred yards away. Could be that his shadower was still on the other side of that ridge.

"Hmmm," Joe said, pensively stretching his lips back

from his teeth. "Have I attracted another possible bush-whacker? Getting all too used to it these days." He waited, staring. Finally, he reined the bay off the trail's right side and up the ridge into heavy timber. "Let's see."

He put Red roughly thirty yards up the mountain and behind a boulder, positioning the mount so that Mannion, still sitting the saddle, could peer around it down to the narrow, sun-dappled trail below.

He and Red waited, horse and rider both staring down at the trail through the trees.

Red lifted his snout, sniffing the wind. He twitched his ears and glanced back at Mannion.

"There's someone back there, isn't there, boy?"

As if understanding the question, the big bay gave his tail a single, resolute switch.

Mannion waited. Birds piped around him. A squirrel chittered angrily from a pine bough. The air was rife with the rich smell of pine needles and forest duff. The sun angling down through the pine crowns burned the back of his neck.

Hoof thuds sounded. Someone was moving along the trail down there at a good trot. Horse and rider came into view, moving from Mannion's left to his right on the trail below, the two figures obscured by the arrow-straight columns of the pines and furs.

But not enough that Mannion couldn't see the rider's glinting spectacles and trimmed beard as well as the crisp bowler hat and fancy, three-piece suit that even out here didn't appear to have a speck of dust on it.

Mayor Charlie McQueen was mounted on a zebra dun. He sat slightly crouched in the saddle, a little awkwardly, leaning too far forward and sort of gritting his teeth, not enjoying the ride at all. No, he wouldn't. Mannion had never known the mayor to ride a horse. He usually drove a small surrey here and there about Del Norte. Mannion had never known him to leave town on horseback.

But here the little, bearded, bespectacled dandy was, riding out in the tall and uncut and not looking damned happy about the punishment the stockman's saddle was giving his tender behind. It would have helped if he'd ridden upright and moved with the movements of his mount. Instead, he was bouncing out of sync with the dun, and the saddle was spanking his ass.

Horse and rider trotted on past Mannion's position, quickly dwindling from view, the thuds of the gelding fading gradually to silence.

"Now, Charlie," Mannion said, raking a gloved thumb across the deep cleft in his chin. "Where are you off to?"

He remembered McQueen's visit with Ray Dumas and Cullen Ventress an hour ago in the San Juan Saloon. And the hasty way the two men had finished their meals and left after Charlie had left.

"Now that there is what I call damned suspicious, Red," Mannion said, reaching forward to caress the horse's left wither, studying the trail below. "What do you think?"

Again, Red gave his tail a resolute switch.

"Yep, yep...I think that's damned suspicious." Mannion nudged the mount forward. "Let's follow the good mayor and see where he's goin'. I have a feelin' we might be more than a little surprised."

A half hour later, Mannion and Red crested a low ridge to see their quarry, McQueen, descending the ridge's other side and heading for a log, tin-roofed cabin sitting in a grassy clearing with its rear wall abutting the forest dropping down from the northern ridge, to Mannion's left. McQueen was about halfway between the ridge Mannion was on and the cabin. There was little doubt he was heading for the cabin—a line shack for one of the area ranches in these parts, most likely.

Mannion backed Red a few feet down the ridge, so they weren't so obviously silhouetted by the sky above and behind them. Mannion watched McQueen rein up in front of the cabin, dismount, tie the reins of his zebra dun to the lone, well-worn hitchrack, then mount the stoop, heading for the front door.

Mannion backed Red farther down the ridge in case McQueen decided to take a gander along his back trail before entering the cabin. Joe turned the mount off the trail's left side and rode up the ridge into heavy timber. He swung right and was soon descending the ridge directly behind the cabin.

When the rear wall of the cabin came into view, Mannion stopped Red, dismounted, and ground reined the mount.

"You stay, boy. Just gonna go see what siren call our good mayor is answering out here in the high-and-rocky, is all. Have a feeling it's gonna be right interesting."

Mannion grabbed his field glasses out of his saddlebags and moved down the slope toward the edge of the forest that all but abutted the cabin's rear wall. "Occupy yourself, now, hear?"

The horse whickered its rueful response.

Mannion stopped near the edge of the forest, dropped to a knee, and scrutinized the area before him with the glasses. An old stable and peeled log corral, as well as a privy, lay to the west of the cabin, to Mannion's left. The corral appeared not only empty but empty a long time, with brush growing tall around the posts and half-ruined rails. The open gate hung askew. A large bush had grown up against one wall of the privy, all but engulfing the little, leaning structure comprised of ancient, gray, vertical pine planks.

He could see no sign of anyone inhabiting the cabin currently except the good mayor of Del Norte.

Strange.

But then the situation lost its strangeness when, not ten minutes later, two riders appeared on the trail left of the cabin, loping their horses. Mannion trained his field glasses on them both and sucked a sharp breath of surprise when, twisting the glasses' focus, he brought into the single, clear field of vision H. Jerome Libby and Ray Dumas.

Both riders pulled up in front of the cabin and were lost to Mannion's view.

Mannion waited, swinging the glasses slowly from right to left and back again...until two other riders appeared, coming from the east, straight out away from the cabin but just far enough right that Mannion could make them out with the glasses.

These two were James Park and Cullen Ventress, Park riding a handsome cream stallion with a charcoal mane and tail. He rode expertly, straight-backed in the saddle and with his crisp, gray Stetson on his handsome head.

When the two riders rode up to the front of the cabin, disappearing from Mannion's view, Joe lowered the glasses and said, "The two leaders of the two competing railroads are meeting out here in the middle of God knows where with the mayor of Del Norte? What in holy *blazes*...?"

Quickly, he returned the glasses to his saddlebags, patted Red reassuringly, then hurried down the rise through the forest. There was only one cracked window in the cabin's back wall. There was a flour sack curtain over it, but it looked thin and tattered with age. Mannion would just have to take a chance that no one would look out the back window and see him.

He had to get down to the cabin.

Quickly, he moved down through the trees, staying low. He gained the back wall then moved along it to the right rear corner. He peered around the corner toward the front. There was one shuttered window between the rear and the cabin's front corner.

Mannion moved toward it, stopped before it and dropped to a knee.

He could clearly hear the men talking inside, McQueen saying, "Well, I didn't call you both out here just so we could all get away, spend a little time together, and play a little cards where the women wouldn't bother us. Believe me, I did not relish the fact of my having to ride all the way out here again either."

"We could have met in town," Libby griped.

"The three of us? *Together?*" McQueen said with a dry chuckle. "Oh, that wouldn't look one bit suspicious!"

"Anyone who saw us likely would have just thought we were negotiating terms," Park said. "You know—a peace settlement of some kind between competing railroads. I have work to do, by God, and so does Jerome!"

"I'll say, I do. I have to keep my men moving—you know, to beat Park to Del Norte!"

Libby and Park had a good laugh.

Mannion scowled and shook his head, utterly baffled by what he was hearing.

These two men weren't really enemies. Hell, no, they'd thrown in together!

"Very funny, gentlemen," McQueen said. "I see no point in taking chances. And, speaking of taking chances, why in blue blazes did your men burn out Mrs. Peterson?

Don't you know how suspicious that makes Park look, since he was trying to buy their land?"

"Mostly because Mannion was inside with her," Park said. "Besides, no one could prove my men had a part in it. Even if they did, it would only convince them all the more of the legitimacy of my track-laying operation. Of course, a railroader is going to burn out a few people who stood in his way. That's the cost of doing business out here!"

"Yeah, I thought it was sort of ingenious myself," Libby said. "That's why my men joined his. His investors now have no doubt he's trying to reach Del Norte before I can."

"What about Roy Peterson?" McQueen wanted to know.

"He got suspicious," Park said. "Jerome and I were riding together, crossing his land. Peterson had a feeling that because I'd offered to pay him so cheaply for his land and wouldn't budge, and because he saw Jerome and I being so friendly, he knew what we were up to. Don't tell me how he knew. The man *looked* dumber than a post. But apparently the ol' rustler had been keeping an eye on both railroads and saw that mine was moving along much slower than Jerome's."

"Yes, odd that such a honyocker could have figured out we were both cheating our investors...and that Park had invested heavily in the Rio Grande Southern Line as opposed to his own...under several aliases, of course."

"We're gonna come away from this rich men," Libby said. "We just have to make sure our investors believe that each line is legit or they'll of course pull out on us instead of investing even more, being the gamblers they are, to see which one reaches Del Norte first."

Libby paused. Mannion could smell cigar smoke

emanating through the cracks in the closed shutter. Libby added, "Don't get your panties in a twist, Charlie. You're gonna take home a goodly amount of money for our little scheme!"

"If Mannion doesn't find out about it," McQueen said. "He's why I called you out here."

"What about him? I thought you said he quit."

"He did quit. But he's got a chip on his shoulder. I know the man. His pride has taken a hit...for now. But by tomorrow, when he's sobered up, he's going to regrow that chip and keep investigating both lines until he figures it out and calls in the feds. Or just takes matters into his own hands and shoots all three of us!"

"Oh, hell," Libby said. "He's only one man. An untethered one at that!"

Libby and Park shared a hearty laugh.

Mannion heard laughter from the front of the cabin. It was then he realized that Dumas and Ventress must be sitting out on the front porch, keeping watch but also listening in on the conversation as Mannion himself was. He'd been so fascinated by the three mucky-mucks' conversation that he'd forgotten all about the two vermin McQueen had sent to fetch them out here.

Only, Dumas and Ventress probably weren't raging mad, as Mannion was...

Joe's blood had fairly turned to burning butane.

What a scheme these three had concocted.

Both men and McQueen defrauding their investors!

"All right, Charlie," Park said. "So, we haven't killed Mannion yet. We will. Don't worry."

"It needs to be done tonight," McQueen said. "In town. Tonight. I suggest you send men tonight. Masked nightriders. While he's good and drunk. Burn down his house. It's been done before. Folks will think it's only another enemy like Whip Helton who came to avenge some past injury. Kill him and burn him out, and that will be the last of him."

"What about his daughter?" Libby said.

McQueen didn't seem to have an answer to that. Mannion heard him only sigh and probably shrug his shoulders.

That cut it.

If Joe waited one minute longer, the top of his head might very well blow off and leave him a babbling idiot. An enraged idiot, but an idiot just the same.

Hardening his jaws, Mannion shucked both big Russians and long-strode to the front of the cabin. He turned the corner. Both Ventress and Dumas were sitting on the edge of the porch, elbows on their knees, smoking.

They both turned to see Joe at the same time.

Both gave startled yelps as they started to rise and slap leather.

Bang! Bang!

Mannion leaped up onto the porch and brushed passed the two men's sagging bodies and kicked in the door, breaking it nearly in two as it slammed back against the cabin's front wall.

The three schemers sat on three sides of the small, round, wooden table before him. McQueen faced him on the table's far side. Libby sat to the left, Park, to the right.

All three men's eyes widened in shock and horror.

McQueen remained seated, stunned, as the other two lurched to their feet, each reaching for fancy poppers strapped to their waists.

"Burn me out and kill my daughter, will ya?" Joe raged.

Neither Libby nor Park's pistols had cleared leather before both of Joe's Russians spoke the language of certain death, blowing first Libby almost literally out of his boots and sending him flying across the cabin and over the potbelly stove to land in a fast-dying heap.

Park was next.

The barrel of his Bisley was just about to clear its holster when Joe's slug punched him straight back and over his chair. He screamed as he fell hard on the earthen floor where he lay with his arms spread, legs hooked over his chair seat, blood bubbling up from high on his belly, turning his white silk shirt and paisley vest dark red.

He stared at the ceiling, blinking rapidly, until Joe shot him again, this time through the head.

Mannion turned both smoking Russians on McQueen, who sat back in his hair, shielding his face with his crossed arms, wailing, "Don't shoot me, Joe! Oh, God, please don't shoot me, Joe!"

He was sobbing, eyes squeezed shut, lips stretched back from his teeth, glasses hanging off his nose.

Mannion gave a bitter laugh.

"Hell, I'm not gonna shoot you, Charlie," he bellowed. "I'm gonna watch the hangman play cat's cradle with your head!"

CODA

EARLY THAT EVENING, JUST AFTER SUPPERTIME, Mannion swung Red off the secondary trail and onto the main trail to Del Norte.

He reined up when he saw a rider coming toward him cross country from the west, silhouetted against the painter's palette of late-day colors bayonetting across the sky, the sun teetering atop the jagged peaks of the San Juans.

Mannion was leading three horses. Over two, Libby and Park's bodies rode belly down across their saddles. On the other one, Charlie McQueen rode astride with his hands cuffed to his saddle horn. He rode with his head hanging in shame, glasses hanging off his nose.

Mannion had left Dumas and Ventress to the carrion eaters. It was better than those two vermin deserved.

Joe sat watching the lean rider ride toward him until the man was near enough that he recognized Stringbean McCallister.

"Good Lord, Deputy," Joe said as horse and rider approached from fifteen feet away and kept coming at a leisurely walk. "I thought you were dead!"

Stringbean's face had been rearranged for him. It looked mighty painful in fact.

Stringbean reined his dun to a halt and gave a grim smile as he leaned forward, resting his arms across his saddle horn. He looked about as weary as any man Joe had ever seen. But there was a prideful glint in his eyes. "I gotta admit, it was touch and go there for a while, Marshal."

"The girl?"

"Safe an' sound in Mexico by now, most like. She took the livery horse. I'll pay for it."

Mannion frowned at him, puzzled. "What about Hidalgo?"

"Dead."

"You kill him?"

"Me an' her. Turns out we made a pretty good team."

Joe stared at his junior deputy, incredulous. "Good God, kid. You did better than I would have done."

"Pshaw!"

Stringbean looked at Charlie McQueen. They mayor continued to sit his horse, head hanging with deep chagrin. He hadn't said a word since Mannion had slapped the cuffs on him. Stringbean looked at the two dead men then turned to Mannion.

"Been busy, I see, Marshal."

"You know how it goes."

"Yeah."

"Can I buy you a drink...Henry?"

Henry J. McCallister smiled, dimpling his cheeks. "I don't normally imbibe, but under the circumstances..."

Mannion chuckled and booted his horse forward. Henry fell in beside him, his coyote dun matching Red stride for stride. A half hour later they rode into the always bustling Del Norte. Joe was met with the usual chorus of morbidly delighted observations, all eyes taking note of the two dead men he was trailing per his usual bloody reputation.

When folks on the street saw Charlie McQueen riding with his hands cuffed, a hush fell, the awful quiet continuing as the riders continued deeper into the town.

Mannion saw a splash of familiar red on the balcony outside Jane's second-floor office, her French doors open behind her, the lace curtains blowing in the breeze. He stopped on the street below her. She stared down at him dubiously, her gaze shifting from Charlie McQueen to the two men riding belly down across their saddles.

When she saw James Park, her cheeks blanched a little. Her eyes crinkled at the corners. Her lips parted but she said nothing before her deeply puzzled gaze returned to Mannion. He said nothing. He gave no expression whatever.

He booted Red ahead and pulled up to the jailhouse. Rio was sitting on the front stoop with Buster on his lap. When Rio saw Stringbean he grinned delightedly, chuckling. When he saw Joe trailing McQueen and the two dead men, he frowned, set Buster on the porch rail to his right, and came down the steps.

He scrutinized the two dead men.

He looked at McQueen, who did not meet his gaze.

He turned to Mannion still sitting his saddle, too weary to move at the moment.

"Been a long day, Rio," he said.

"I see that." Rio removed the badge from his shirt, reached up, and pinned it to Joe's. "Here, you best take this back. It's awful heavy for a potbellied old cuss like myself."

He smiled up at Mannion.

Joe smiled back at him.

A LOOK AT: LONNIE GENTRY AND THE CURSE OF SKULL CANYON

A LONNIE GENTRY DUO

Western action and adventure author Peter Brandvold's iconic Lonnie Gentry series comes together like a stick of dynamite and a match to blow readers away!

In book one, *Lonnie Gentry*, life has not been easy for young cowboy Lonnie Gentry. He and his mother live alone, working hard on their remote Colorado mountain ranch. Now the thirteen-year-old must travel over perilous mountains to return money stolen by his mother's outlaw boyfriend. It's a man's job. And it's going to take a man – and the woman the man loves – to see it through.

In *The Curse of Skull Canyon*, everyone in the Never Summer Mountains knows about the ancient Indian curse on Skull Canyon in the highest, remotest reaches of the range, not far from the ranch young Lonnie Gentry shares with his mother and infant half-brother.

When a man's agonized wail lures him into the canyon, he finds a youth only a few years older than himself dying from a gunshot wound. Later, when savage men pour into the remote canyon, apparently searching for something they're willing to kill for, Lonnie learns the extent of Skull Canyon's horror.

AVAILABLE NOW

Peter Brandvold grew up in the great state of North Dakota in the 1960's and '70s, when television westerns were as popular as shows about hoarders and shark tanks are now, and western paperbacks were as popular as *Game of Thrones*.

Brandvold watched every western series on television at the time. He grew up riding horses and herding cows on the farms of his grandfather and many friends who owned livestock.

Brandvold's imagination has always lived and will always live in the West. He is the author of over a hundred lightning-fast action westerns under his own name and his pen name, Frank Leslie.